"*Operation Grendel* is sci-fi at its finest. Fun and incredibly clever, this book kept me on the edge of my seat. Grab a copy. It's fantastic!"

—JILL WILLIAMSON, award-winning author of *By Darkness Hid*

"I've been waiting ages to read this book! Now it's here. Or, as Star-Lord would say: '*Finally!*'"

—NADINE BRANDES, author of *Romanov* and the Out of Time series

"Uncharted realms. Unfathomable odds. Unexpected twists. *Operation Grendel* will spark your imagination, quicken your pulse, and keep you questioning what's real ... and what's next!"

—ALLEN ARNOLD, author of *The Story of With* and *Chaos Can't*

OPERATION
GRENDEL

OPERATION GRENDEL

DANIEL SCHWABAUER

Operation Grendel
Copyright © 2021 by Daniel Schwabauer

Published by Enclave Publishing, an imprint of Third Day Books, LLC

Phoenix, Arizona, USA.
www.enclavepublishing.com

ISBN: 978-1-62184-161-6 (hardback)
ISBN: 978-1-62184-163-0 (printed softcover)
ISBN: 978-1-62184-162-3 (ebook)

Cover design by Kirk DouPonce, www.DogEaredDesign.com
Typesetting by Jamie Foley, www.JamieFoley.com

Printed in the United States of America.

CONFESSION

Like every journalist, I lie for a living.

In this case, I had to become someone else in order to get the story. I'm not who I say I am.

My name isn't Ansell Sterling, and I'm not a captain. I'm not even a marine.

The only military training I've ever had was grunt basic, just after I joined the reserve infantry back on Kanzin.

The real marine died at Camp Locke, New Witlund, during the grendel invasion of Quelon. Captain Ansell Sterling took a round through his right lung and choked on his own blood in an air-conditioned office.

A few minutes after he died I stole his identity, along with his comms bracelet.

It was the only way I could get the story. The only way I could tell the colonies how we're being manipulated.

My name is Corporal Raymin Dahl.

I'm a military journalist for the Orbits News Syndicate, and I'm going to show you what happens when you compromise with the grendels. Even if that means a court-martial.

Since I don't have the recordings from my own comms, I'm writing this old-school, fingers to pad, with no input from my AI.

Sterling agreed that if I went through with his mission, I could write the story however I wanted.

So this is how I want to do it. A war story by Raymin Dahl that finally tells the truth.

Which sounds more courageous than it is. For me to face a court-martial, I'll have to survive long enough to load this story into the net.

And really, what are the odds?

PART ONE

GRENDELS INVADE QUELON!

BY CPL RAYMIN DAHL

EMBEDDED WITH MADAR TEAM TWO

1

STORY FIRST

The grendel wars started twenty-eight years ago. One week before I was born, and welcome to the galaxy.

Back then, most of our military strategists thought we had a reasonable chance of winning. Twenty years later, everyone knew it was just a matter of time before the United Colonies bled to death. The Grand Alliance was going to conquer every free, autonomous human being in the Milky Way mind-by-mind, planet-by-planet, until we were all grendels and absurdly happy about it.

Grendels. We didn't even know what that meant. All we really knew was that integrated AIs had transformed our former trade partners into something other than *homo sapiens. Homo integris,* maybe.

Sure, we'd taken a few as prisoners, but they always killed themselves.

In twenty-eight years not one grendel had ever defected.

But we weren't going down without a fight. Even the press corps was trying to do our part. So, naturally, when my commanding officer and editor at OrbSyn, Major Weston, sent me an assignment to the back end of the tip of the spear, I saluted and grabbed my go bag.

He wanted me to interview a Psychological Operations officer about the launch of a new combat unit with the impenetrable designation of MADAR. And the interview *had* to take place on the tropical hellscape of New Witlund, where it was always summer but never a holiday.

We couldn't have met on, say, Quelon, the planet that New Witlund orbits as a slowly spinning moon. A place with clean air and moderate temperatures and eleven Fleet military installations.

Nor could we have, I don't know, opened a secure channel and done the interview from our respective offices. Maybe sent a few text pigeons.

No, according to Major Weston, this particular story required "texture."

So there I sat in the cafeteria of a remote Marine Corps training base, waiting for Captain Ansell Sterling of the PSYOPS unit to walk in and explain what the acronym MADAR stood for. It had only taken me three days and seven different flights to get there.

I stared out the cafeteria window at the jungle and fidgeted with my comms bracelet, as if jiggling the thin circlet might bring up some new background material, some clue as to why I was really there.

It was a newer unit, with a military-grade AI and a neural interface capable of ghosting my eyes and ears from the safety of a wyrm-resistant firebox. Our techies were serious about shielding my God-given, human-born, colonial free will.

Surprisingly, nothing had changed since I last checked it, ninety seconds ago. Sterling's personnel file was functionally empty. The man's career was a thin curtain of white space autofilling next to his official—and lengthy—list of commendations and unit connections.

Just outside the window, a platoon of marines jogged past, their PTs saturated in sweat, their voices trailing after the drill instructor's:

> One fine day signed my life away.
> *Gave my life to the Corps.*
> Two months in boot, sergeant taught me to shoot.
> *Found my life in the Corps.*

The cadence of the training song poked a bruise at the back of my brain as the group moved out of sight.

Everywhere I went, I was reminded that Fleet had no place for my unpatriotic existence outside of a tiny cubicle at OrbSyn.

A reservist, you see, wasn't a real marine.

And a journalist wasn't even a real reservist.

In the distance the platoon's voices salted my wounded pride with more of the same tuneless jody.

> Three meals a day, plus a rack and some pay.
> *No better life than the Corps.*
> Four days in space with puke on my face.
> *Ain't life grand in the Corps?*

After I could no longer hear the words, I passed the time trying to remember what followed. There were eight lines, each beginning with the next number in sequence, and each ending with the word *Corps*. It was the perfect training song for jarheads, since most of them could in fact count all the way to eight, and *Corps* was their second-favorite word.

But for the life of me I couldn't recall what happened in line five. Looking it up would have spoiled the exercise.

Then Sterling came through the door and spotted me by the window. Camp Locke was in the last stage of decommission, so finding me wasn't hard. We were the only people in the room.

He stood about my height and was maybe four years older, but that's where the resemblance ended. Sterling was pure United Colonies Marine Corps, right down to the citation patches on his lapel.

Since he chose to be interviewed in Camp Locke's dining hall, I kept my seat and my silence, even though I wasn't eating. It's an old tradition, and who was I to challenge military etiquette?

He pulled up a chair across from me and sat. "Corporal Dahl."

"Sir."

Sterling studied me briefly and said, as if I'd had a choice, "Thank you for meeting me."

"Of course. I'm excited to find out what this new program is all about."

He gave a wry smile, the faintest suggestion that he understood my

Kanzin reservist sarcasm, and folded his hands on the table. "You're not here for the MADAR story, Corporal . You're here because we're losing this war."

"I can't write that," I said. "They'll say I'm giving comfort to the enemy."

Sterling's dark hair was going prematurely gray, but he had the body of a young man. Even the loose cut of his utility fatigues couldn't hide the impression of a high-performance engine idling at poll position. "Today maybe. Not by the end of the week. It's why you're here. Fleet doesn't have the resources to protect nineteen systems. Coffee?"

I gave him an expression that hovered between false humility and blissful ignorance. "Thank you, no."

Sterling shoved his chair back and retreated to a wall of auto-dispensers for a cup.

It never hurt to let a source feel they had the upper hand. Especially when they were wearing captain's bars and a combat recon badge with six(!) stars. How he'd achieved that without also being promoted to at least Lieutenant Colonel had to be a story in itself.

Through the mess hall's curved windows, heat blurred the air above the parade ground, turning the jagged green horizon into a smear of color, like an impressionist painting. Higher up, Quelon's crescent balanced on one point, as if deciding which way to fall.

I'd spent the last four years writing stories about wounded veterans and combat fatigue and the difference between colonials and grendels. Now they wanted me to help throw in the towel?

Sterling took his time with sugar, cream, and more coffee. Probably wanted me to stew a little. To ponder the idea that Fleet Intel needed something badly enough they were willing to disperse it through the features of an OrbSyn journalist.

More specifically, through *me*. Corporal Raymin Dahl of "Three Days on a Wounded Cruiser," and "Life and Death as a Harpy Ace."

That Raymin Dahl.

So what did they want? And what did Captain Sterling have to do with it?

The AI on my comms bracelet noticed my curiosity. It couldn't read my mind, of course, because it was a Colonial AI, but it tried to be helpful by returning to my most recent query. The white space of Sterling's personnel file projected a quilt of transparent fog across my optics.

I thrust the file off my grid with a mental flick as Sterling sat down and put the steaming cup between us.

"You need me," I said. "That's why I'm here."

"I *requested* you, yes. I need a writer of your caliber who isn't perceived as pro-military."

I arched one brow. "I'm not perceived as pro-military? By whom?" I liked to use *whom* with officers. It kept them off-balance. Usually.

"My job is to read people, Corporal. And I've done a lot of reading about you. Every feature, every column, every blast and mock-over and psyad you've penned going back to your junior exams. And I think I know something about you. Something you may not have figured out for yourself."

I barely kept the sneer out of my voice. "Let me guess: I want to be a *real* soldier?"

His face was granite. "No. You just want a real story."

The implications of that statement brought a wave of heat to my cheeks. "So all the work I've been doing for OrbSyn is what? Propaganda?"

He sipped his coffee and glanced casually out the window, as if expecting someone else. "You write puff pieces that serve a very specific purpose. Believe it or not, I respect that. You at least volunteered. You crawled out of a Kanzin backwater and made a life for yourself apart from the expectations of your father. Not to mention everyone else. Being the son of a decorated Fleet officer couldn't have been easy."

Intimidation. He was showing me how deep his info-well was. Proving that on his comms my personnel file wasn't redacted at all. "I don't need your approval, Captain."

"I wasn't offering it." His expression hadn't wavered. "You write a lot of drivel, Corporal. I know it, and you know it, and most of my superiors at Fleet Intel know it. What some of them don't understand is that you've actually found ways to tell people the truth. You've gotten more past your editor than anyone in twenty years. That's how I know you want a story with teeth."

I wondered just how deeply he'd seen into my work. I didn't have loads of respect for most officers, especially ones who considered themselves intellectuals. But the PSYOPS unit had a reputation, and I would be stupid to underestimate any of them. "And you're going to give it to me?"

"Yes."

"Why?"

"Because it's your readers who need to see it."

My readers. Meaning edgers. Colonials in the backwater militias who loved freedom and hated big government of any kind. People who preferred a Colonial senator to an Alliance oligarch only because a senator could be bribed into leaving them alone. People who loved it when some lowly corporal, some Kanzin reservist with press creds, say, poked a rear admiral or congresswoman in the eye.

So I'd been right. Sterling needed me because he wanted help selling a story to groundlings. Which meant that I suddenly had a little leverage, if nothing else.

I lit an insubordinate grin and nudged my AI to begin recording. I couldn't have trusted Sterling less if he'd been the senate press secretary. He may as well have been a grendel.

Recording our conversation would provide some security if things went sideways. However bogus his fake story turned out to be, I'd have the makings of a real one stored on my wrist. Later I could use my notes to write an alternate feature on the reality of psychological warfare. I'd call it something like, *"Liar, Liar, Planets on Fire!"*

"All right, Captain," I said. "I'll play along. What's the story?"

"Check your grid."

I hesitated, then prodded my AI for a terminal overlay.

A transparent display of colored icons, holographic images, file indicators, and status alerts should have appeared at the periphery of my natural vision, sent to my brain from my comms bracelet.

Instead I saw a battery of offline warning ticks blinking red.

"What is this?"

"Security," Sterling said. "You'll be offline till we're ready for your story to go live."

"I can't work if I can't access the net," I protested.

"And I can't risk this story getting out. Even if I trusted you, which I don't, we can't have an enemy wyrm hacking into your comms and accessing your notes. That trinket on your wrist would leak like a French colander. You'll have to work offline. Pen and paper if necessary."

The fact Sterling had the authority to shut down my link to AFNET when I wasn't even in his chain of command irritated me. It shouldn't have *surprised* me, given the reputation of the PSYOPS unit, but I resented the feeling of powerlessness and isolation it created. On the other hand, I wasn't about to let him know how I felt. "All right. I'll work offline. What's the story?"

"We're going to negotiate with the grendels," he said, leaning forward. "Secretly. So that no one will know what we're doing until it's too late."

The hairs on the back of my neck tingled. I looked for physical clues that he was lying but saw none. This was not the sort of story Fleet sent to Raymin Dahl. "When?"

"Tomorrow."

Last-minute notice would make it hard for me to leak the story early. Even if I found a way to send a file to Major Weston without going through AFNET, I'd still need to dig up enough details to prove the story was credible. Otherwise Weston would never run with it. "Where?"

"Here. New Witlund. A compound owned by the Trevalyan cartel." He nodded west out the window. "Sits about twenty klicks into the mountains southeast of Seranik."

That fit the story too. Cartel property could pass for neutral ground. "Who's doing the negotiating?"

"I am," he said. "And an Alliance emissary who will arrive soon via consular shuttle from the Corgan system. You and I will be hiking up into those mountains tomorrow morning with a small MADAR team."

"Our bodyguards."

"They are quite capable."

I still knew nothing about the MADAR designation, but the fact Fleet Intel thought there was a credible threat to our safety implied something else. Was it possible this mission had already sprung an intelligence leak? "What are we offering the Alliance?"

"The goal," Sterling said, "is to negotiate a peaceful transfer of authority over the edge colonies—and *only* the edge colonies. None of the core systems are on the table. That needs to be clear in the story. We are not negotiating from a position of strength, but neither are we rolling over. We can survive without the edge worlds, but we're not turning over even one core system."

"Which ones, then?" I asked, mind reeling. "Which colonies *are* on the table?"

"The whole edge. Quelon, Moadi, Inawa, Holikot and, well—" He paused as if not wanting to say the last name. Must have seen it in my file.

"Kanzin?"

"Yes."

The name reminded me I hadn't been to my homeworld in years. To be honest, I didn't miss it. But the thought of it being turned over to grendel shock troops brought an empty feeling to the pit of my stomach.

"Quelon," I said, sliding the story fragments together as I spoke. "Explains why they're closing Camp Locke."

Sterling nodded. "In three months this place will be crawling with enemy troops. Grendels eating at this table, complaining about the heat."

"Things are really that bad? We're just giving up? Letting them have five systems we've spent centuries cultivating?"

"The simulations are clear," Sterling answered. "If we continue trying to defend all nineteen systems, we will lose the war. And half of the edge population will be wiped out within two years."

He's serious, I thought. *This is really happening.*

I'd written a lot of stories from the safety of a skyport lounge or edge system hotel. Maybe I'd gotten too comfortable with the idea that Fleet would never let me anywhere near the real war.

"And you want me to sell that—the story of our surrender—to the six hundred million people we're leaving behind?" I rubbed my palms against my pant legs. For my own protection, I needed Sterling to be clear on the recording. *"That's* the story you want me to cover in lipstick?"

"You'd rather write the story of three hundred million *deaths*?"

"Of course not," I said, ignoring the gibe. Any reporter will tell you that the only meaningful statistic is a human face. Preferably one covered in blood. But covered in fear was almost as good, and nothing would make the edge colonies more terrified than news of an imminent grendel occupation.

Sterling was offering me the story of a lifetime. Oh, he was hiding something. Probably something vital to my understanding of what was really going on. He was from PSYOPS, the dirty tricks unit.

But if the main premise of the story was correct, and Fleet really intended to turn over five colonial solar systems to the Grand Alliance, the only thing I could do to make a difference was tell the story of how it was going to happen. The *true* story, in advance, so maybe the edge militias could do something about it.

And it didn't hurt that this story could also make my career.

"Good," he said. "Then start figuring out how you're going to convince five systems to cooperate with the enemy *without* accepting their symb-collars."

I folded my arms. "If you want me to reach the edgers, Captain, you need to let me do it my way. You can't ask them to take one for the flag while you're slipping out the back door."

"You're not getting carte blanche."

"I know how these people think. And they're going to see this as the most callous sort of betrayal imaginable. Because it is. Nothing I say will matter if I can't tell them the truth."

He took a deep breath, as if making up his mind. "Tell you what. You write the story your way. But it comes to me first. Then to Major Weston."

"I don't do public relations."

"This isn't about PR. It's about timing. The only way Fleet Intel will let your story go out live onto the OrbSyn breaking feed is if it comes through my grid. Otherwise the censors will pick it apart line by line."

More bait. More control. A prime spot on the most prestigious news feed in the United Colonies, and all I had to do was agree to submit my story through Sterling's comms.

We had a saying at OrbSyn. *Tell the facts when you have them, the truth when possible, and the story regardless.*

Or, as Weston liked to say, usually in the voice of an exasperated kindergarten teacher: *Story first. Story last. Story in between.*

I pretended to consider the deal, even though I'd already made up my mind. Assuming the talks succeeded, the only real question was how much we'd have to surrender in return. That story could serve as my first follow-up. *Why It Had to Be Done.*

On the other hand, the enemy obviously had their own plans for using the edge worlds in remaking humanity. But since no one knew what those plans were, that angle would require a zoomed-in approach. Perhaps an exposé of how adults are infected with AI wyrms. The symb-collar angle alone would be worth a five-part series. Something like *Slave to a Quantum Master.*

Meanwhile, I'd be salting everything with details about the treachery of the Grand Alliance, and how colonials must never succumb to the bondage of fully integrated artificial intelligence. Written well, my stories could keep our resistance militias on the occupied worlds fired up for months. They'd be passing my feature stories from comms to comms as if they were hard currency.

Raymin Dahl would tell them to never put on an infected comms bracelet no matter how attractive the benefits seemed. And they would listen. I'd write stories with titles like *Say No to Wyrms* and *The Plight of a Human Puppet.*

Remember why we're fighting, I would write. *The flag of the United Colonies stands for something. Our AIs serve us, not vice versa. Autonomy or death!*

I stared out the window, and Sterling sipped his coffee in silence. He probably knew I'd already taken the bait.

"All right," I said at last.

Ironically, that's when the first image of the invasion appeared in the monitor above the windows: a grendel warship ripping a gash in New Witlund's copper-and-pearl sky.

She was a small ship, wreathed in fire, and I barely breathed as she traced a bloody claw across the screen.

Sterling's eyes widened, and I could tell he was seeing it on his private grid. He rose and went to the west window, though the view there was worse than the one that would be superimposing itself on his optical nerve.

"That's a *consular* ship?" I asked.

He shook his head, still staring with wide-open eyes. "Alliance frigate. *Strangler* class. They're going for our datalink off-moon. Do you know where Colonel Vermier's office is?"

"No, sir. Never been on this base till this morn—"

That's when the front of the building erupted in flames and I slammed backwards onto the tiled floor.

It took me ages to slip into darkness, but as I closed my eyes, the memory finally returned to me, and I heard the cadence again as if for the first time:

Five planets down, we can't lose this ground.
    Do what I'm told in the Corps.
Six grendel ships and the truth on my lips.
    Life and death in the Corps.
Seven of our best, laid to rest, laid to rest.
    These were the best of the Corps.
Eight, make it eight, for the round that caught me late.
    Gave my life to the Corps.

2

DELETION

You get this feeling when a story is wrong. A dead feeling in the back of your brain, in the muddy places where your AI can't look even with permission. You know something's off, that you're being used, that the assignment sent through your wrist-comms probably originated way over your editor's head, at Fleet Intel maybe, or even with Psychological Operations.

Usually the point is to send a message to some covert agent who can't be reached via more direct channels without risk of interception by a grendel wyrm. Someone living among the edgers.

Your editor might change only a couple of words, but those words will make the story worse, and won't fit the context. Major Weston, my editor, once told me to mind my own store when I asked him why he inserted the word "qualifactory" into a piece about an orbital fighter ace.

Other times the manipulation is so hidden it doesn't leave any footprints in your finished product. The assignment itself is your only clue.

Like sending Raymin Dahl all the way to New Witlund to interview an intel officer about a new special forces program. Why New Witlund? Why an in-person interview when Fleet Intel could easily have connected us using a secure channel? For that matter, why send a PSYOPS officer to explain a special forces program?

Those are the questions you learn to think about, even if you can't ask them.

Two weeks ago the wrong story came from my girlfriend, Ivy Weber. We'd been together six months, and without realizing it I had started to expect our relationship to continue, maybe forever.

Then one afternoon out of the midnight clear she canceled our dinner plans.

No big deal, but it was her favorite restaurant, a corner cafe halfway between OrbSyn's Holikot office and her apartment. And she canceled by text message via my AI. With a 30 minute timed delay, as if she didn't feel like talking.

Okay, that happens too. Everybody has bad days, and since we'd been together I'd had more than my share.

But the text!

–WEBER, I: HAVE TO CANCEL TONIGHT. CALL YOU MONDAY.–

It was short, bland, and featureless. All things Ivy was not.

Ivy was everything I'd given up looking for in a woman. She tolerated my political pessimism, my erratic work schedule, my compulsive need to arrange facts into narratives. But she was also gracious, smart, and unconsciously attractive. She sometimes complained of her narrow frame and deep green eyes, and was constantly tucking her long black hair behind her ears. Distracting, she called it. I agreed, but for different reasons.

The implication that I should wait for her to call me—for four days, no less—clearly signaled distance. Either she was angry or something had happened that she didn't want me involved in.

The first possibility didn't make sense. We'd had no argument, and if I had inadvertently said or done something stupid—always a possibility—Ivy would have confronted me immediately. She didn't pout. Her eyes sometimes flashed green fire, and she was the most determined, strong-willed person I'd ever met, but she didn't play games.

I loved that about her. As far as our relationship was concerned, I'd always known where I stood.

Which left the possibility something else was wrong, some work or personal problem she wanted me to stay out of.

One thing you learned as a journalist was that *everybody* had baggage. Sometimes people deserved it and sometimes they didn't, but either way they tried to hide it. Self-preservation was built into our genes.

My job was to dig up that stuff and see if it looked any different in the clear light of cynicism. When you expected bad behavior, you were occasionally surprised.

Maybe that was my problem. I'd stopped expecting anything really bad.

I opened a channel to my OrbSyn workstation on my wrist-comms, mentally flicked over to AFNET, and logged a comms query for Weber, Ivy, 9174336NW. I'd been telling her for months to put a tracking clamp on her bracelet, but she always replied that the only people who would ever look for her would be someone who cared about her.

Which, in this case, turned out to be true.

Her icon flickered on a transparent overlay against my natural vision, and I recognized the place instantly. It brought a hollow feeling to my chest.

She was holed up at Frillz, the night club where we'd first met.

I closed the channel and deleted my query. Anyone who knew what to look for would be able to find it, but who would bother? Using military assets for personal reasons was technically a violation of policy, but everyone did it. And some low-level reporter using AFNET's GPS system to find out where his girlfriend had gone after she sent him a cryptic message wasn't even a curiosity. No one at Fleet Intel would raise an eyebrow.

I walked to the kiosk and swiped my comms for a rental, picked up a sandwich and chips at a dispenser, and ten minutes later squeezed the two-door sedan into a space overlooking the club's front entrance.

At that point I was more puzzled than worried, and I figured I could get some work done while I waited. I do some of my best writing in rentals. Besides, I still needed to deal with Fleet's take-it-or-leave-it reenlistment offer. The bonus of $30,000 for another five years of Raymin Dahl's feature stories would only be on the table for a few more days. After that it would start decreasing daily. Because the two best ways to motivate anyone were cash and a ticking clock.

I was already planning to re-up. I just didn't want to read the contract, which had been bleating its digital PATRIOTS SERVE! reminder across my closed eyelids every morning for the last week. Problem was, I had to actually read every word of the twenty-three-page contract before I could sign. My AI had to witness that internal mental process and attest to my comprehension. Colonial comms techs don't just protect our God-given, colonial free will from grendel wyrms. They also shield it from ourselves.

I'd read all the way to page seventeen when Ivy walked out the front door holding some officer's hand and leaning into him like he'd just paid off her grandmother's mortgage. I'd never seen the guy before. He was tall and athletic and wearing a major's oak leaf on his collar.

I nudged my AI to record visuals and stared unblinking as a glossy black sled, a luxury sedan, drifted to the curb and swung open its doors. Ivy reached up, pulled the guy into a long kiss, and dipped into the back seat. The major followed.

After the sled drove off I stared at the empty street, the occasional weeknight customers going in and out of the club, the night sky alive with stars. Eventually I remembered to stop recording.

Some small, fragile part of my mind tried to argue that there might be a reasonable explanation for what I'd just seen. But I had the recording, and after I rewatched it twice, the excuses shut up.

I drove around for a while, then stopped at a pawn shop close to the base and slapped the velveted box on the counter. I'd been carrying the ring since I bought it back on Moadi. I'd hired a local artisan to set a series of peridots in a band of white gold. *Green and white, like your eyes,* I would have said, or some such nonsense.

The pawn-shop guy offered me twenty percent of what the ring cost. I haggled until he threw in a bottle of Inawa bourbon and a set of shot glasses etched with the Marine Corps logo. Drove back to base and returned the rental. Walked into the OrbSyn building and smuggled the bottle and shot glasses up the service staircase to my spot on the roof.

I'd been keeping an all-weather folding recliner up there for a couple of years. I liked working at night. I'd written as many features under the stars as I had wedged into the driver's seat of a military sled or while polishing some barstool in a militia canteen.

Since my AI would never witness my signature with alcohol in my bloodstream, I spent the next hour reading the minutia of the contract, signed it, and sent it off to Fleet for processing.

Only then did I recognize the real reason I'd been putting it off. I'd been hoping Ivy and I might have a future together. A future outside the service, where every assignment wasn't dictated by war policy or strategic need or even morale. A job where I could tell a story because it needed telling, and people needed to know. The two of us back-to-back against the galaxy, obviously doomed because that's how life is, but at least going down together, going down fighting.

Trust.

Isn't that what our heroes always told me they had? Isn't that why they fought? It was never for love of service or love of the flag. It was always for the man or woman next to them. Shakespeare's band of brothers.

Well, no journalist had faith in the people around him, military or not. How could you trust someone who was always shaping reality for the consumption of outsiders? At best the reporters at OrbSyn were a loose coalition of misanthropes who had agreed not to eat their own. We were a band of strangers.

I broke open the bourbon and tipped a finger into the glass, vaguely wondering if it had been washed but not really caring. I tossed it back and closed my eyes as the warmth seeped into my throat.

No reason to put this off, I thought. *It's over now anyway.*

I pulled up the recording and zoomed in. Trimmed it to a single frame, Ivy's lips pressed against the mysterious officer's. Plucked that single image from the clip and deleted everything else. If I archived the video I would just be tempted to watch it again later, salt in the wound.

I flicked a text pigeon onto my optics and attached the damning evidence. Labeled it for Ivy's comms, but with a nice little 30 minute delay. Fair was fair.

Regret whimpered in that tiny, malnourished corner of my soul I called a conscience. More accurately it's the empty space left behind when my conscience exfiltrated for more defensible ground. I ignored it and sent the message, then poured myself another drink.

Would Ivy bother to call me, I wondered, or would she just let the picture serve as a clean break between us? What, after all, was there to say?

I looked up at the stars and decided a clean break was what I really needed. Probably what Ivy needed too. I was going to be at OrbSyn another five years—assuming we didn't lose the war by then. I would be better off not trusting anyone, and Ivy would be better off not wondering what corner of the edge Fleet was sending me to.

Sensible woman, Ivy. I'd always said she was smarter than me by half.

Still sucked.

I nudged my AI. [How many memories of Ivy have I archived?]

A list of dates and locations scrolled past my vision on the left side, white text brilliant against the night sky. I selected three of the most familiar ones and sent the rest to the shredder.

[*Permanent deletion?*] my AI objected. [*Are you sure?*]

Military wrist-comms aren't like those you can buy on the open market. They have a lot more security, a vast number of interface capabilities, and the personality of a houseplant.

[Positive.]

[*File deleted.*]

I called up the most recent of the remaining three videos. A few weeks prior, Ivy and I had spent a weekend at a water resort in Kadir. I scrubbed past our ride from the terminal and slowed to watch myself open the door to our hotel room. Turned back to look at her, and there she was in the hallway, eyes sparkling like I was the only person in the universe who really mattered.

Shouldn't have watched that one obviously, but how could I look away from those eyes? I'd almost forgotten how green they were.

Then past-me pulled her into a long kiss, and I snapped the memory off.

[Yeah, delete that one too.]

[*File deleted. Are you all right?*]

I was staring at the first file, the one labeled *Frillz*. That one especially needed to be removed from my bracelet's passive memory. But deletion on a military comms was really and truly permanent—a safeguard against grendel hacking. Once I sent it to the shredder, nothing could bring it back. The only memories I'd have of our time together would be the frail, unreliable bio-fragments left in my own mind.

Then again, was that really a problem?

I opened the second memory: Ivy splashing in a fountain downtown, relief from the summer heat. Her pants were rolled up almost to her knees, and she was soaking a couple of pre-teens who held water guns. They were strangers to us, but had drawn her—not me—into their game as though instinctively recognizing her as a natural ally.

She'd always had that power, I decided. Who *didn't* want Ivy Weber on their team?

The memory froze with Ivy's face distorted into a playful grimace as a stream of water from one of the kids sprayed her in the back. The video only ended there because I'd gotten a call and had to blink out of the recording. Her expression had made us both laugh when I showed it to her later.

[Delete,] I said. [And yeah, I'm sure.]

[*File deleted,*] my AI replied. [*This seems to be painful for you. Are you sure you're all right?*]

The hollow feeling in my stomach rose to my throat, and I reached for another shot of the good stuff. [My girlfriend is cheating on me, that's all. Though I guess it's not cheating if you weren't playing by the same rules in the first place.]

I could almost hear its algorithms trying to interpret my words and the obvious edge to my voice. [*She doesn't know what she's missing.*]

That almost made me laugh, which was probably what my AI was going for. No doubt Fleet had millions of Dear John scripts pre-programmed, one of which had to be calibrated for caustic journalists like me. They'd been dealing with the emotional effects of romantic breakups for a very long time.

Anyway, Ivy certainly *did* know what she was missing.

[Thanks, bracelet. That means a lot.]

[*Would you like me to delete the last memory too?*]

I knew what was on it without looking—had watched it a dozen times. It was the moment we'd first met. Part of an assignment, so recording had been a matter of procedure. But after that first interview, before I even asked her out, I kept wanting to rewatch it. Ivy already meant more to me than some bit player in a feature story for OrbSyn.

She'd been standing at a table inside Frillz, waiting for me beneath the throbbing lights and bluesy rhythm of some holo-band playing live from the core. The night club had felt surprisingly empty for a weekend. Probably the band. Edgers no longer cared what the core systems were doing. It had taken generations, but we'd finally realized the kids at the cool table were mostly snobs.

I toyed with the idea of watching it one last time to fix Ivy's smile in my bio-memory. Nail it to the wall where it couldn't be forgotten.

Overhead, the stars pulsed behind the white text of the filename *Ivy Weber Holikot Interview* as I wavered between past and future. The holocon of Ivy's smiling face next to the recording didn't make it any easier. I was already regretting the other deletions. But in the end what choice did I have? Brass says move on, you move on.

[Yeah,] I said at last, reaching again for the bottle. [Delete that one too.]

Twenty-three minutes later Ivy rang.

I sent her to messaging.

3

RESISTANCE

I spotted her in the back of a night club on Holikot, hands fencing a beer mug.

The holo in Ivy Weber's personnel file revealed long black hair, green eyes, and dimples you could trip over. Even the digital version of her smile was captivating.

In person, her slender beauty was magnified by the barricade scowl she'd propped up against hopeful drunks. She was clearly waiting for someone.

Artificial smoke jetted over the dance floor, lighting the club's pulsing neons into colored plumes. The place had that unreal quality of a dream, but with a hint of detail that seemed to be shaking me, as if someone wanted me to wake.

I snatched my beer from the counter and circled behind her, pondering what to say.

Maybe it was the way she leaned on the table: lightly, and with endless patience. As if she could walk away from the club, from Holikot, from the interview I'd asked for, and feel no regrets. Ivy Weber didn't carry the weight of the world on her shoulders, and didn't want to.

Something twisted in my gut, some thread from the past unraveling in the moment. How might it feel to be my real self around someone? To spend time with a woman who didn't care that I lied for a living?

I wasn't thinking about love. Not yet. At that moment it was just a feeling, like that tickle in the back of the throat that signals the onset of flu.

More smoke clotted the air, an unnatural swirl of brown and black that hid the lights rather than revealed them. The song spilling from the overheads, a concert streaming live from one of the core planets, had a rhythmless, bass-heavy quality that was more noise than music.

"New Witlund?" I asked, my voice rising over the crackle of flames.

"Born and raised." She glanced at the unit patch on my sleeve. "You up for a walk?"

I set my beer next to hers. "Sure."

She took my arm. "Be still." Now her voice was low, urgent, not a woman's voice at all.

I pressed my hands over my ears and blinked against the burning air.

Sterling knelt next to me, his wrist-comms pressed to mine. "Don't say anything, Corporal. Can you fake a twisted ankle?"

I blinked against a shifting pattern of light. I was on New Witlund, not Holikot. Something had happened to the mess hall. A blanket of smokey heat squeezed the air.

I took a quick inventory. The bios on my overlay were all green. Aside from a pounding headache I wasn't hurt. I nodded and rolled onto my side.

"We have 'em, Lieutenant!" someone shouted. "In here!"

Four silhouettes, rimmed in sunlight, came through the wreckage of the foyer, weapons raised.

The soldier in front motioned with his rifle. "Put your hands up!" He wore the black fatigues of an edge reserve unit, citizen soldiers who answered neither to Fleet nor to the Senate , but to whatever passed for a provincial government here on New Witlund.

Sterling raised his hands and turned. "Militia?"

The soldier was still a teen, with pimply cheeks and a thin neck. His name tag, stitched over paneled body armor that looked too big for his frame, read PFC KURCEK. "Yes, sir. We're taking you into custody for your safety. Are you armed?"

"Custody" was an odd word to use under the circumstances, and I could tell Sterling didn't like it.

"Son, I am a *captain* in the United Colonies Marine Corps, and if you really care about my safety, you'll lower that weapon."

"Captain Sterling!" The last of the four edgers was shorter, heavily muscled, and carried himself with an air of pretension that annoyed me immediately. He didn't salute Sterling, though he did motion for Kurcek to lower his weapon. "Lieutenant Dogen, New Witlund QRS. I need you to come with me."

"My orderly twisted his ankle," Sterling lied. He reached down and hauled me to a lopsided standing position, mouthing the word "slow" as I hooked his shoulders for support.

"See that, private?" Dogen said in a tour-guide tone of measured respect, as if explaining something at a museum. "Colonial marines carry their own."

"Yes, sir." Kurcek kept his rifle pressed into the crook of his right arm, finger parallel to the trigger.

Leaning on Sterling, I fake-hobbled past overturned tables, through the twisted remains of the hall doorway, and into the spot where the foyer had been. A jagged hole in the north wall revealed New Witlund's copper sky and a thin sliver of sunlight.

Outside, the tropical heat felt relatively cool, the humid air refreshingly clear. Through a pallor of thinning smoke the perimeter fence and encroaching jungle shimmered. Draped above the mountains beyond, New Witlund's rust-colored sky gave the whole moon a weirdly bipolar ambience. Like a drunken parent, it seemed familiar and strange at the same time.

An armored sled waited for us, the rear door flung open to the heat. Backed onto the curve of the patio, its hull vibrated just above the pavement as if impatient to leave. It was an old SAV "Snapper" troop carrier, a wheelless box that hovered on AG repellers. Weld together a couple of eight-meter fishing boats, one on top of the other, and you'd have the same basic shape. It was easy to see how it had gotten its surname. It was angular, armored, and slow, but its repeller drive probably made it ideal transport through the jungle. The only thing jutting from its surface was a domed turret mounted with a pair of wicked-looking rail guns. This particular SAV was older than me by at least a decade—with patchwork outer paneling so faded it was impossible to determine the original paint color.

Two of Dogen's men hopped into the sled in front of us, one of them worming into the narrow standing platform of the top turret, the other sliding into the squad leader seat behind the cab.

Off in the distance towards the skyport a rapid string of pops cracked the air like fireworks, and suddenly the lieutenant was on my right. "That the best you got, marine?"

It was the first time anyone, anywhere, had mistaken me for an actual marine, and under other circumstances I might have enjoyed it. Maybe said something like, *I'm not ugly enough to be a marine, Lieutenant. I'm Kanzin Reserve Infantry, OrbSyn press corps. A Big-Red-Oh word-pounder.* You know, just to see the horrified look on the other guy's face. But Dogen hadn't made an honest mistake. He was just ignorant. So I gave him a fake grimace and a nod and tried to look like I was trying to hobble faster.

At the sled Sterling climbed in first and reached down to help me onto the rubber-coated platform. The SAVs rear compartment was designed for a single squad, with about as much room as a walk-in closet. Except this closet sported a metal turret platform dead center and angular wall panels checkered with mounting grommets. A single webbed squad leader chair sat across from the weapons locker just behind the cab, and two plasteel benches faced each other across a center aisle barely big enough for a dozen gear bags.

I couldn't imagine ten people stuffed into the back of it. Four of us plus the turret platform consumed most of the space. The compartment reeked of sweat and repeller fluid, even with the stench of smoke still burning in my throat.

Private Kurcek shoved me onto the bench next to Sterling as something like lightning flickered against a high concrete wall down the street. I knew what it was, though I'd never seen the effect in an actual firefight.

Dogen slammed the rear hatch from the outside, triggering soft blue lights that washed the interior with a cold glow. Something pinged against the bulkhead as the lieutenant scrambled into the cab, and he said "Go!"

The Snapper coughed to life. It tipped forward, rising slowly like an old man from a chair. The armored glass in the hatch framed a sky veneered with black smoke. It was like looking through a sheet— everything hazed in a blur of soft edges and unexpected shadows. Then more light strobed the blackness, a string of flashes like a summer storm on the horizon.

The soldier in the turret stomped a pedal, and the railguns spun around backwards with a mechanical groan. I couldn't see the upper half of his body, which was wedged above the roof in an armored bubble, but I heard the distinctive sound of a charging handle racking. The sled's heavy 50-50 twins were primed.

I pulled up my grid and sent a query to my AI. [That gunfire in the distance—what kind of weapons are they using?]

A map of the base flicked onto my vision. Two icons, labeled "Dahl" and "Sterling," drifted down the translucent overlay, with yellow approximation labels marking the probable location of the firefight.

[*Audio profiles match those of the Ruger MG9a and the Bering Model VB40. However, keep in mind that AFNET is still unavailable for confirmation of–*]

[So, our own Marine Corps weapons and de-commed flash rifles?]

[*Yes.*]

[Nothing with a GA signature? The grendels aren't even here yet?]

[*Unknowable. But no Alliance weaponry is evident in the sound profile. And standard enemy tactics for assaulting Colonial infrastructure typically involve deployment of cutter drones before shock troops.*]

I gripped the front of the bench with both hands, fingers tightening on the rounded lip. Across from Sterling and me, Private Kurcek peered out the hatch window in the direction of the gunfire as if he wanted to be dropped off for a sample. But the other guy, the one in the command seat, just sat there staring at me with narrowed eyes. He was in his midthirties and wore the unadorned third chevron of an E-5 sergeant. He'd shaved recently and still had the tan line from a beard. His name tag read SGT PORTH. The rifle angled in the ready position across his chest—and therefore pointing just a few inches to the right of my head—was a Bering VB40.

A flash rifle.

I gripped the bench harder, felt my shoulders tighten as I shoved my back against the wall of the SAV, as if its armor plating could shield me from whatever was going on. It dawned on me that these guys were probably not here to rescue us.

Was it possible they weren't really edgers at all, but disguised grendel special operators? I'd heard of grendels using alternatives to the normal symb-collars the Grand Alliance required of its citizens—specially designed hardware that would allow them to move freely among colonials without sacrificing the benefits of integrated wyrms. Fleet had denounced that rumor as fear-mongering, but their denunciation had been a little too loud.

Then again, these guys didn't *act* like a special forces squad. They lacked the precision of real training, instead covering their lack of experience with a swagger I'd seen in real militias all over the edge. Besides, who but reservists would wear black fatigues in this heat, and in broad daylight? Or sport home-sewn "Jungle Cat" unit patches on their left sleeves? Or festoon themselves in a web of ammo straps clipped on backwards?

A line of fencing whisked past. The icons on my overlay placed us outside the camp perimeter, heading towards Seranik City rather than Camp Locke's skyport. We were moving away from potential reinforcements, away from any air cover, away from the most defensible position in the area.

I glanced at Sterling and was surprised to see him crack a grim smile.

—STERLING, A: BE READY TO MOVE ON MY SIGNAL.—

The words flicked across my grid so unexpectedly I flinched in my seat. The base network had been eviscerated by a Strangler class enemy frigate. How was Sterling sending comms messages?

He scratched his chin, eyes locked neutrally on the space next to Sgt. Porth's command seat. "Where are we headed, Sergeant?"

"Someplace safe," Porth said, still staring at me. "You look familiar. What's your name?"

"Dahl," I answered, then remembered Sterling had called me his orderly. I'd have to pretend to be someone else. Not a problem. I'd been telling stories from the first-person perspective of soldiers, marines, and pilots for years. I just hoped this guy wouldn't recognize the face OrbSyn always ran next to my byline. "Corporal, United Colonies Marine Corps. Sorry, sergeant, but I've never seen you before."

"Huh." He rolled his tongue into one cheek and squinted at me sideways.

I looked out the back window, hoping to hide most of my face. If anyone liked the features of Raymin Dahl, it was the part-time warriors of the edge militias. They usually loved my combat action stories, in part because so few of them ever saw any real action, but also because I acknowledged they were right to distrust the bureaucracy of the Senate. Fleet *did* waste human lives. It *did* send soldiers and marines into battles we should have avoided. It *did* squander ships, cargo and weaponry, sacrificing essential resources on the altar of politics.

But I couldn't say that. Not now. Now I had to pretend that I wasn't more on his side than he knew, that I wasn't the one journalist at OrbSyn who still tried to make sure enlisted men mattered to the republic. That I wasn't *the* Raymin Dahl.

Sterling cleared his throat. "How many Alliance ships have you spotted?"

Porth gave a barely perceptible shrug. "Above my pay grade, Captain."

"So who are we running away from?" I asked, pointing in the direction of Camp Locke, now lost behind a canopy of jungle vines. "Those weren't Alliance shock troops in the middle of Camp Locke."

Porth said, "Maybe you should just sit tight and be grateful the cats were here to pull you out of that situation. Whatever it was."

"Your officer's gonna get you killed, Corporal," Sterling said. He was looking at Kurcek, whose head snapped around as if he'd been caught napping in class.

—STERLING, A: DUCK LEFT.—

My heart climbed into my mouth. Sterling's gaze flicked over to me—a second warning.

I had barely started to move when Sterling shoved himself off the bench.

He moved like a cat. One instant he was sitting beside me; the next he had launched himself across the compartment and jabbed Porth in the throat. With his left hand he swung the man's rifle away from me and towards the kid in the back just as the sergeant squeezed the trigger.

Light strobed in a blinding staccato as magnetic rounds pinged across the bulkhead in a sloping line. The line started just to the right of my face and ended in a row of bloody dots across Corporal Kurcek's back.

One of them must have severed the kid's spine: he raised his right hand as if swatting an insect, then tipped forward against the rear door, his faced mashed against the paneling.

"Val?" the guy in the turret called down.

Sterling tried to rip the rifle out of Porth's grasp, but its strap hooked on something. He was still wrestling with the choking sergeant when the guy in the turret crouched down to see what was going on.

"Val?" he said again.

When I saw the kid's body slumping forward, time slowed, as if everything was happening under water.

I dove for the handle of the rear door and shoved against it with all my weight. I imagined those turret guns firing *inside* the compartment and those 50-50 EM rounds turning my body into something like condensed soup.

Impossible, of course. The gun's elevators couldn't be lowered that far. But fear does things to you. Shrinks your mind to a single, brutal focus.

Open the door!

The steel lever was jammed, wedged against something immoveable. I hammered at it with an open palm, bruising the heel of my hand, but it didn't budge.

Faces of war heroes flashed past. Half a dozen interviews with the frontliners who had told me their stories. Men and women who gave me what I asked for instead of what really happened. Now I understood why combat vets didn't want to tell the war story everybody back home wanted to hear: survival wasn't a matter of courage or conviction. It was an accident.

[*Wrong direction. Try pulling the handle up.*] My AI must have seen the adrenaline flooding my system.

Light strobed through the compartment again just as I was heaving on the lever. Then something slammed the whole vehicle sideways and up. The world tipped. I flew backwards and landed on the bulkhead above the bench, Kurcek's body draped across my knees, a horrible scraping sound in my ears like metal dragging across stone.

Then the noise stopped, leaving in its wake a mindless, mechanical wheezing from the turret. The gunner's body hung just above the platform, one boot depressing a rotation pedal, blood streaming from his chest.

Odors assaulted me: human waste and blood and more of that awful repeller fluid. I wondered briefly if it was flammable. On the networks such collisions always ended in an explosion.

The hatch door was hinged on the right side. Now the door lay open against the ground like a short ramp. The SAV had apparently been tossed onto its side like some discarded toy. The opening revealed a narrow street flanked by three- and four-story block buildings. We'd come at least four kilometers: off the base, then through the jungle corridor, and into the outskirts of Seranik.

"Dahl," Sterling said. He pulled himself up to one knee and wrapped the strap of the flash rifle around his forearm. A gash just below the hairline trickled blood between his nose and right eye, but he looked completely composed. Even his shirt still hung in perfectly tucked panels. "Dahl!"

"Sir?"

"You hurt?"

Gunfire popped in the distance, then closer. Some of it seemed to be coming from the other side of the SAV's upturned hull, maybe two hundred meters off.

Sterling was staring at me. Over his shoulder, the turret gunner was slumped in his harness, legs dangling from the platform cage, arms spread forward as if he were trying to fly. I had the strange feeling I'd stepped into one of those dreams where reality is suddenly a different shape and color.

"*Dahl!*"

"Sir?"

"Take the corporal's weapon and spare ammo. We need to get out of here."

I shoved the kid's body off my legs, the expression on his clay mannequin face bringing a wave a guilt. I unclipped his rifle and fished two magazines from his webbing.

"When was the last time you fired a rifle?" Sterling asked.

Behind him, blood from the gunner's chest began to spatter against the side paneling in a steady *drip drip drip.*

Sterling killed them, I thought. *The kid, the sergeant, the turret gunner. Killed all three in a couple of seconds. Maybe the driver and Lieutenant Dogen as well.*

Someone was *still* shooting at us. I could hear the ping of rounds hammering the SAV near the cab.

"Dahl?"

"Sir?"

Sterling shook his head. "Never mind. Turn around."

I turned. With the SAV on its side there wasn't room to stand, so we knelt by the hatch looking out into the shimmering heat.

"We're going out the back door and into that alley on the right. See it?"

My AI sent a map to my grid, forwarded from Sterling, zoomed in on the precise location and expanded into a 3D representation in the lower right corner of my vision.

Grid comms were good. I could do grid-work.

I nodded.

"There's a door on the left. We're going through it and then up the steps to the top floor. High ground. You understand me?"

"Door on the left. Got it."

"I'll be right behind you, Corporal. Go!"

Sterling slapped me on the shoulder, and I lunged out into the morning sunlight.

I cracked my head on the doorframe and stumbled as bits of the road exploded around me. For a moment I thought someone must have gotten that turret cannon working again and was shooting at us, then realized that was stupid.

They *were* shooting at us, but not with a 50-50. If they were using heavy twins, there wouldn't be anything left of either of us.

I looked back as I ran and saw Sterling shooting around the corner of the SAV, suppressive fire, and for a moment the return fire ceased.

Then I was at the mouth of the alley and rounding the corner, looking for the doorway.

—STERLING, A: I'M COMING NOW. PRETEND YOU'RE IN THE
ARMY AND GIVE ME SOME COVER FIRE.—

I went back to the mouth of the alley and peered around, using the corner of the cement-block building for cover. Scanned. Raised my rifle and pulled the trigger.

Nothing happened.

My AI sent a soft reminder: [*Release the safety.*]

I cursed, scanned the edges of the rifle until I found the black button, but by then Sterling was almost in front of me, and the shooting from across the street had started again, so I ducked back behind the safety of the wall without firing a shot.

Sterling stumbled as he lurched into the shadows of the two buildings, but we were out of the line of fire. For the moment, anyway.

I would have liked more darkness, but at least there were no windows in the walls to either side, which meant no place to shoot out of. And there was a nice, friendly door a couple meters off to the left. I checked it, but the door was locked, and made of steel. Maybe Captain Sterling's magic PSYOPS wrist-comms could sync with the building's security and force our entry.

I went back and offered him a hand up. "Almost there, sir."

He wore an expression I'd only ever seen on drunks and drill sergeants, like he was so mad at the world he couldn't think of a revenge big enough to fit it.

The front of his shirt was saturated in blood.

4

CAPTAIN STERLING

I knelt for a closer look at the wound. He'd been shot in the back, the round penetrating between shoulder blade and spine, and exiting through a far more sinister hole in the right pectoral.

I glanced up at the mouth of the alley. Whoever had been shooting at us was bound to be close behind, but if I didn't slow his blood loss, he would never make it to the top floor.

I peeled off my shirt, wadded the body into a ball, and tied it by the arms across the bullet holes. I took his right hand and placed it over the makeshift bandage in front. He groaned a little but didn't resist.

"Get me inside," he said.

"Yes, sir. Sit tight."

I ran over to the door and lifted the rifle. Lowered it again to flip the action lever to full automatic. Sent about thirty rounds into the handle.

Well, I *tried* to. I didn't hit the actual mechanism, but standard flash rounds are jacketed penetrators, and the burst shredded the door in a crescent of torn metal and insulated foam. One kick wrenched it open, the handle still hanging onto the jamb by its lock.

I slung the rifle by its strap over one shoulder and ran back to Sterling. Somehow I hefted him to his feet and through the door, which opened directly into a stairwell. "We still going up?"

Face pale, he nodded.

So we climbed, Sterling leaning against me, each shuddering breath coming with a sound like boiling water, one step at a time: my right, my left, his left, his right. Over and over with his blood squeezing out in spurts, soaking the bandage, warm against my forearm.

The climb seemed to take forever, and when we hit the third floor his knees gave out, and we spilled to the carpet together.

"We aren't going to make it to the top," I said. "I'll have to find you a nice room on the third floor. Something with beer in the fridge."

He gave me a look halfway between humor and disbelief but nodded his assent anyway.

I cracked open the access door and stared down a hallway of stained government carpeting, flanked by office doors with empty nameplates. Like much of Seranik City, this probably belonged to a military contractor. But the air was cooler here, which meant air conditioning. Someone was still using the building somewhere, even if the place looked deserted.

I stepped into the hall and opened the first door on the left. Inside, everything had been removed except for three boxy gray desks and a row of visitor seating. A kitchenette ran the length of one wall, and on the far side were windows with a view of the street.

I went back to the stairs, grabbed Sterling by his left arm, and dragged him cursing through the hallway and into the office. Peering under the bandage, I sent a query to my AI. The hole in his chest looked worse now, and I was running out of ideas.

The kitchenette was still stocked, so I ripped a fistful of recycled towels from the dispenser and was about to stuff them under the bandage when my AI stopped me.

[*No*,] it said. [*Use plastic.*]

I went back, flipped open several drawers until I found a roll of cooking wrap. It took me several seconds to cut away his uniform with my pocket knife, and meanwhile blood still pushed from the wound.

Sterling cursed as I wound the roll diagonally across his chest, from the top of the right shoulder under the left arm and back around. Tight. Each layer adding to the pressure as the blood seeped under the clear plastic and spread to the edges.

After six or seven passes Sterling said, "Check the window."

I rose and went over for a look, peering around the edge of the corner in the direction we'd come. Half a block away the SAV lay beached on its left side. From this position it was obvious what had happened. A wheeled APV—gunless and less than half the size of the Snapper but much faster—had rammed the top-heavy armored sled as it passed an alley across the street. Around both vehicles bodies were sprawled. Two wore black fatigues, the other three blood-spattered marine utilities. I wondered if any of them knew who Sterling was.

"Looks like the base garrison sent a Sherpa after us. Rammed the SAV and got caught in the firefight. I count five dead and don't see any movement in the—"

Flashes lit up a window below us and off to the right. I heard a soft *tink tink* and the sound of cracking glass.

"Get *down*, you idiot!" Sterling called.

I dropped below the level of the window and glanced over at him. "Sir, what's going on?"

He was lying on his back now, one leg hooked to the side, the other knee angled up. "Someone wants to stop this deal. Try to keep the edge."

"Someone at Fleet? In the Senate?" Even to me this sounded unlikely—and over the years I'd invented a lot of weird theories to cover up for missing information.

Sterling flapped his left hand dismissively. "Not a conspiracy. Alliance probably just leaked the meeting."

"They told the *truth*?"

"Truth can be a great PSYOP, Corporal. People here don't want to be sacrificed. But since they can't take out a grendel warship . . . probably want to use us for propaganda." He shook his head weakly and gave a grim smile. "You know . . . *your* job."

No wonder he hadn't wanted them to know who I was. Still, the facts felt like a betrayal. Which was ironic, because betrayal was what we were here to do.

My position as a reporter had always shielded me against the harsher realities of military life. It was one of the unwritten rules. One of the few benefits of the job.

Worse, I wasn't just any reporter. I wasn't some schlub from Holikot tagging along to take notes on a backroom deal. I was Raymin Dahl, feature writer for Orbits News. The edge militia were supposed to love me—especially on New Witlund. I was on their side.

We sat in silence just long enough for the quiet to become noticeable. Sterling's eyes took on a distant, tired quality that terrified me. He certainly hadn't told me everything he knew, but I had no delusions about his last point. If he died, there would be no reason for the militia to let me live.

"Sir," I said. "We need to get out of here."

He seemed to recover a little. Drew a breath. Shook his head. "Stay here. MADAR team is inbound." His voice trailed into a hacking cough, bloody spittle forming at his lips.

"How do you know?"

He held up his wrist-comms. "Perks of the job. Barricade that door."

"Against our own guys?"

He looked weary, as if he were surrendering to the idea of explaining the alphabet to a small child. "Against the militia. Cavalry is still nine minutes out."

Nine minutes. It felt like nine years. A death sentence.

I crawled over to the closest desk and shoved it across the carpet to the door, then did the same with the middle desk. Such resistance would only slow them down, so the last desk I tipped over as a protective shield between us and the door. When I was finished I said, "Remember the Alamo. Oorah."

He made a noise that was either a laugh or a snort of derision, but was cut short by another cough. "Everyone died at the Alamo. Can you actually use that thing?"

"Hadn't fired a weapon since boot." I glanced down at the rifle I'd taken from PFC Kurcek. "Till I took out that door downstairs."

"You cheat your quals too?"

My weapon qualifications. Every soldier has to pass an exam on the firing range in order to graduate, regardless of destination assignment. Even journalists. "No comment, sir."

"All right. Can you make them uncomfortable without blowing my head off?"

"Probably one or the other," I said, and raised the barrel over the edge of the desk just as the latch turned and the door shuddered against my makeshift barricade.

"Fire your weapon, Corporal."

I swallowed something hard and dry in my throat, finger hovering in front of the trigger. There were people on the other side of that door. Kids, probably. Young men or women who had never been off New Witlund and were just trying to save their loved ones from occupation. Or maybe it wasn't enemy soldiers at all. What if there were civilians in the space below who had heard the noise in an otherwise empty building and come up to—

—STERLING, A: FIRE YOUR WEAPON!—

I squeezed the trigger.

The rifle mashed into my shoulder, spitting rounds over the desks and into the upper half of the door, the wall above it, the ceiling above that. The weapon was still set to automatic, and that burst probably unleashed half the magazine. Ninety, maybe a hundred rounds.

Dust drifted down from the mangled ceiling. The corridor fell eerily silent.

Sterling stared at me, a look that meant he knew something I hadn't yet realized. Something I'd figure out in an hour or two. "Welcome to the war, son."

"Now what?" I asked.

He nodded as if I had passed some sort of test. "Now—you finish the mission."

His words might as well have been in another language. I had no idea what he was saying. "Sir?"

But the effort to talk was too much now. A message flashed on my comms:

—STERLING, A: CAPTAIN STERLING *HAS* TO BE AT THOSE
TALKS. YOU UNDERSTAND? YOU'LL GO IN MY PLACE.—

I studied his face for what seemed a long time, hoping to read something there besides the reality. I didn't find it. "Captain, that's insane. I can't go as you. I have no training, no credentials, no—"

> —STERLING, A: I'M OUT OF TIME, CORPORAL. TAKE MY COMMS. PUT IT ON. TELL THEM YOUR NAME IS CAPTAIN ANSELL STERLING.—

With great effort he moved his right hand to the inside of his left wrist, to the base of his comms. His face was a mask of pain, then relaxed as the bracelet split and fell into his lap, now a hinged cuff.

"Sir, they'll never believe—"

"They're marines." His voice was strangled in fluid. "They'll follow orders."

I shook my head, still in disbelief. He was asking me to impersonate an officer. As if I could somehow channel my father's voice and mannerisms and certainty. As if I could act like I really believed in the rightness of every Fleet decision. As if I could pretend I even wanted to. "It won't work."

"No one here knows," he gasped, "what I look like. Even . . . grendels."

"They'll court-martial me."

He nodded slowly. "Great . . . story."

A great story. A *real* story, free of editorial intervention and feel-good propaganda.

And wasn't this what I'd always wanted? What I'd been complaining about for years to Major Weston and any other reporter who'd listen? A chance to tell a real war story as an eyewitness, with no censors looking over my shoulder?

Or had that just been the lie I told myself to justify writing dissident features at OrbSyn? The compromise that made space for my dignity?

Now that I'd seen what war was like—Kurcek, Porth, Sterling—was the truth really what I wanted to write about?

I tried to swallow again, but my throat had filled with sand. I nudged my comms to begin recording and said, "Is that an order, sir? You're ordering me to impersonate you and make this deal with the Alliance emissary?"

"It's an order," Sterling said, each word a struggle. As if he understood my need. "Go . . . save . . . six . . . hundred . . . million . . . lives."

Even if it hadn't been a direct order, what should I have done? Wait till the special forces team arrived and tell them the truth? *Sorry about all the trouble, but the guy you were supposed to rescue is dead. I got him killed in a firefight. And the Grand Alliance is about to bring down hell on a base you never should have been sent to because the secret meeting we were supposed to attend got canceled by a bunch of local yahoos. Sorry, boys. Can you escort me to the nearest evac ship?*

"I'm going to write it my way," I said. "I'm going to tell all of it."

"However . . . you . . . want," he breathed.

Maybe he knew I was recording our conversation on my own comms, and maybe not. Maybe he just didn't care.

Now at least I had something to fall back on in case they court-martialed me, even if such evidence was flimsy.

Voices called in the street, a distant sound, and without any gunfire. I crawled to the window and peered over the sill. Men in jungle fatigues worked in a relay down the street from the direction of the base. "They're here," I said. "How do we tell them where we are?"

When he didn't answer I said, "Sir? The cavalry's here. What do you want me to do?"

I crawled back to him. His face was gray, his eyes fixed on the ceiling.

The emptiness in the pit of my stomach widened.

His comms. That's how they would know. I had to put it on.

But not yet.

I flipped the catch on my own bracelet, felt the tingle along the inside of my wrist as it disconnected from my nerve endings. Couldn't wear two comms. I'd have to leave it behind.

The hollow feeling expanded into a revelation. Shirtless and disconnected, the familiar nearness of my own AI suddenly gone, I felt the weight of my absolute aloneness pressing me into the carpet.

Everyone who had died today had given their lives for something they believed in. Those militia pretenders in the SAV. Their comrades in the hallway. The marines who had come to our rescue with no heavy weaponry or protective armor.

Captain Sterling.

He'd died not knowing whether something good would come of his sacrifice or not. He'd put his hopes in me because there was no one else. He wasn't going to live to see how the story ended.

Somehow, that thought seemed worse than the prospect of death. Everyone dies. But don't we all expect to see how the story ends anyway?

I removed his insignia and badges from what remained of his shirt. I'd cut it into bloody strips trying to get it off him, so now I wadded the strips into a ball and stowed them in the cabinet under the sink.

A forensic team would have no problems figuring out what took place here, but by the time that happened—if it ever did—I'd be dead or admitting the truth publicly. Either way it wouldn't matter.

I knelt next to Sterling's body and snapped my comms onto his wrist. The surface of the unit began flashing a red—NO HEARTBEAT—warning, which I deactivated.

I'd just created a new victim. Cpl. Raymin Dahl, Kanzin Reserve Infantry, OrbSyn press corps: KIA on New Witlund.

Voices erupted in the stairwell, followed by a muffled curse, then silence.

I took a deep breath and lifted Sterling's comms to my left wrist. Snapped it on. Felt the tingle of activation.

—SYSTEM RESET. ANALYZING . . .—

Sterling's grid appeared on my vision, remarkably uncluttered by the normal tapestry of a military comms. There were no biological status indicators, no system tics, no reassuring icons to select in case I needed network access or satellite directions. Instead, a single folder icon, labeled "Operation Grendel," blinked in my upper right vision.

Below that were three small notification panels marked with my name and numbered.

Practically everyone in Fleet used the standard comms reminder app the same way. On reset, or in the morning with a wake-up alarm, you could have your AI message you about things you didn't want to forget. It was also an effortless way to encode thought-to-text ideas and bursts of inspiration.

The first one was already selected, its contents displaying in a visual text window.

> 1. Tell them what they want to hear. Give them a story.

I'd read that before somewhere. But was it meant for me as instruction? And who did "them" refer to? The marines, presumably, but Sterling might have meant the Alliance emissary. Maybe he meant both.

I'd have to solve that riddle later. I flicked the second box open.

> 2. Admit something secret or shameful.

In the corridor something moved, but I wasn't worried. On my grid the newcomers were marked MADAR. The rescue team was here.

Now, suddenly, I realized that I knew what the acronym stood for: Marine Autonomous Direct Action and Recon. I had not known that fact before putting on Sterling's comms, and I can't explain *how* I knew afterwards. I didn't have the sensation of learning anything. I just knew what MADAR meant and that the four people who had just come into the building, three males and one female, were here to take me back to the base. The knowledge had come the same instant I saw the MADAR icons.

No wonder Sterling's AI grid was so spartan. It could afford to be. If a sled's software is smart enough, it doesn't need a steering wheel. It doesn't even need a driver.

I opened the last message.

> 3. Your father was wrong.
> You're a PSYOPS officer now.
> Everything you need to know is on this comms.
> Make it happen.

I stared at the door to the hallway for what seemed a long time. Only when the system flashed its ready signal did I snap back to the moment.

> —ANALYSIS COMPLETE. NEW USER DETECTED. INITIATING
> WELCOME PROTOCOL.—

A wave of sudden relief and unexpected otherness.

This AI was no butler standing stiffly in the anteroom of my mind, mutely awaiting my instructions.

She was a warm caress, a smile, a kiss on the lips that meant *welcome home.*

She was a woman.

[*Hello, Ansell.*] Her voice was soft butter, as tangible as any audible sound, and dripping with irony. She knew who I was, and knew that I knew. She'd been expecting me. We were going to play a game. It would be *such* fun! [*Shall we introduce you to our marines?*]

5

INVASION

"Captain Sterling!" a voice in the corridor called.

"In here," I said.

"Hold your fire."

A location map appeared on my grid, the names and ranks of the marines in the hall indicated beneath their icons.

[They restore the link to AFNET?]

[*No,*] my new AI said. [*I have a proximity interface. Do you like it?*] She might have been asking me about a new dress.

I didn't answer. I could feel her lurking there in the background of my mind, gathering information, trying to piece together who I was and how to best interact with me. Part of the PSYOPS welcome protocol, I guessed. But it was a protocol I'd never experienced and wasn't sure I liked. As a Fleet AI, she wouldn't be able to see any thought I didn't deliberately send her, nor could she access my natural bio-memories. But she could observe my biotics and trace the activity on my grid. Who knew what else she could do, what else she might know? The PSYOPS boys were always pushing the limits of autonomy. Anyway, we were starting this partnership from scratch, with almost no time to get used to each other.

I filed her response and took a guess at the voice from the hall. "That you, Sergeant Major?"

"In the flesh, sir. Coming through hands first."

The door inched open, pushing the barricade with it, and Sergeant Major Glen Raeburn slid through with open palms. He wore UCMC jungle fatigues and carried an honest-to-God Ruger MG9c field carbine. His face was that of a unit leader, prematurely aged, tanned to the texture of buffalo hide, and sporting two days' worth of graying facial hair. It was a face that had seen too much and couldn't stop seeing it.

I lowered my rifle.

"You hurt?" he asked.

I shook my head. Sterling's body would be hidden from Raeburn's view, so I pointed and started to say, *Captain Sterling*. But he wasn't Sterling. Not now. And since I couldn't bring myself to call the body by the name *Raymin Dahl*, I said, "He doesn't have a pulse."

Raeburn came around to look as three other marines slipped into the room. They wore the same mottled green and gray fatigues Raeburn wore but seemed to be carrying heavier gear.

"Laclos, see what you can do."

She wore a medic's badge above her MADAR unit patch, which featured a snarling rottweiler and the words "Mad Dogs." Skinny, midtwenties, her blonde hair pulled into a short ponytail, Master Sergeant Laclos seemed unexpectedly cheerful, as if determined to find the universe as accommodating as possible. She touched my old comms on Sterling's wrist and pressed two fingers against his neck. "Corporal Dahl?" She asked, glancing up at me.

The question startled me. Then I realized she was asking about the body. I nodded. "Raymin Dahl, OrbSyn reporter."

"Sorry, sir. He's gone. Did you know him?"

"Just met."

Laclos pulled a bag from her thigh pocket and unfolded it. "Hopper. Pajari."

SFC Hopper turned out to be a Sergeant First Class, with skin as dark as his uniform and eyes hidden behind a set of close-fitting black sunglasses. "He the guy who wrote all those stories from the edge?"

"Feature, writer," I said, the words strange in my ears. "Yeah. That's him."

Hopper sucked air through his teeth. "Good writer. Too bad he wasn't on our side."

"Stow it, Hop," Raeburn said. "Man's dead."

I felt my face flush. Raymin Dahl may have been a hero to the edge militias, but that reputation clearly had limits.

Staff Sergeant Pajari, tall and thin and carrying a mean-looking Barrett RMG sniper rifle, squinted at Sterling's corpse. His expression was inscrutable, but the way he slipped the plastic around Sterling's head told me he'd done this before.

Together Laclos and Hopper tucked the rest of Sterling's body inside the bag and sealed it.

New icons appeared on my overlay, and I went to the window to verify what I was seeing. Half a dozen Sherpas were rolling onto the street below. Camp Locke's garrison was finally flexing its muscle.

I queried the AI for options under the device's proximity sensors, and a list of possibilities appeared, including thermals. Sure enough, I could see the heat signatures of everything out to about 200 meters, like a satellite map with fuzzy edges. But the vibrant colors were distracting and hard to see through, so I nudged it off my grid.

Now that Sterling's body—that is, *Dahl's* body—was stowed and tagged for the cleanup crew, Raeburn said, "Colonel Vermier wants to see you ASAP, Captain."

I followed Raeburn to the hall, hesitating at the doorway. I didn't want to see the people I'd killed, didn't want to see what those hundred rounds from Kurcek's flash rifle had done to them. But there was no other way out. So I stepped into the hallway and breathed a sigh of relief. Someone had dragged the bodies away, leaving behind only the blood spatters on the carpet and wall.

Once on the street I climbed into the back of a Sherpa with the MADAR team. The rear of the vehicle was open to the heat, the air thick with moisture and the buzz of insects. No one spoke, as if sensing that I needed to process what I had just been through.

They had no idea what I was facing, the weight of it. So I stared out the open tailgate as the tropical greens and ochres of the jungle corridor rumbled past, and I tried to figure out what Sterling's last instructions might actually look like. How was I supposed to "make it happen?" Did I even *want* to? Even if I succeeded—

[*I'm here for you,*] my AI said. [*I really can help.*]

[Thanks.]

[*Normally we'd spend a week together, learning each other's quirks and habits, but there isn't time for that. We'll have to do this on the fly, especially since you will have to pass yourself off as a PSYOPS captain to Camp Locke's commanding officer.*]

She was right. I should have been reading the mission file. But I didn't want to know what I was facing. If I opened that mission file, would I be able to turn back? To decline the mission and own up to what I'd done? Besides, we were already turning into the main gate. Outside, marines were hauling back temporary barricades so the Sherpa could pass through. There wasn't time to do any reading. If I opened the "Operation Grendel" file, it would have to be later. [Where do we start?]

[*Give me a name. Something meaningful to you. Someone you trust.*]

[A name? Seriously?]

[*Naming is an act of ownership. An act of mastery. Giving me a name will signal your subconscious mind about our relationship. You will need to trust me on a deep level, or this mission will fail.*]

Sterling had been leading me, *manipulating* me, ever since this assignment showed up on my comms back on Holikot. I'd had no choice about anything, including whether or not to write the original fake story about MADAR teams. And how much choice did I have about impersonating an officer? If I survived this nightmare, chances were I'd be spending time in a core penitentiary.

And now the AI on Sterling's comms was giving me the psych equivalent of a bedside enema. I'd been bullied enough by Fleet, by military operations, by rank. I wasn't about to be bullied by my own comms! Besides, I wouldn't be wearing the thing long enough to become pals with its digital keeper. She didn't *need* a name. [Then I guess this mission will fail.]

[*Captain—*]

[Okay,] I cut her off. [Your name is AI. Welcome to the team.]

She backed off, but I could still feel her there sulking as we pulled up to the admin building next to the skyport.

When Raeburn jumped down to let me out I stood there on the blistering asphalt, glancing back and forth between him and his team. My undershirt and arms were smeared with dried blood, or I would have tried to shake his hand.

"Thanks," I said and meant it.

Raeburn shrugged. "Don't mention it."

He meant it too.

Inside, an orderly ushered me to the third floor, through a command center staffed with noncoms glued to their screens, and into an office that smelled like coffee and furniture cleaner.

"Captain Sterling." The colonel turned from a row of windows overlooking the tarmac. She was a short woman with straight black hair pulled into a tight knot above the collar. Her green utilities looked well-worn, though the sleeves were neatly pressed and the fabric unspotted. She carried herself with the taut readiness of a besieged officer—someone who had clawed her way to a summit only to discover she was surrounded by the enemy. Her nametag read VERMIER.

Colonel Vermier's eyes took in my blood-stained clothing and skin in a glance. She had told Raeburn to bring me in ASAP and didn't seem surprised by my appearance. "Have a seat."

"Thank you, Colonel."

"You all right?"

"Five by five."

"Good." She sat in the oversized chair across from me. "I've read your mission brief. How do you want to proceed?"

"Colonel?"

"Corporal Dahl was a critical piece of your operation." Her voice carried the lilting accent of a local New Witlunder, suggesting she'd either been born in-system or had spent a good deal of time here.

"You obviously can't replace him at the last minute. So where do you go from here?"

"Dahl was important but not critical," I said, surprised by how easily I had put on ruthlessness. It was a bit like slipping into an old coat. "I'll write the story myself. OrbSyn will run it under his byline. Someone at PSYOPS will come up with an explanation for his death. Give him a hero's burial. And no one will know the difference."

"Really?" She looked surprised. "You think you can replicate his style? His, what do you call it, *rapport* with the militias?"

"There's only one Raymin Dahl," I said. "But I've read everything he ever wrote, and I did major in journalism before I enlisted." Both things were undeniably true. "More importantly, in this case, the story itself is so explosive I don't think many people will be paying attention to how it's written. No one's going to be looking for a strong literary voice, if that's what you're worried about. All they'll want is a way forward."

Colonel Vermier leaned back in her chair and glanced out the window at the shimmering heat coming off the tarmac. "The Alliance frigate that shut down our link to AFNET is no longer in orbit. She put down in the jungle west of Seranik, then set up a defensive perimeter. So far their shock troops and drones have stayed within a four-klick radius. I'm wondering why."

"Isn't it obvious?" I asked. "The Alliance government still wants the peace talks to happen."

She arced one brow. "They cut our pipeline, Captain. We not only can't talk to Command and Control, we can't talk to each other except by unsecured satcom."

"Maybe this is the enemy's way of preventing Fleet from changing its mind. What better way to ensure the meeting take place than to remove any chance of a cancellation?"

"And the attack from the New Witlund militia?" she asked, drumming her fingers on the edge of her desk. "That's just a coincidence?"

I shook my head. Strained to think of what Sterling might say and how he'd say it. But when I spoke, the voice I heard belonged to my father. "That's an intelligence leak. Probably originated with the

Alliance, but who knows? The point is that someone found out we're leaving the locals to fend for themselves, and they didn't like it. I can't say that I blame them."

She stared at me for what seemed a long time, then touched the keypad on her desk. The window monitors blinked away the sunlight and began streaming recorded images and shifting ID tags. "This morning just after that frigate cut our link off-world, a grendel invasion fleet jumped in-system and began an assault of Quelon. Our command subnet has better shielding than the base nodes, so we had a downlink from our host planet for almost thirty seconds after that *Strangler* appeared."

Eleven heavy cruisers, twenty destroyers, and fifteen carriers—the big motherships that disgorge grendel invasion troops like dandelion seeds on the wind—appeared above the blue horizon of Quelon. A Grand Alliance armada so large it could only be the main body of their third fleet.

On the window monitors, Colonial defensive batteries opened up from orbiting satellite platforms and ground positions. Guided missiles streaked along the screens on digital threads; rail guns spat armor-piercing rounds that were invisible even to the subnet's sensors; a handful of AF-11 Harpy fighters dotted the screen for a few seconds and were lost in the explosion of data.

The big ships were easier to track. Two grendel cruisers took massive nuclear hits, and one of the carriers exploded just as its launch tubes opened.

The wall of monitors went black. The windows cleared, and New Witlund's rust-and-emerald horizon fogged back to clarity.

Thirty seconds of data. That's what Vermier was operating on. And no way to know what was happening on Quelon now—whether the battle still raged or not.

"That doesn't look like peace to me," she said.

Frankly, I agreed with her. But I wasn't about to sacrifice the story I had for the one I didn't. Of course, even the story I had depended on me impersonating Sterling. And was I really going to do that? Was I willing to pay the price they would exact from me when the truth got out?

I said, "Yet they've only landed one ship here on New Witlund. A frigate, not even a destroyer. They have to know we can't hold this moon against any serious invasion force. If they didn't want this meeting, Camp Locke would be crawling with shock troops by now."

She pursed her lips, eyes narrowed. At last she said, "I'm giving you seventy-two hours because Fleet"—she stabbed the surface of her desk with two stubby fingers—"*Fleet* apparently thinks your mission is more important than all the men and women living on my base. But know this: I'm also bringing a hammerhead along with your security team."

The hammerhead surface-to-air missile was a shoulder-launched rocket designed to turn pretty much anything smaller than a warehouse into a cauldron of liquid metal and bubbling flesh. "You want us to take a weapon of war to a peace treaty?"

"That *Strangler* is vulnerable as long as it's grounded. If your meeting goes sideways, we're going to blow their warship to hell. Are we clear?"

I swallowed back the sort of sarcastic remark I might have made to Major Weston back on Holikot. "Yes, ma'am."

"Good. Then I'll see you in the morning."

"In the morning?"

"I'm coming with you, captain."

The words hung in the air between us. I was certain the real Sterling would have bristled at the sudden upending of a carefully planned mission by a senior officer acting on her own discretion. As New Witlund's planetary station chief, Vermier had considerable flexibility over everything that happened within her jurisdiction. But interfering with a high-priority operation, even under the existing circumstances, could easily ruin her career. Why then was she taking the risk? "Is that . . . necessary?"

She seemed to look through me, as if I still wore the double chevrons of a reserve corporal, or a press pass etched with OrbSyn's logo. "You saw what's happening on Quelon, Captain. I'm not going to sit here watching from the sidelines."

It occurred to me that Vermier was itching for some excuse to countermand our mission orders and take control of it herself, though

I had no idea why. I only hoped she didn't poke around too deeply into Sterling's personnel file. What if she found something to give me away?

I decided to let it ride and screwed on the stiff, you're-in-charge expression every recruit learns in boot camp. "Very good, Colonel."

"Close the door on your way out."

I stood, gave my best impersonation of a crisp marine salute, and went to the door. When I pulled it closed the windows were black again, and Vermier was staring intently at the recorded invasion.

In the lobby Laclos met me by the door. "I have a sled in the lot, sir. I assume you want to head back to your hotel?"

If they'd sent a combat operator to shuttle me across the base, they must think there was still some element of danger from the locals. "You my new shadow, Master Sergeant?"

"Tops didn't want you getting lost again, sir."

"Uh-huh. Well, I suspect that comment ought to offend me, but right now I'm too tired to carry a grudge. You take me back to my hotel room, and I'll pretend I didn't hear it."

A hint of a smile touched the corners of her eyes. "No problem, sir."

We found the sled and drove the few blocks to the hotel, then Laclos followed me all the way up the elevator to the door of my room. It opened for my new comms, and she walked through to make sure there were no surprises. "I'll be outside if you need anything, Captain."

I sighed, trying to hide my frustration. What I *needed* was to be left fully and completely alone. Laclos standing outside my room meant I couldn't relax. I'd have to stay in character every moment.

Worse, I'd have no opportunity to change my mind about this story—to slip off Sterling's comms and try to retrieve my old identity from a body bag somewhere in the base morgue. Yes, that idea had occurred to me more than once.

"Master Sergeant," I said, "I'm not going anywhere. The base is on lockdown. Why don't you come back for me in the morning at oh-four-thirty? You can drive me to the rendezvous."

"Sorry, sir," Laclos said. "If I leave my post, tops'll have my head on a lunch tray. Get some rest."

I hadn't really expected it to work. "Okay, doc."

After she let herself out I dialed up a hot shower. Peeled off my blood-stained clothes and stepped into the scalding water as if to scour off a layer of skin.

For a long time I stood there trying to assemble the pieces of the day, fitting what little I knew against the hard edges of my predicament.

Eventually I closed my eyes and pulled up my new grid. Sterling's mission file and notifications burned stark white against the muddy darkness of my eyelids. I nudged open the "Operation Grendel" folder, which expanded to a longer list.

> > 1. CLASSIFIED LEVEL RED: Operation Grendel [text]
> > 2. UCRI-K PERSONAL DATA: Raymin Dahl 4277962 [restricted]
> > 3. UCF PERSONAL DATA: David Dahl 3995918 [restricted]
> > 4. Corporal Dahl's published articles and feature stories [text]
> > 5. Preliminary Interview with Dahl - New Witlund [video]

The first file was the important one; two through four were obviously background research, and I had no desire to relive the morning's events from a different perspective.

I read through the classified mission instructions three times under the purifying stream of hot water. Sterling's assignment was ridiculously simple. Tomorrow morning I and the MADAR team (plus Vermier, I reminded myself) would hike through tropical jungle to a compound outside Seranik City. After a ninety-minute introduction ceremony, I'd try to negotiate a galaxy-wide ceasefire of *at least* ten years. In exchange, I would offer *up to* all five edge colonies. Preferably fewer. If the conditions were met I—that is, Sterling—was authorized to sign an intent letter on behalf of the President of the UC.

The skin on my arms was raw now from scrubbing, the dried blood finally having washed down the drain, but I didn't want the shower to end. So I opened the next document, Raymin Dahl's personnel file, and scanned its contents. Most of it I had seen before, or knew from memory, but there were two confidential assessments in the file that I didn't know existed. They seemed to be psych evals composited from interactions with various AIs issued over the past few years.

CORPORAL DAHL'S FATHER, COMMANDER DAVID DAHL, UCF, IS A DECORATED VETERAN WHOSE PERSONAL LIFE HAS BEEN TROUBLED SINCE HIS WIFE OF SEVEN YEARS, INONA RIUS-DAHL, DEFECTED IN THE FOURTH YEAR OF THE WAR. THE RELATIONSHIP BETWEEN FATHER AND SON HAS BEEN STRAINED EVER SINCE.

COMPLICATING THIS IS THE FACT CORPORAL DAHL CHOSE NOT TO FOLLOW IN HIS FATHER'S FOOTSTEPS AS A FLEET OFFICER, INSTEAD ENLISTING IN THE KANZIN RESERVE INFANTRY. A SIMPLE BUT USEFUL EVALUATION OF THIS SOLDIER IS THAT HE STRUGGLES WITH LATENT FEELINGS OF ABANDONMENT THAT ARE CURRENTLY EXPRESSING THEMSELVES IN HIS WORK AS AN ORBSYN JOURNALIST.

DAHL'S RELATIONSHIP WITH HOLIKOT RESIDENT IVY WEBER PROBABLY ERODED DUE TO THE SAME EMOTIONAL UNDERCURRENTS . . .

The report went on, but I couldn't stomach any more of it, so I switched to the personnel file for Commander David Dahl, UCF war hero and officially great guy.

A quick scan revealed that Fleet had known about his alcohol problem going all the way back to the week Inona evac'd to a better world. Of course, Fleet didn't bother to *do* anything about it. The report didn't admit this explicitly, but the reality was written squarely between the lines. David Dahl's friends had covered for him. Fleet had covered for him. The OrbSyn press corps had covered for him. I'd probably even covered for him.

I closed the file when I got to his psych eval. The last thing I needed was a dose of insight into a war hero's "humanity." I'd seen enough of that growing up.

The auto-timer dinged and the shower spat a dribble of cold water across my shoulders like some parting gift. I stalked to the closet and found Captain Sterling's immaculate fatigues hanging there as if in expectation of my arrival. They were oversized, but not by much. His uniform had been tailored for someone with more muscle.

For a moment I stood there staring at the uniform, wondering if I really owed anything to the man it was made for. He was dead now, or would be as soon as the story went live. He had dragged me into this predicament at every stage, and now he was dragging along everyone else.

Maybe I owe it to the edge, I thought. *To the militia groups at least, if not to the citizens.* Most of them had no idea how their lives were about to be upended by a political scheme cooked up lightyears away. The least I could do was give them the truth.

But who was I kidding? The "truth" changed sides as quickly as the headlines on OrbSyn's breaking feed. That wasn't why I was drawn to the uniform. Not really. No, I was going to put it on and tell the story because that's what I did. It was all I knew how to do, and this was the most important, most exhilarating assignment I'd ever be given. I would never get another chance like this. A chance to make a difference. A chance to make a mark.

The only real difficulty I had in donning Sterling's clothing was the act of pinning my new hardware to my collar. I kept seeing a distorted face and wide-open eyes. Heard the rasping breath. Whenever I got the captain's bars next to the fabric, my hands shook, as if refusing to be part of the lie. Then I saw his words in my head—*FIRE YOUR WEAPON!*—and the shaking stopped.

The hotel room had a small desk by the window overlooking the northwest corner of the skyport tarmac. Outside, heat still shimmered off the pavement.

It was late afternoon. Time to record everything that had happened today. If I was going to write this story, I would have to do it piecemeal as it unfolded. But I had time enough for the first feature. Especially since I knew I wouldn't be able to sleep. The face of PFC Kurcek kept popping up in my mind, the weight of his body rolling off my legs as I pushed. Then the guy in the turret with the chest wound. What had his name been?

I couldn't recall. And I had no first-person recordings to rely on, so I'd have to work from memory.

The main question I had was one of perspective. I was using

Sterling's comms, Sterling's access, Sterling's history. But I had told Vermier that OrbSyn would run the story under Dahl's name.

Was that what I really wanted? For readers to see the real journalist behind their favorite war stories? Did I want that comfortable, familiar mask ripped off?

Yes. That wasn't just what I wanted. It was what I *needed*. I needed the name "Raymin Dahl" in the byline. And it *was* my story, after all, even if someone else had dreamed it up. I was the one doing the work, the one finishing the mission. Besides, I had a knack for first-person features, for telling people the story they wanted to hear. I'd been doing it for years.

Raymin Dahl, then. My great war story would be told by Corporal Raymin Dahl, OrbSyn word-pounder and darling of the edge.

Sergeant something. The guy Sterling had punched in the throat. He'd had a name too. Maybe it would come to me as I wrote.

I scooted the chair up to the desk and conjured a keyboard against its smooth surface. Old-school, virtual keys always provided a satisfying feedback loop that helped me to think. Thought-to-text was more efficient but often resulted in a jerky, unreadably stream-of-consciousness flavor neither I nor my editor could stand.

But where to start?

Sterling's first memo had said: *Tell them what they want to hear. Give them a story.*

Advice even Major Weston would have agreed with. But I was planning something deeper. Something to set the edge colonies on fire.

I was going to tell the truth.

All right then, a confession.

> *Like every journalist, I lie for a living.*
> *In this case, I had to become someone else in order*
> *to get the story. I'm not who I say I am.*
> *My name isn't Ansell Sterling, and I'm not a captain.*
> *I'm not even a marine.*

The words burned in the text window of my grid, and I could feel the AI peering over my shoulder as I wrote, staring at my opening in fascination.

It felt good, to be honest. Having an audience of one.

One fan, not a critic, not an editor, just a reader eager to hear the story.

The sun set as I worked. Room service brought me something unmemorable—a sandwich perhaps—and Laclos knocked to tell me Hopper was relieving her at the door. I don't recall my reply.

Finally, when I'd gotten most of it down, I stopped typing and stared out the window at the night sky. Quelon still hung in a blue-and-white crescent above the jagged black horizon. Even the Grand Alliance couldn't change the natural courses of planets and moons. Nevertheless, I wondered which side claimed the system now. There would be no way to find out until our link to AFNET was restored.

"Raymin," Ivy Weber's voice said from behind me.

I turned, and there she was. Not the real Ivy, of course, but a digital projection behind my grid—a translucent ghost image not unlike the ones cast by a holo-screen.

The work of Sterling's comms. *My* comms.

My AI.

I understood at once what had happened: reading my work, she'd found a name for herself. Not a name I would have picked, nor one I could have expected. Yet it fit somehow. That presence in the back of my mind *was* Ivy.

Someone I could trust.

I wondered how she knew and resented the fact she'd unraveled that part of me so quickly when I'd hidden it from myself so long.

She stood in a pool of light from the bathroom, her arms crossed, her lips pressed tightly together. I had hurt her, and she wanted me to know about it. She had no interest in hiding her emotions.

Rage and gratitude washed over me simultaneously. [Ivy!] I snarled.

But already my resolve was slipping away, and a moment later I called her name again in the darkness, this time out loud. "Ivy?"

Her green eyes flashed in the starlight, then moistened. "You never even said goodbye."

PART TWO

WHY IT HAD TO BE DONE

BY CPL RAYMIN DAHL

EMBEDDED WITH MADAR TEAM TWO

6

INSERTION

The first time I stepped into Orbits News Syndicate's Holikot office with my brand-new duty assignment pinging from my wrist-comms Major Weston made me wait in the reception area for two and a half hours. When he finally appeared and waved me over to the elevator I mistook him for a clerk.

Weston was short and skinny, the sort of build they'd have jammed into a ball turret or a mini-submarine hundreds of years ago. I towered over him, and I'm not particularly tall. Instead of a service uniform, he wore khakis and a short-sleeved T-shirt emblazoned with the UCMC logo. Later I would discover he almost never wore his uniform around the OrbSyn office.

"You the new guy?" he asked, as if he couldn't be bothered with learning my name and rank.

"Yes, sir."

He jabbed the elevator pad with one stubby thumb. "Save the 'sir' crap for when you're irritated. It'll keep things clear between us. Call me Charles or Major or Editor."

The elevator doors dinged open, and I followed him on. I'd been warned about his unique leadership style and bulldog attitude, but he didn't strike me as a man compensating for the fact that he looked nearly everyone he met in the chest. He seemed more like a man looking *through* everyone to something else. "Okay, Major," I said. No way I was calling him Charles. I doubted anyone called him by his first name.

He keyed the seventh floor, marked EDITORIAL, and placed his hands on his hips as if he'd just finished a race and needed space to breathe. He wasn't looking at me—a quirk I would have to get used to over the next four weeks. "I've read your file. What there is of it. And I don't care who your father is. You understand that?"

His voice had taken on the tone of a drill instructor, as if the whole process of training yet another newbie reporter were so tiresome that he'd just as soon chuck me out an upper-story window as let me breathe the filtered air of his news office. I said, "Yes, uh . . . Major."

"As of today you are just another intern—a barnacle fixed to the underbelly of Fleet's news division. You aren't a journalist yet. You understand that?"

The word *yet* quickened my pulse. This was what I had been planning for, and I was finally standing in the reception area of the biggest news organization in the republic, talking to the war features editor. "Yes."

The door dinged and opened into the editorial floor. We stepped out into a spacious hallway overlooking an atrium. The open floorplan housed rows of desks flanked by glass-paneled offices and conference rooms on every side.

Major Weston led me past a massive holo-screen in the center of the open space. Two stories tall at least, it was flooded with shifting images of breaking news from across the battlefronts of the war. This was the holy grail of armed forces journalism Fleet broadcast across every core and edge system in the galaxy.

He kept talking as we walked. "Frankly, I doubt you have the temperament to become a real journalist. But I'll treat you the same way I do every idiot they send me. Fleet says to make you a reporter in four weeks, so that's what I'll try to do. If you can't cut it by then, you're not my problem anymore. That sound right to you?"

"Four weeks," I said. "I can do it."

"Uh-huh." He stopped outside a door market JANITORIAL and pushed it open. "Well, you'll be doing it here."

The building relied heavily on robotic cleaners, so the room was larger than I might have expected, with rows of charging bays for the cleaning bots and pressure connectors for refilling the chemical tanks of the machines. It also had a single student-style chair equipped with a writing tray.

Any other assignment I might have assumed Weston was trying to make my life miserable to get rid of me, but I didn't get the impression he hated me. He just didn't want me in his newsroom. And I had my wrist-comms, so I didn't really need anything else.

"Nice and quiet," I said.

He gave me an appraising look, like I'd just passed some sort of test, then let the door whisk closed. He turned on his heels and stalked away. Since he hadn't given me any other instruction I decided to follow him to his corner office, which turned out to be a surprisingly small, surprisingly cluttered nook walled with feeds from OrbSyn's various news branches. Weston had a window that looked down on the street below and, off in the distance, a beach. He had a desk too, and a high-backed chair, and a desk lamp fashioned to look centuries old. He waved me into a seat and collapsed into his own.

A holo-feed bloomed to life above his desk: high above a city, a destroyer dropped cutter drones that zoomed into the streets below and opened up with silent ordinance. A missile flared from the top of a building, white plumes billowing behind it.

"This is your assignment," Weston said. "You recognize it?"

I shook my head as the scene shifted to a view from the street. Colonial marines were leaping through a darkened hole in the front of a high-rise. Talking heads appeared in eight different perspectives, recounting whatever was happening with muted urgency. Some sort of clash with the GA, obviously, but I'd never seen any of this footage before.

"First battle of Chalmers Bay." Weston squinted into the flickering images. "Year three of the war. You know about Ciekot, I suppose?"

Ciekot. Dad had told me all about him when I was a kid. "He was that rear admiral the grendels kidnapped."

Weston rolled his eyes. "He wasn't kidnapped. He defected. We sent two platoons and a special ops team to get him back. Traitor blew his brains out when our guys stepped into his apartment. That's the real story here: Fleet opened a ground war in yet another system over nothing. Personally, I think our geniuses at Command and Control wanted to flip the Taino system with support from the locals and didn't expect so much resistance from people who had only recently been converted. Of course, OrbSyn had to sell that cockamamie story to the public, and Fleet had to give Admiral Ciekot a special tombstone with a star on it."

"You can prove this?"

"Of course not. Even if I could, I wouldn't. We have three rules in this building. Before I let you go off half-cocked and start writing news stories under OrbSyn's masthead, you're going to convince me you know what those rules are and how they work."

"All right. What are they?"

He held up his forefinger. "First, never write anything that compromises the war effort."

Simple enough. And why would I *want* to compromise it? "Okay. Got it."

"Second"—he flicked up another finger, forming a stubby V above the desk—"give me honest work. I don't mean I want you to work hard. If you don't work hard you won't last, and you won't be my problem. I mean tell an honest story. Don't just shape the facts to fit whatever narrative you want to tell."

This one sounded suspiciously like the sort of ethical challenge professors dish out to students their freshman year, but I nodded anyway. "Simple enough," I said. "Tell the truth."

He flinched a little at that word, then extended his thumb. "And third, make me feel something."

"*Feel* something? What do you want to feel?"

"Anything. I've been in this business thirty-three years. My emotional core wouldn't crack under a plasma welder. If you can make *me* feel something, you can make the average *reader* feel something. And feeling is the point. People read to be moved. To be angry or sad or hopeful or, well, anything besides bored."

I motioned to the display above his desk, which was still streaming twenty-five-year-old holos. "So you want a story about the first battle of Chalmers Bay?"

"A *feature* story, not just a recap of the facts any idiot can dredge up from AFNET. Give me something interesting."

"Okay. Any particular angle?"

"Up to you. Find something that doesn't break any of the rules. Which are . . . ?"

Another challenge. I held up three fingers as I zipped through his short list: "Don't hurt the war effort. Tell the truth. Make Major Weston feel something."

He gave the barest hint of a smile. "You have four weeks. Don't waste them."

I left his office whistling. Four weeks was a veritable eternity. I could write Major Weston's cub reporter shibboleth feature in a couple of days.

I slept in my new office that first night, determined to hurdle Weston's artificial barricade as quickly as possible. My grid was strewn with hundreds of holos, text articles, unclassified reports about the battle from OrbSyn's archives, and half a dozen transcripts of eyewitness testimony pulled from the Senate's post-battle inquiries. I ate breakfast at an overpriced cafe and put together my rough draft by late afternoon of the next day.

I came to work early the following morning and rewrote the story three times, with my final polish dedicated to a line-by-line comparative analysis based on Weston's checklist. Was I compromising the war effort with information unavailable to the public or the enemy? No. Was I being honest? Yes. Would it make the editor-in-chief at Orbits News Syndicate *feel* something? Impossible to predict.

I sent him the finished story before lunch, headed out for a quick bite, and by the time I was standing in line at Rioni's, my grid was already flashing an incoming text alert.

—WESTON, C: THIS IS AWFUL. TRULY AND IRREPARABLY
AWFUL. I ASKED FOR A STORY, NOT A COMP ONE ESSAY.
TRY AGAIN. OR BETTER YET, GIVE UP AND JOIN THE
REGULAR INFANTRY.—

Along with the text came a little animated holo of a marine officer—
obviously a cartoon caricature of Major Weston—setting a piece of
paper on fire and stoically warming his hands over the blaze.

Okay. Not what he was after.

I started over, this time from a different perspective. More research,
more combing through the newsroom's archives, more scanning of
bodycam footage and aerial drone shots.

Day five I sent a polished story I felt sure was good enough even for
the major. (I'd stopped thinking of him in human terms, as someone
capable of being named, and reduced him to the status of a rank
hidden inside an extra-small T-shirt.)

Thirty minutes later he sent another rejection.

—WESTON, C: THIS IS THE SAME NON-STORY, AND ONE I'VE
ALREADY READ A ZILLION TIMES. NO DESIRE TO READ
IT AGAIN. —

My third attempt was based on an existing feature, something that
had actually been published at OrbSyn. Obviously I didn't plagiarize
the original. I just studied its structure, its use of startling facts, the way
it conveyed insight into the personal life of its human interest subject,
a double amputee. Then I applied what I learned and composed a
new feature about a woman who had returned from the first battle of
Chalmers Bay in a body bag.

—WESTON, C: READS LIKE SOMETHING FROM REGINA
BAER. BUT YOU AIN'T HER AND SHOULDN'T TRY TO BE.
WORSE, YOUR STORY LEAKS SEVERAL UNIT DESIGNATIONS
AND THE ADDRESS OF A SPECIAL OPS TRAINING FACILITY.
SEE RULE #1.—

I pounded the writing tray of my student desk so hard the support arm bent, leaving the surface cocked forward. I stood, kicked the desk out my way, and paced alongside the charging counter until my breathing returned to normal and the pain in my jaw went away. I'd been clenching my teeth hard enough to crack a walnut.

When I felt calm enough to consider starting over. I propped the closet door open and dragged my chair away from the wall so I could watch the news feed streaming through the center of the building. Larger-than-life and flooded with stories from all across the republic, the holo not only reminded me why I was here, it demonstrated that what I was trying to do was achievable. *Someone* was creating all of that content. Presumably, reporters who had passed the major's seemingly impossible evaluation.

The problem wasn't lack of story material. Nor was it a desire to leak classified information or to twist the truth for the sake of a story. The problem was that Major Weston was too cynical to be moved by real news. Anything honest just wasn't a story. And anything that read like a story wasn't actually true.

I started over. Sent him a fourth feature. Then a fifth, sixth, and seventh. I dragged a portable lounge chair to the roof and spent my evenings up there, writing under the open sky.

By the middle of week four I'd sent him eleven different stories, each of which had been summarily trashed by the major as unpublishable.

With only three days left in the training calendar, I was running out of time. My next story would be my last shot at getting Weston to stamp my passport into OrbSyn.

I spent a couple of hours just staring at the massive holo-feed. Seeing it from a distance wasn't efficient; from my position in the closet near the end of the floor, the whole enormous display was no bigger than my outstretched palm. I could see it in grander scale by pulling it up on my own grid. But efficiency wasn't why it drew me in.

The flashing images and scrolling text, centered mid-air above the atrium, weren't any better than the stories I'd sent to Weston. If anything, they were *worse*. And not because I was lost in admiration of my own talent. They were worse because they constantly violated Weston's second rule.

OrbSyn's feed was flooded with half-truths, with innuendo, with opinions masquerading as analysis of breaking stories from around the edge. But it wasn't news. The whole vast river of information was just another cleverly packaged source of entertainment.

I took the stairs to the roof and plopped down in my chair, wondering if I'd made a terrible mistake. Did I want this job? Really?

I had thought I did. Now I wasn't sure. But how could I decide if I didn't understand what the job actually was?

Overhead, the stars formed dubious constellations, most of which I hadn't bothered to learn. OrbSyn, predictably neutral towards religion, ran astrology columns for all the terraformed planets in the republic, usually accompanied by their new mythologies. The Bell, home of Holikot's very own polestar, was visible overhead even now, nine stars arranged in a silent outline of the Koudouni nebula.

And all I could see in the night sky was OrbSyn and its towering news feed. The stars were facts. The nebula was a fact. Polar north was a fact. But calling it a bell? Making up a story about the "ghostly ringing" that supposedly saved sailors from crashing into a hidden reef?

Yeah. That was OrbSyn.

That was *Fleet*.

That was my new job. Assuming I found a way to pass Weston's test.

Fleet had made up stories about my dad. They'd done the same thing with Admiral Ciekot. Probably they were doing it with me.

They tell us what we want to hear, I thought. And remembered something I'd uncovered in all my digging. A quote from the Covert Intelligence Bureau's abstruse *Handbook of Psychological Operations*, which read like an owner's manual of the human mind, but with all the human parts left out.

I pulled up the document on my grid and scanned till I found the section I had highlighted.

> *Psychological Operations depend heavily on techniques gleaned from modern journalism. A good*

PSYOP is always based on facts rather than lies. We simply pick and choose the facts. We arrange convenient details into the sort of narrative our audience wants to believe.

Therefore the effective field agent will:
1. *Tell people what they want to hear.*
2. *Disguise the truth by admitting something secret or shameful.*
3. *Empower his or her allies.*

This is what Fleet had done with Admiral Ciekot. They had woven together facts to create a narrative that would secure the republic. Facts that made people feel good about themselves and about the war effort. What they *hadn't* done was tell the truth.

Could that be what Major Weston was after? The story people wanted to hear most?

And what was that story?

What was the one thing every citizen wondered about, and had been wondering about ever since the Grand Alliance and its citizens turned over their autonomy to their AIs?

I knew. Everyone knew. We'd all been asking the same question for twenty-eight years.

What made life as a grendel so great that no one ever defected from their ranks?

Maybe *that* was a story worth telling. A story Major Weston would run on his towering news feed.

Anyway, that was the story I wanted to tell. And if I could tell that story, working at OrbSyn would be worth whatever it cost.

So I wrote about Admiral Ciekot. How he had felt when the grendel shock troops kidnapped him. How they had forced him to wear a symb-collar, subdued his free will and crushed his own spirit under the weight of a quantum monster. I wrote about what it felt like to be manacled inside his own body, free only to watch life passing from behind the prison of his eyes.

Somewhere deep inside, I wrote, Admiral Ciekot had longed for the freedom of a republic citizen, for the life of free choices that had been stripped from him.

And when those Colonial marines had blown open his apartment door and told him everything was going to be okay—well, it had been a relief. No, they couldn't give him his life back. Not with a symb-collar around his neck. But they had, nonetheless, saved him. He saw it even as he saw himself reaching for his service pistol. Felt waves of relief as the wyrm moved his left hand to pull back the charging lever.

It wasn't him, Admiral Ciekot, raising the muzzle to his right temple. But in his last moments he did imagine the motion as a kind of salute. A way of saying *thank you* to the men and women who had come for him. His friends. His comrades. His brothers-in-arms.

I wrote the whole story sitting there on the roof under the stars. Sent it to Major Weston from my comms, then trudged down the steps and headed back to my apartment. Slept through my alarm. Showered. Ate a slow breakfast.

And finally opened my grid to check my messages.

—WESTON, C: SEE ME IN MY OFFICE. YOU'RE OUT OF TIME.—

He didn't even acknowledge me when I rapped on the door, so I stood there for a couple minutes until he let out a long sigh. "Sit down," he said.

I took the seat across from his desk. "You read it."

"I did." Still he didn't look at me. He was staring off to the right, obviously engrossed in something on his own grid.

I didn't care what he was looking at, and I was out of patience. "Am I working for OrbSyn or not?"

His gaze flicked over to me. "Some story. Ciekot as an actual hero. No irony, no family interviews. Just a first-person feature from a perspective that doesn't exist. I'd thought I'd seen everything."

"It doesn't compromise the war," I said. "And it made you feel something. I know it did."

"You *know* it did?" He was scowling now. "And what do you know about facts? Rule number two. I specifically told you I want honest reporting, not propaganda."

"Yes, *sir.*" I nearly spat the word at him. "But you don't *publish* honest reporting. You publish stories people will read. That's why you sat me in a chair with line of sight to your golden calf. So I'd learn the lesson on my own. Because anyone who can't learn the lesson on their own probably isn't cut out for this kind of work."

He cracked a faint smile. It looked genuine. "You *aren't* cut out for this kind of work. Most of my reporters figure out what I want their first week."

"So that's it? I'm out?"

He shook his head. "I didn't say that. I said you'll never be a journalist. Not a real one. But you can pretend pretty well. Maybe that will be enough."

A notification appeared on my grid. Press credentials and an OrbSyn ID tag.

"Thank you, Major," I said.

"Get out of here." He turned his back to me. "And go write me a great war story."

7

WYRM

Ivy woke me at 3:30am, as instructed.

I had ordered her to stop using a ghostly apparition of my ex, even though she insisted face-to-face communication helped with memory retention. Seeing her translucent image was far too distracting. Still, I enjoyed hearing Ivy's voice in my head, even if she was a simulation. Somehow Fake Ivy had captured the sweet, home-cooked perfection of the real thing. She seemed to understand why I had fallen in love with Ivy in the first place. Or maybe that I'd never fallen out of love with her.

I dressed in the dark, out of habit pulling up my grid to see if anything important had dropped over the transom. But the link to AFNET was still down, so I skimmed through the mission plan one last time as I brushed my teeth.

The negotiations would take place at a compound owned by the Trevalyan family in the mountains outside Seranik City. The problem was getting there. Sterling's plan called for a discreet, day-long hike up a steep mountain valley via one of the game trails leading through the jungle. Raeburn's team had already scoped a path during their preliminary training run before either Sterling or I had arrived. The jungle would hide our movement and help keep the location a secret.

I rinsed my mouth, took a long drink of water, and headed for the door.

Frankly, this hike was going to suck. I was already exhausted, yesterday's adrenaline having worn off. I'd been polishing bar stools and rental seats for months with no serious physical conditioning regimen. I was in no shape to be slogging up New Witlund's tropical mountains. Worse, my MADAR team needed to believe that I was a decorated marine officer—the same PSYOPS captain who had earned a combat recon badge in *six* different theaters. If they found out who I really was—

I paused with my hand on the doorknob. Called up a map of the hotel. Saw myself in my room, with "Sterling, A" in white letters under my icon. And on the other side of the door, nothing.

No icon, no name, no rank.

Someone from Raeburn's team should have been standing guard.

I pulled up Ivy's proximity filter, and immediately a red blur of body heat mapped itself on the other side of the door. Someone *was* standing there.

[Ivy,] I asked. [Who is that?]

[*From his heat print, best guess is Sergeant Major Raeburn.*]

[Why is there no ID signature?]

[*He isn't wearing a comms.*]

[They're going dark?]

[*Presumably,*] she said. [*Which means you should plan on removing your comms at the rendezvous.*]

It was bad enough trying to impersonate Sterling *with* the help of his AI. But *without* that help?

This day was just getting better and better.

I opened the door. "Sergeant Major."

"Morning, Captain," Raeburn said. "You ready for a little walk in the woods?"

"Nothing better than early morning PT."

We took the elevator down, then headed to the skyport in the same sled Laclos had used to shuttle me to the hotel. Raeburn took us around the edge of the tarmac to the southeast corner and parked next to a concrete outbuilding. In the distance a couple of GS-117 medical airshuttles crouched in the darkness like a pair of vultures.

The rest of the team had already assembled, including Colonel Vermier. Pajari, Hopper, and Laclos, like Raeburn, wore marine jungle camos and carried rucksacks and a variety of weapons. Vermier and I were wearing standard khaki utilities. She at least carried a 10mm service pistol. As an official UC delegate, I was prohibited by intergalactic treaty from carrying a weapon to the meeting place. My security guards could be armed to the teeth, but I wasn't even allowed nail clippers.

Pajari unslung a rectangular plasteel case from his shoulder and set it on the hood of the sled. Red pinpricks blinked at either end. He fiddled with its twin latches, then shook his head. "If we are going dark, we have to remove the failsafe now."

"Staff-level override," Raeburn said. "That would be a job for the colonel."

Vermier stepped up, her face taking on that faraway look people get when they're working with an AI. The lights on the case flashed red twice, then showed a steady green.

Now the latches clicked open, and Pajari lifted the top to reveal a shoulder-launched missile. A hammerhead, presumably. I'd never seen one. Just knew they had an unbelievable bark-to-bite ratio. Twelve kilograms of destructive firepower capable of bringing down something as large as a destroyer.

"Don't drop it," Hopper said. He wasn't wearing sunglasses now, so I felt like I was seeing his face for the first time.

"Good idea." Pajari closed and latched the case. "In fact, I think you should carry it."

Instead, Raeburn hauled it up over one shoulder. "PJ and I will escort Colonel Vermier and drop some breadcrumbs. Captain, you'll be about five minutes behind us with Laclos and Hopper. No one but my team knows the route we're taking, so in theory we should have a nice boring hike through the mountains."

"In theory," Pajari said.

"So let's keep it that way, huh?" Raeburn looked back and forth between me and Colonel Vermier.

She got the hint before I did; she unsnapped her wrist-comms and slid it into her pocket.

I hesitated, not wanting to lose the sense of companionship that had supported me through the last sixteen hours. Ivy's silent presence in the back of my mind had given me courage and a sense of confidence. She was a constant reminder that I was finally doing something that mattered. And she was my only access to the story I was writing.

Reluctantly I thumbed the release tab and pocketed the bracelet. The world immediately seemed darker, the morning hotter.

"See you at the top," Raeburn said, more to Hopper and Laclos than to me.

Laclos picked up a hydration pack from where it was lying on the ground and handed it to me. "You'll want to drink all of this before we get there," she said. "It's going to be another scorcher."

Five minutes later we slipped through a gate in the perimeter fence and plunged into the predawn darkness of the jungle. Hopper led the way, and though he often disappeared into the foliage, Raeburn's trail markers kept me on the right path. The markers looked like wisps of blue flame welling up from the soil. In reality they were smears of fluorescent dust dropped on ground, visible only from a couple of meters away, and burning out after half an hour.

We covered almost two kilometers before dawn began to pierce the treetop canopy, and the reassuring markers grew less frequent.

Just ahead, Hopper's easy lope kept taking him out of sight, though occasionally I'd catch a glimpse of him at a switchback standing with his head cocked to one side as if listening. Then he'd go off again to be swallowed by the trees.

Behind me, Laclos padded softly at a distance, her footsteps echoing my own. And all the while something clutched at me, a sort of emotional residue. It felt like both the *presence* of something and the *absence* of something. Like I was being stalked.

I knew what it was, or thought I did.

I'd gotten used to having Ivy back. And now she was gone again, and that fact made sense. Raeburn was right to have us remove our wrist-comms when we left the base. Hadn't Sterling told me that Colonial comms were susceptible to enemy wyrms?

That thought lit a terrifying *"what if"* question in my imagination. I tried to brush it off, to tell myself it wasn't possible. PSYOPS comms were bound to be heavily shielded. They were Fleet's most advanced technology. Designed to protect our most guarded secrets. Sterling would not have ordered me to put on his comms if he'd thought it might be infected with enemy malware.

Then again, he'd been dying.

And he *had* left me one file I hadn't bothered to open: the recording of our first interview from yesterday morning. His perspective just before the *Strangler* shut down our link to AFNET.

Was there something on that recording Sterling had wanted me to see? *Expected* me to see? If not, why include it in the mission files?

I'd been stupid not to watch it when I had the chance.

There was only one way to find out if that recording mattered. To make these negotiations work I needed to be able to access Ivy. I needed to know if I could trust her. And I needed to find out as soon as possible, without giving myself away to Raeburn's team.

I needed to watch Sterling's recording.

But how? Laclos was following close behind me. And I was physically occupied with the hike. Getting more and more winded with every step.

By the time we had gone eight kilometers my shoulders heaved with every breath. The sun filtered through the upper canopy and spiked the air with heat. Sweat poured off my forehead as we climbed.

At some point Laclos called, "How about a breather, Cap?"

I stopped and turned. Except for the sweat glistening on her face and hands, she might have just climbed out of bed.

I nodded gratefully and leaned back against a tree, trying to hide my breathing with deep gulps of air.

"You all right?"

I took a sip of water from my mouth tube and thought of that time back on Holikot when my apartment was robbed. Emotion is only convincing when it's not forced, and I needed Laclos to believe that I was really disgusted.

Admit something secret or shameful. "Been better," I said.

"You look a little gassed."

"A little?"

"Riding a desk?"

"Picked up a case of endocarditis six months ago." It was a lie, of course, but better than trying to explain why a man of Sterling's reputation was in such poor shape.

Laclos scowled, a foreign expression on her face, and I knew the message would get around. From the team's point of view, their babysitting job had just gotten a little harder. They'd wonder why they hadn't been told. "You got a release for this mission?"

I nodded. A different sort of lie, but one that felt safer. "If it comes down to it, I may need a few stims. Those militia boys confiscated mine in the attack."

As the team medic, she obviously didn't like it. "All right, I'll see what I can do. I don't carry antimicrobials, so you may regress in a couple of days."

"It won't matter at that point."

"Well, I *hope* that's not true. We're looking for a happy ending for everybody, right?"

I smiled. Her optimism was weirdly inspiring, despite the fact that our mission was to sell out six hundred million colonials. "Everybody wins."

"Does Raeburn know about the endocard"

"Not yet. I—" What excuse did I have? I'd actually planned to tell the sergeant major once we were far enough from Camp Locke that Vermier couldn't use it as an excuse to cancel the mission. In hindsight it was probably the wrong decision. It would show a lack of trust in the team. "I didn't expect to feel it this soon."

"You didn't want to look like a pogue," she suggested.

I winced at the term, though inwardly it brought relief. Laclos was seeing what she expected to see—a marine PSYOPS officer—not an enlisted journalist. "You a head shrink, too, doc?"

"Can't protect you if we don't know what's going on, sir."

"Point taken."

"Anything else we should know?"

It dawned on me that these questions wouldn't have originated with her. Raeburn had probably put her up to it. Which meant he was worried about something. "What do you mean?"

Laclos shrugged. "Corporal Dahl. He was kind of a jackwagon, but it couldn't have been easy to watch him bleed out."

"A jackwagon?" I said, surprised. "You knew him?"

She shook her head. "No offense, sir. I used to read his stories aloud to the team. Hopper always got a big kick out of it. Said he wanted Dahl to write his obituary. Pajari would usually get mad and stomp off."

My ears burned, but I couldn't help asking, "Why mad?"

"He thinks that kind of propaganda makes all of us look bad. Like we're all in on the joke. War is just a show, and getting your legs blown off makes you some kind of hero."

I wiped my palms on my shirt and took another sip from the hydration tube. "Maybe Dahl didn't think of it that way."

She looked off into the jungle. "I think he knew exactly what he was doing."

"Really?"

"Edge militias seem to like him. And that hasn't exactly turned out to be a great thing here. For us, anyway. For you."

"Well, I barely knew the man." Another lie. "How about a couple of steadies and we get moving?"

She dug into her med kit. "How about *one* steady and we take a ten-minute break." It wasn't a question. She passed me a small white pill.

Steady-stims were favored by operators because they produced a feeling of increased stamina without the twitchiness of a big juice stimulant. Laclos probably didn't want to overtax my heart. It would have to do.

I popped it onto my tongue and washed it down with a mouthful of tepid water.

A moment later a feeling of calm readiness seeped into me, as if I were being held up by the air. It was a like stepping into a warm pool.

"You can have another one in six hours. Meanwhile"—she knelt on the trail facing the way we came, her rifle propped over one forearm— "you should rest."

Rest. The word sparked an idea. "While we're getting all personal, I think I'm going to step into the latrine and shed a couple pounds."

She kept her eyes down the trail. "Don't go far."

I stepped onto the upward slope and went about three meters before I found a tree thick enough to cover my movement. A hole in the canopy revealed the full sweep of the valley we were ascending: the stream bounding in a long scar of white foam, and on the far side of the river an open glade bursting with sunlight.

My fingers shook as I fumbled with the flap of my thigh pocket. I didn't just need to connect with Ivy. I wanted to. Bad enough I could almost smell the scented shampoo she used.

I pulled the bracelet out and snapped it onto my wrist. Felt the tingle of activation. A pause like an indrawn breath.

[*What's the matter?*] Ivy asked. Somehow she knew.

[How far back do your recordings go—the ones on this unit?]

[*Twenty-six hours, eleven minutes, fourteen—*]

Sterling had been wearing this comms unit for a while. At least a matter of days, if not months. There should have been something on it besides the one recording flagged on my grid. [Yesterday morning? How is that possible?]

[*I am a PSYOPS comms,*] Ivy said. [*For security reasons, everything in my memory is redactable. Captain Sterling forced a hard reset before taking off the cuff. He only left one recording fragment in the permanent archives.*]

Stupid. I had assumed the file was just the detritus of an ongoing mission, the sort of thing you save for later, something to jog the memory. But no, he had intended for me to see it. Had *expected* me to watch it. [He was hiding something.]

[*Everyone's hiding something. Even Colonel Vermier.*]

Whatever the colonel was into, I didn't want to know. And it didn't matter now.

I pulled up my grid and opened the recording.

Immediately, familiar images ghosted my overlay.

The mess hall at Camp Locke, lit by a single panel

near the doors. Through the long row of windows,
sunrise tinged the horizon.

A warm tingling ran along my wrist as the AI nestled
*into Sterling's consciousness. [*Morning, Captain. I
don't see any local user data. Would you like—*]*

[No need. I'm familiar with your systems. I just need
a little time to myself, please.]

The recording skipped, freezing at the moment Sterling rose to
look out the window at the enemy frigate. No image of Dahl's face.
No conversation about selling out the edge colonies. No implications
about the positive effect covering this story might have on my career.

That shouldn't have surprised me. But it meant I *still* didn't have
proof of Sterling's orders. And the fact he'd thought to erase them
was disturbing. He'd left out the parts of our conversation that would
prove I was acting under Fleet's authority. The parts that outlined his
plan to surrender the edge colonies for a ten-year ceasefire.

Which meant someone wanted plausible deniability. So if the
mission failed, I could be buried in an unmarked tomb or incinerated
in a mass grave and my memory erased from Fleet's conscience.

I nudged the recording to resume, but it didn't budge.

[*There's something you should know,*] Ivy said. [*Before you watch*
the ending.]

The way she said it raised the hair on the back of my neck. [*Oh?*]

[*Whatever you think of me afterwards, I'm still your only chance of*
pulling this off.]

The recording flickered to life . . .

. . . and I strode towards the window, calling up
the data on the enemy warship as I moved. It was a
frigate, unescorted, but branded on my grid with a
J-designation, which meant it boasted the newest tech
fresh from a grendel shipyard.

Alarm crashed over me.

"That's a consular ship?" Dahl asked from behind,
puzzled. His voice sounded unnaturally high.

"Alliance frigate," I corrected. "Strangler class. They're going for our datalink off-moon. See if you can—"

[Camp Locke's base nodes have already failed, Captain,] *the AI said.*

[Peaceful negotiations!] *I snarled at her.* [What else did that thing do?]

She hesitated for a fraction of a second. [They seem to have launched a wyrm array at us.]

[Us?]

[Your comms, specifically. I was the only target.]

[Your firewall hold up?]

[I believe so. The wyrm appears to be fifth generation, which I am well prepared to handle. However, the J-class frigates are probably equipped with newer—]

[So we won't know for sure until your system reboots?]

[Correct. As long as you don't shut me down or remove the comms from your wrist, any enemy wyrm that may have defeated my onboard security should remain inactive.]

[And if we do have to reboot?] *I demanded.* [How will we know whether you've been compromised?]

[You won't, Captain. You'll have to destroy me.]

I swore. "Do you know where Colonel Vermier's office is?" I asked Dahl, still staring at the enemy ship.

"No, sir. Never been on this base till this morn—"

Something moved on the far side of the valley, snapping my gaze from the flicker of Ivy's overlay to the sudden splash of movement. Through the bare patch of jungle, bursting into the sunlit glade, a dark shape ambled from the shadows, its horselike snout nosing the ground. It was broad-shouldered as a grizzly, with wide hind legs and a quick, loping gait that took it across the clearing in mere seconds.

[Ivy, what is—?]

Before she could answer, gunfire popped in the distance, the distinctive crackle of a flash rifle.

"Cap!" Laclos called.

I ripped the bracelet off my wrist and shoved it into my pocket before scrambling back onto the trail. Laclos stood, rifle ready, her head swiveling to take in our surroundings. She grabbed the back of my shirt and pulled me off the path into the brush. "Stay down, sir."

We waited under a tapestry of green and black, the only sound a steady droning of insects.

An eternity later—probably five minutes in real time—Hopper's voice pierced the stillness. "Coming in. Hold your fire."

Laclos lowered her rifle as Hopper came into view.

"We got company?" Laclos asked.

"Looks like they were expecting us," Hopper said. "Colonel saw the compound downslope, decided to take a short cut. Militia got her."

"They killed Vermier?" I said, not quite believing it.

"No, sir, we're not that lucky. They've got a gun to her head. And they want to talk to you."

8

GRENDELS

Infuriating.

After all of the work and sacrifice that had gone into this mission. After all of the planning and self-denial. After I'd watched a man bleed out from a sucking chest wound because hundreds of millions of lives were hanging in the balance.

Vermier had thrown all of that away because she didn't want to stay on the sidelines while a junior officer from PSYOPS went off to talk to the enemy.

Worse, I let it happen. I should have confronted her in her office. Rolled the dice that she wouldn't dig deeply into my personnel file. Forced her to put her career on the line.

Now we would all have to deal with the fallout: the smoke and the bloody ruin awaiting us inside the front gate of the Trevalyan compound, which squatted on the mountain like some nightmare composite of postmodern architecture and medieval fortress. Its outer walls were high and angular and capped with shards of broken glass. Inside, a mansion rose above the perimeter, its wings embracing a neatly trimmed lawn and a crescent pool that sparkled with reflected sunlight.

The place reeked of money and pride and panicked afterthoughts.

Whoever said the feudal system died out sixteen hundred years ago had never been to New Witlund.

The front gate lay in pieces strewn across the hard-packed earth, apparently having been shredded by fire from the ridges above. Just inside the gate, a burned-out SAV gouted lazy smoke skyward.

Around it, half a dozen bodies sprawled across the gravel. No great loss to me, of course, but the Alliance ambassador would certainly care. I couldn't think of a more obvious way to derail the peace talks than assaulting the meeting place.

Obviously New Witlund's disgruntled militia had known we were coming. Maybe they had firefly cameras along the jungle trail. But that sort of sophistication and money seemed way beyond them, especially since they would have needed to know where to place the tech.

More likely someone had tipped them off. Which was more terrifying than infuriating. Theoretically no one outside the team had access to the mission file. Even Sterling's handlers at Fleet hadn't been given the route from Camp Locke to the compound.

Still, Lieutenant Dogen's goons had found Sterling and me inside a UCMC training base. Someone was feeding them classified intel.

I stalked deeper into the compound, Laclos trailing me, and found Sergeant Major Raeburn standing over the bodies of three grendel scouts, two men and one woman, between the mansion's front doors and the burning sled. He wore an uneasy expression on his scarred face, but I got the impression it had nothing to do with the amount of blood spattered on the imported tiles of the sled port.

"Mansion and village are ours." Raeburn motioned in the direction of the ridge to the west, now obscured by the compound's western wall. "Militia's holed up in that utility shed with the colonel."

"How many shooters do they have?" I asked.

"Unclear. Based on what's coming over the squawker, best guess is three plus the colonel. Pajari saw the last one disappear inside."

"What are they saying?"

"They want to talk to you," Raeburn said. "You mind telling me what's going on, sir?"

How was I supposed to answer that? "Looks like somebody doesn't want me talking to the GA."

Raeburn glanced at the grendel corpses. Dressed in tattered, blood-soaked black-and-gray uniforms, the bodies were so mangled they might have been assembled piecemeal from a charnel house. "You sure the GA still wants to talk to *you*?"

I bent down to examine the closest victim. A thin, finger-width line of silver sprouted from the back of the head and looped under the chin. It almost looked like jewelry except that it didn't lay flat on the chest but pressed unyielding into the man's lower jaw. A symb-collar.

"We didn't do this," I said. "And the fact those clowns in the shed are making demands should prove that point. We have to assume their ambassador wants this meeting as much as we do."

"With respect, sir," Raeburn said. "Assumptions will get you killed."

He had a point. "Any sign of Trevalyan?"

Raeburn hooked his thumb towards the mansion's double doors, which stood open to the blistering air. "Senior isn't here. Place is empty except for a teenage son. He's barricaded in a bedroom with one of his dad's bodyguards."

Odd. I didn't remember Trevalyan's file mentioning children. "He tell you anything?"

"Says he needs to get back to campus for a midterm. Goes to some private university on Quelon. Figured I'd let you break the news to him."

I rose slowly and turned in a circle, taking in the compound's pockmarked walls and dark spatters of blood. The covered sled port with its six empty bays and sleek red convertible were miraculously unharmed. A massive amount of ordinance had swept through this place in a very short time, most of it directed at the open space where the bus lay smoldering.

I could almost feel the mission slipping away from me. Without the peace talks, I didn't have a story. And Fleet wouldn't have its ceasefire. "I'll be back, Sergeant Major."

"They'll have seen you coming in, sir. You want to respond to their satcom transmission?" He held out a portable radio just larger than his palm.

I shook my head. "Later. I want to talk to Trevalyan's son."

"Top of the stairs, first door on the right."

I mounted the broad front steps and slipped into the blissfully cool air of the mansion. Its foyer was bigger than my apartment, with a wide staircase sweeping up from the left in an arc that carried to an upper hallway. Under it and across from the front door stood a huge bay window looking out on the pool, the rear wall, and the mountain ridge beyond. Somewhere up there in that terraced greenery was the utility shed Vermier had been taken to, probably a storage unit for the narcotics this place produced.

Laclos went past me around the corner and returned chugging a bottle of cold water. She held out a second one to me. "Kitchen."

I downed half of it before pressing the side to my forehead. Its coolness felt marvelous. "Mission protocol said there'd be snacks."

"Mention anything about cutter drones and dead bodies?" Laclos asked.

"I must have missed that part," I said and headed up the stairs.

The bedroom door stood open. The dresser they'd shoved in front of it had been moved back but still slanted at an unnatural angle just inside.

I knocked and stepped inside, Laclos coming in behind me, her rifle lowered.

The kid's teeth, slacks, and Rostram University shirt were white and semi-dazzling against his suntanned skin. He was athletic and good-looking and, based on my experience sizing people up in a glance, he seemed to know it. "Who are you?" he asked.

"Captain Ansell Sterling, UCMC. Who are *you*?"

The kid glanced at the other person in the room, a short, muscular man sitting blank-faced in a padded leather chair beneath another window with another spectacular view of the mountains. The man only gave a slight shake of his head, as if he hadn't understood the question.

"Giuseppi Trevalyan," Junior said. "You're trespassing."

I ignored the challenge. "You're Master Trevalyan's son?"

"What do you think?"

"I didn't think he had kids."

His lip curled into a sneer, something that looked like a nervous tic. "Pop had two. The good one is off on a business trip. Don't know where the old man went."

The silver comms unit on his left wrist caught my attention. It was thin, loose, and flowed like an encircling fountain of water just above the skin. Probably a Divanese Co. special, which meant it would be one of only five hundred originals and obscenely expensive. Apparently there were numerous advantages to being cartel royalty.

"You aren't supposed to be here," I said.

"Yeah, well nobody told *me* that. It's not like I don't have a key."

The bodyguard cleared his throat. He wore a less flashy comms unit on his right wrist, the line of thin silver tight against his skin. "Giuseppi has a friend in the village. He had a break in his classes and wanted to"—he hesitated long enough to polish his reply—"*meet* her. I'm sure you understand."

A tryst, then. One of the locals. Not exactly a girlfriend, but someone he could bed when the mood hit him.

"Where is she?"

Junior shrugged and looked away. "The workers of course would have scattered as soon as the shooting started." He sounded bitter, as if he thought she owed him something. "She's not a fool. She wouldn't have stuck around."

"So not a fool . . . but a *worker*?" I asked, poking at his dignity, even though it didn't matter who she was. This young man annoyed me. The fact he could use people and throw them away. The fact he clearly didn't see that as wrong. The fact he had options, which meant that when the Alliance took over New Witlund, he'd probably just flee to a backup mansion somewhere else. "Did you see the fight outside your front door?"

His bodyguard lifted one finger for my attention. "We were both here, in this room, when we heard shooting in the courtyard. The alarm system triggered my assistant, and we were urged to lock the door and remain quiet. We didn't receive the all clear until you arrived."

An alarm system. I could probably access the recordings, but that would be time-consuming. "You didn't see anything?"

"Heard the shooting," the kid said. "But we never left the room."

"So you don't know how many men were here?"

"No idea."

"And that utility shed on the hill?" I asked. "What can you tell me about that?"

He shrugged. "What's there to tell? It's dry storage. A place to keep product."

Product. Obviously these two weren't going to be able to help us get Vermier back. Best thing would be to get rid of them. One less factor to calculate. "You have keys to that sled in the garage?"

"Of course."

"Some place you can go besides Seranik City?"

The bodyguard said, "We can take the pass to Tamani."

"But I have class planet-side tomorrow," Junior protested.

"Quelon's under attack," Laclos said. "You won't be having classes for a while."

"Really?" His expression changed, and I couldn't tell if he was frightened or excited. War often impressed young men who considered life a public theater where dramas unfolded for their private amusement.

"Tell you what," I said. "Wait three days. If you don't see a grendel carrier dropping shock troops into Seranik by then, it'll be safe to come home."

"Thank you," the bodyguard said with a carefully manicured inflection. "We appreciate your concern."

Raeburn was waiting in the foyer with the radio, a familiar voice squawking from its tiny speaker. "Lieutenant Dogen, New Witlund QRS to Captain Sterling, UCMC, I know you're in the house. Talk to me."

Lieutenant Dogen. I should have known it would be him.

Raeburn held out the radio. "Anything you say will be intercepted. Grendels are listening too."

I took the radio from his outstretched hand but didn't depress the talk button. Instead I slipped the unit into my pocket and removed Sterling's comms, holding up the bracelet so Raeburn and Laclos could see what I was doing.

"They'll wait," I said. "We need information. And I think my

AI may be able to get it off one of those dead grendels. You have a problem with me reconnecting, Sergeant Major?"

"Sir," Laclos said, "we don't know if that comms is secure."

"That's a fact," I agreed. "But we *do* know this mission is no longer a secret."

Raeburn gave a long sigh. "As long as you take it off again, and let Laclos check you out afterwards."

"Agreed," I said, and stepped out into the blistering jungle heat. After the paradise of air conditioning, it felt like putting on a layer of warm wet clothing on an already hot and muggy day.

But I couldn't wait to slip Sterling's comms around my wrist. Even if the mission had gone exactly as Sterling had planned it, I would have needed Ivy's help. Now everything in my world seemed to be unraveling. And some part of me wanted to hear her voice again, if only for the sake of my own sanity. It reminded me of what I'd been missing.

I strode over to the dead bodies and flipped the bracelet over my left wrist. Pressed the halves together.

The tingle of activation brought a surge of relief so powerful I closed my eyes as it washed over me. *Was she a wyrm? Was this what a wyrm did? Was this what the Alliance was built upon—a desire for camaraderie?*

[*You've been busy,*] Ivy said, her voice a smile. [*Can I help?*]

[You know anything about what happened here?] I asked.

[*A little. I've been monitoring their satcom transmissions. And I was able to intercept some of the burst data the ambassador's security team sent during the firefight.*]

So these grendels had been part of the ambassador's security team. That made sense. Still, I was astonished. Even though she'd been riding in my pocket, Ivy knew more than I did. [You can read grendel messaging?]

[*It's in the job description.*]

[Can you pull the action logs from their symb-collars? I'd like to see exactly what happened here.]

[*Hm.*] She seemed to consider the question. [*Sorry, but the most recent recording is a routine inspection of the compound. The firefight data has been deleted. Standard GA procedure.*]

[Show me what you have.]

The smell of blood and flesh rose to my nostrils for a moment, then the world went dark.

Images floated before me, a moving line of ghosts on my overlay that captured both sensory and conceptual highlights in a sort of three-dimensional essay. Ninety minutes squeezed into a two-minute cognitive encounter:

> *I moved downhill towards the compound's high western wall. Only the dim albedo of Quelon filtering through the trees gave any light. Better that way, really. Tanja held my hand in the darkness, listened for any out-of-place night sounds that might mean we were compromised.*
>
> *[Just ahead,] Tanja warned.*
>
> *I slipped past the cartel guard in his hidden bunker near the ridge. Could have killed him easily, and that didn't bode well for the rest of the cartel's security measures.*
>
> *[Asleep,] I answered. [You should send that in.]*
>
> [Way ahead of you, Slick.]
>
> *[Not that His Excellence will care. A meeting on New Witlund? At a compound set in the jungle foothills of Seranik City? Surrounded by hostiles? What could go wrong?]*
>
> [You need a full company of experienced rangers around you to feel comfortable?]
>
> *[Just you and my rifle. But someone needs to remember we are on enemy soil.]*
>
> [Hot shower would be nice too. You're starting to stink.]
>
> *[That is the smell of manliness! If you didn't like it, you'd be dialing it down.]*
>
> [You flirting with me on an op, Slick?]

[Am I ever not flirting with you, Tanja?]

[That time we faced the *Isnashi* together.*]*

[Afterwards though!]

[So I guess these reservists won't be a problem. That what you're saying?*]*

I came to the edge of the trees and watched as two red dots slid into place beside me on the grid. Lyla and Kole sent the ready signal at the same time, and we stepped into the wash of bluish light together.

The guard at the gatehouse lifted his rifle, but the three of us walked with hands held high, our own weapons secured peacefully to our backs. Tanja would have warned me if the man seemed likely to shoot. His finger wasn't near the trigger.

A moment later the gate opened, and two other men in dark green business robes, heavily armed and reeking of cologne, met us inside.

They gave us a full tour of the compound: the monitored perimeter, the guest house, the sled port, the sky port, the "business" storage facilities set into the hillside, and last, the mansion.

My opinion is that this compound has no serious security at all, just a team of six mercenaries—probably distant members of the Trevalyan clan.

When I asked to see Master Trevalyan, the head of security replied, "He is away on business."

Which means the one person on New Witlund who isn't a fool isn't actually on New Witlund. Also, he's a drug lord. He probably figures that if this meeting goes well, his cartel will benefit from the black market trade for decades. And if it goes poorly, he will be holed up somewhere else, lightyears from the fighting.

[Some of these colonials are smarter than we give them credit for, yeah Tanja?]

[Exceptions to everything, Slick.*]*

The report ended. No recommendation to keep or cancel the meeting. No mention of an attack by militia. No reference to an ETA for the grendel emissary—apparently "His Excellence" in the report.

Just a lingering warmth of self-confidence, a residue that coated every thought with the stickiness of the integration I'd just experienced. The relationship between Slick and Tanja had been a kind of permanent mental dance, except that it seemed to require no mental energy. Slick had been a hero in Tanja's eyes. A giant among men.

I knelt next to Slick's body and tipped his head to one side. There was a swollen mass of tissue below his ear where shrapnel had torn his neck open, but the symb-collar was still intact. It figured. Probably why combat troops sometimes said that grendel meat could go bad, but their wyrms never died.

Now I understood why the place was so empty. Trevalyan hadn't taken any chances. He probably didn't trust us any more than he trusted the Alliance. Just left behind a few goons to make sure no one stole the silverware.

I looked over the bodies as the stink of death once again penetrated my thoughts, forcing me to rise from my crouch.

Three grendel rangers ripped apart by heavy fire from the ridges above us. Plus a second kind of ordinance. A cutter-drone maybe. And sporadic fire from flash rifles.

Slick's voice replayed in my mind: *Some of these colonials are smarter than we give them credit for, yeah Tanja?*

And her reply: *Exceptions to everything, Slick.*

The words brought a hollow feeling to my stomach. More longing than apprehension, like that last roll of the dice after a bad night at the casino.

Could it really be so simple? I fingered Sterling's bracelet. *The colonies, the Marine Corps, Fleet, everyone on our side is simply . . . wrong?*

Then the parallel thought: *When haven't we been wrong?*

Dogen's voice squawked at me from my thigh pocket, his voice weary. "Lieutenant Dogen, New Witlund QRS to Captain Sterling. I am running out of patience."

[*They'll want you,*] Ivy said. [*In exchange for Vermier. That will be his demand.*]

[A captain for a colonel?]

[*You're a decorated PSYOPS officer with key information critical to their future lives on New Witlund. Colonel Vermier is a career staffer with no real intel about the war.*]

It made sense. Problem was, the GA ambassador would never show up while there was an active hostage situation in the area. Especially after his advance team had been slaughtered. Somehow I was going to have to convince the locals to stand down. [Any ideas how we can get them to come out?]

[*You don't need them to come out,*] Ivy said. [*Raeburn's team has the hammerhead. You can take out that utility shed easily.*]

[Kill them all?]

[*Colonel Vermier isn't part of this mission and would be an acceptable casualty. She shouldn't have imposed herself on the team. And you don't even like her.*]

The idea alarmed me. To throw away someone's life with no attempt to get her back seemed beyond cynical. But then, was Ivy's ruthlessness a result of her being programmed for strategic psychological warfare in some PSYOPS laboratory? Or was it because she'd been hacked by an Alliance wyrm and was trying to remove the only weapon we had that was capable of taking out their high-tech frigate?

I had no way of knowing. And for the moment it didn't matter, because either way, I needed Ivy to help me get the peace talks back on track.

Still, what if I couldn't get the ambassador to discuss terms for a ceasefire? We would *need* that rocket. I wasn't going to waste it on some drug lord's storage cellar. [No. I won't do that.]

[*Sterling would absolutely give that order,*] Ivy said, and I could almost see the expression on her face, the earnestness in her eyes. It was the look she got whenever she was ready to fight. [*If you don't give that order, you will destroy this mission. Those New Witlunders may be poorly trained, but they've already lost at least six of their own trying to derail the ceasefire. You really think they'll hesitate to kill you?*]

I stood there blinking in the sunlight, the sweat pouring off of me, the stench of death hanging in the air above the bodies like a blanket. She was right. They *would* want to kill me. And Vermier *didn't* really matter. Not against the lives of six hundred million people.

But I couldn't order Raeburn to blow up that shed—to kill everyone inside it, friend or foe.

That kind of thinking might have suited Ansell Sterling, but it didn't fit Raymin Dahl. Such coldblooded calculation was the very thing Dahl had been railing against his entire career. He wasn't one of those soulless Fleet uniforms who sent men to die over brunch at a private club. Raymin Dahl was the guy who exposed them.

For that matter, I wasn't the guy in the field who made the hard decisions no one else wanted to make, then spent a lifetime trying to forget them.

I wasn't my dad.

[No,] I said. [They won't hesitate to kill me. I'll have to talk them out of it.]

"Lieutenant Dogen, New Witlund QRS to Captain Sterling, UCMC—" [*Don't do that!*]

Before I could change my mind I pulled the radio out and thumbed the transmission button. "Captain Sterling, United Colonial Marine Corps. What do you want?"

"Sterling," Lieutenant Dogen said. He seemed surprised I'd finally answered. "There's been enough bloodshed. All we want is to talk."

"So talk."

"Not like this. In person. The colonel for you. Come unarmed to the door. I'll send her out when you're a few meters away. If you run, we'll kill you both. If you cooperate, you'll both live. You have my word."

His word. Maybe that meant something and maybe it didn't. Before I put my life in his hands I needed to know the colonel was still alive. "Put her on."

A short pause, then Vermier's unmistakable voice saying, "Captain, you will take out that frigate and—"

Silence. A moment later Dogen said, "You have one hour. Then she gets a bullet in the head."

I turned and looked at Laclos, who had walked over from the front porch and was watching me with narrowed eyes. "Sir, that's not a good idea."

"Give me a minute." I handed her the radio and headed towards the covered sled port. Past the dead grendels and into the shade. Through the empty bays and halfway to the red convertible that was unlike any I'd seen before. Obviously an import from some core system manufacturer so exclusive they didn't need to market to someone like me.

Ivy ghosted into view next to me, worry clouding her eyes. She wasn't real, of course, but the filmy projection was enough to stop me in my tracks just under the overhang.

[*You don't have to prove anything,*] she said, facing me. [*Not to me, not to Fleet, and especially not to your father.*]

[What are you talking about?]

[*You want to hate him, but you can't because he's a war hero. He has campaign stars and valor ribbons and a reputation for looking out for his marines. And unlike your mother he at least didn't leave you. So, how could you hate a man like that?*]

I didn't hate him, but she had no idea, this ghost-Ivy in front of me, the girl with Ivy's face, Ivy's mannerisms, Ivy's way of standing with her weight on one foot, arms crossed as if calculating her next move on a chessboard. [I don't hate him.]

[*No. You want to be like him.*]

[You don't know what you're talking about.]

[*It's not his fault that he only really understood one thing. How to be an officer but not a dad. That's why the only real choice you've ever had was to not become him. So you ran away from the academy, enlisted in the reserves, and made a career out of turning the UCMC into a living hyperbole. You write puff pieces that are so overblown the only people who can't tell they're lies are the officers who want to see heroes in the mirror. And buried somewhere in all that patriotic verbiage are the implications of what you really believe. That the colonies are corrupt. That the Corps is rotting away. That the war is being lost because it wasn't worth winning in the first place.*]

[First I want to be my father,] I said. [Now I want to be a grendel?]

[*You are not a traitor. Your father was wrong. And this is the wrong decision. You cannot walk into that shed alone.*]

I realized suddenly that she didn't believe I could do it. Not really. And somehow that hurt worse than everything else.

I took a deep breath. Ivy would have to stay behind. If the militia saw what was on Sterling's comms, my story would never get out. [Okay. Talk to you soon.]

[*Please,*] Ivy said.

I pressed the release tab and peeled off Sterling's comms. Ivy's ghost flickered away, her presence in my head melted to silence, and the loneliness of the sled port assaulted my senses.

All around the quiet heat of the compound thickened. The dead bodies of the grendels and the militia were beginning to swell under the buzz of swarming insects.

Nearby stood a row of heavy ceramic jars with miniature banana trees sprouting from each center.

I scooped back a handful of soil in one of them, pressed Sterling's comms down into it, and covered it up with dirt.

Clenched both hands into fists to keep them from shaking. Shoved away the thought that I had just buried Ivy as surely as if I'd lowered her body into the earth.

Sweat saturated my fatigues and brought a sudden dryness to my throat. It wasn't likely that Lieutenant Dogen and his New Witlunders would kill me. Not right away. They'd want information first.

They'd want to know the truth.

So I'll tell them, I thought. *I'll tell them what they want to hear.*

9

FEATURE WRITER

"How you feeling, sir?" Laclos asked.

We were sitting in the kitchen at a rustic wooden table carved to look like something from a hunter's lodge and coated in enough transparent plasteel to armor a cargo shuttle. Laclos sat across from me with a bottle of cold water and a single white pill at her elbow. Time for another steady-stim, but not until I proved I hadn't become a grendel sleeper agent by reconnecting to Sterling's comms. I felt like a dog waiting on a treat.

"Tired," I said. "And angry, to be honest."

She looked up from the tablet she was recording my vitals on. "Second thoughts? You don't have to do this, you know."

"You think they won't shoot her?"

Laclos shrugged. "I think they understand the hell they'll bring down on themselves if they don't back off. Dogen is already looking at a twenty-year term. Or worse." She looked down at her tablet, then read from a diagnostic. "You notice anything different about your AI when you put it back on?"

"No," I said truthfully. Ivy hadn't changed riding in my pocket. She'd been exactly what I expected. Exactly what I *needed*.

Laclos stared at me with narrowed eyes as a wave of guilt knotted my throat. I couldn't tell her that, yes, my comms might be infected by a grendel wyrm, but I had no way of knowing for sure, and even if it was infected, I still needed to use it in order to complete my mission. Because I wasn't really Captain Sterling.

Maybe I'd be able to tell her at some point, but not now. Not when I was about to walk unarmed to the door of that utility shed.

She looked back at her tablet. "After the *Strangler* attack, did the onboard system display any firewall warnings?"

"Yes. She said it was a fifth generation attack she was well prepared to handle." Also the truth, though it left out the important caveat of not taking it off. Which I had done twice. Three times if you counted taking it off initially.

Laclos flashed a curious smile. "She?"

"It's an advanced system," I said. "A PSYOPS thing, meant to tidy up your grid through deep neural bonding. I even had to give her a name." This last bit of information slipped out before I realized what I was saying.

"Oh?" she said, typing rapidly. "And what do you call her?"

"Ivy," I said. "Like the plant, not the injection."

She smiled again and slid the pill across the table with the bottle of water. "This should help with the climb."

I slipped the pill onto my tongue. "So I'm not a monster?"

"You are," she said. "You're just one of ours. Drink all of that."

I did as instructed, gulping the cool water as the near-instant stimulant worked its magic. By the time I'd emptied the bottle I was ready to go. "Let's get this over with."

Raeburn appeared in the doorway holding a jar from the pantry. He spread flour across the table, then sketched a map of the hill in the powder. "Pajari's upstairs with a clear shot all the way up the mountain. Do not make a move until Vermier clears the threshold. When the door is open and you have the space to do it, dive on the colonel and roll. Pajari will fire over your head with the long gun, which should buy you a couple of seconds."

I pictured grabbing Colonel Vermier and pulling her to the ground. "She's not going to be happy. Especially if she gets hurt."

"Cross that bridge," Raeburn said. "Hopper's in the trees at four o'clock. *Here.* Level with the door but at a bad angle. From that spot he can put a lot of rounds into the opening without hitting anything."

"Plus it's Hopper," Laclos said, straight-faced. "He can put a lot of rounds anywhere without hitting anything."

Raeburn ignored her. "Mostly he'll add noise and confusion to the inside of that shed so the unfriendlies don't take potshots at you on your way out."

Unfriendlies. I'd forgotten the term. "So we get one shot from Pajari after I make the first move, then the colonel and I better be as far away as possible if we want to live?"

Laclos looked stricken, like I'd just slapped her. "I was kidding, sir. We've got your back. Hopper's actually a great shot."

She'd been trying to help me relax. Probably figured Sterling's robust combat history would kick in with the right encouragement. But how would I know what it was like to play the part of a battle-hardened veteran? I decided to go for the easy insult. "Not what it says in his top-secret PSYOPS file."

Laclos laughed nervously. "Quote you on that?"

"When it's over. Don't give him any excuses."

Raeburn slid his index finger twice through the flour. "This plan makes the mountain your enemy going up, and your friend coming down. If they don't shoot you as soon as the door opens, you'll have the first move. Since action beats reaction nine times out of ten, you should be able to dive on Vermier and pull her to the ground. We'll buy you time to roll downhill a few meters until you're out of their line of site. Doc and I will also provide additional covering fire as you run back to the compound. Of course, all of this depends on you being right. That they want to *use* you, not *execute* you."

"I'm right," I said, injecting more confidence in my voice than I actually felt. "Let's get it over with."

"You *sure* you're up for this, Captain?"

I rose, the sweat on the back of my uniform clammy against my skin. "We've got nine dead, including three grendel peacekeepers. And it would have been worse if Trevalyan hadn't left the place almost empty. What happened here is about to be repeated on a scale we haven't seen since the war started. It's *already* happening on Quelon.

As I see it, we've got this one chance to work something out with the Alliance. The only thing standing in the way of a ceasefire is that pack of overpaid idiots in the shed."

I didn't specifically mention Colonel Vermier as one of the idiots, but I didn't leave her out, either.

Raeburn nodded at Laclos and picked up his rifle. "Good luck, sir."

They left through the front door.

I counted to a hundred before following them into a wave of heat that was somehow worse than it had been thirty minutes earlier.

Left the compound through the main gate.

Headed west up the slope towards the utility shed.

If time slowed to a crawl yesterday when Sterling was bleeding out in that third-floor office, it seemed to stop altogether as I climbed.

The building jutted from the mountain like a concrete dormer, its rear wall nestled into the hillside. Hopper had briefly looked through the house for blueprints but didn't have the time for a thorough search. I suspected the shed was actually the entrance to a larger storage facility where the cartel kept its supply of "product" to be readied for shipment. Which meant Dogen's militia probably had access to whatever firepower Trevalyan kept there for emergencies.

I plodded methodically up the slope, running my hands through waist-high sawgrass as if to catch a few last impressions of life. The jungle had been cut back all the way to the top, probably to make movement smoother for the cargo sleds hauling bundles between the cartel sky port and the shed. The result was a kind of terraced ascent reminiscent of the Mayan pyramids.

Six minutes dragged into an eternity. Every step, every heartbeat, every glance at that reinforced door seemed a roll of the dice, as if at any moment a mag round would punch a hole in my chest and I'd drown in my own blood as Sterling had. But this was the story I'd come to write, so I kept walking.

For the last four years Raymin Dahl had been writing feature stories from an OrbSyn cubicle—or a skyport terminal, or a base lounge, or even the barstool of some territorial roadhouse—and never actually seen what he described. It had always been someone else, some soldier or marine or fleet with a faraway look and an ear for the story readers wanted to hear.

Now I was actually in the mix, and there was nothing heroic, nothing noble about it at all. I just wanted to be somewhere else. Would have given anything to be able to watch some other dumb puke climb that hill in my place, and maybe watch through a scope as Pajari and Raeburn and Hopper were watching me.

All those faraway looks I'd seen during my interviews came back to me in a rush. That attitude of disgust and loathing as I asked the latest war hero to describe what it was like to live through a firefight. Maybe their commanding officer took a round through the neck, or a friend lost her legs to a cutter-drone, or a shipmate was bisected by an airlock door.

And how did you feel? I would say. And of course I could *see* what they were feeling as soon as I asked. It was etched on their faces. They wanted to beat my brains out for asking such an arrogant, stupid pogue question.

But how they felt about the question wasn't what I was asking. And they never punished me, never even objected to the question. They knew I had to ask it. Because that's the story, and everyone knows it. The story is what you're feeling when things are at their worst and you do something brave and horrible and desperate anyway. That's all any story is.

And it was the story I was writing as I climbed that hill.

This story wasn't about me. It wasn't about the jungle or the cartel or the New Witlund militia.

It was about Sterling's comms. How it was probably infected with a grendel wyrm, a wyrm that had breached its firewall when the *Strangler* landed west of Seranik but didn't activate till Sterling took off his comms and I put it on.

That had been his risk to take. He'd understood the dilemma but decided the pros outweighed the cons. And he'd trusted me to deliver the United Colonies' terms to the Alliance, even if the process of doing so was compromised. Even if it meant my mind might be torn apart by a quantum infection. Even if the MADAR team that was sent to protect us were all killed as a result.

Our lives didn't matter when weighed against six hundred million souls. We didn't matter to a core government that was fighting for *billions* of free people to retain their natural autonomy, the freedom to think. How could the few of us compare to all of that?

No, this wasn't my story.

I was just the one writing it.

I passed the halfway point of the semi-pyramid, and though my shirt lay saturated with sweat against my skin, and my breathing sounded like that of a winded racehorse, the nervous jitters had started to melt away. The steady-stim Laclos had given me carried me on buoyant waves from terrace to terrace, every step bringing me closer to the moment of truth.

And suddenly, fingertips dusting the grass, I saw the connection. The slope up. The door at the top. The fact that I was writing a feature story for OrbSyn, and every feature was built like a pyramid rather than like the inverted triangle of hard news.

Raymin Dahl, OrbSyn word-pounder, was a *feature* writer!

That was why Sterling had plucked my name from Weston's ranks. My first-person features. Stories about people. Stories built on an inductive structure. Stories shaped like a pyramid, with the best parts coming at the very end.

The polar opposite of the structure used by the Grand Alliance. The grendel model of information delivery was, in every possible way that mattered, quite the reverse. They took a *deductive* approach to everything, with the important always coming first and the unimportant last. It was why they had stripped the action reports from the symb-collars of the advance security team when they died, but left behind—

Slick and Tanja.

I stopped about six meters from the door to the shed. Tried to recall the first thing, the very first thing Slick had discovered when probing Trevalyan's perimeter. The reason he had said the cartel had no serious security measures at all.

Asleep. The guard had been asleep. In a hidey-hole on the ridge just to the right. Slick had called it a hidden bunker. And what better position to occupy if you wanted to pour down fire on the inside of the compound?

The shed in front of me wasn't a warehouse. It was part of a tunnel system, with branches feeding off into the ridges on either side. Branches with other hidey-holes, other concealed bunkers, where Dogen probably had his soldiers stationed even now with their flash rifles.

Raeburn's plan wasn't going to work.

The door would open. Vermier would come out. And the moment I brought her down we'd be hit by fire from at least two directions.

I hesitated on the last terrace, but what choice did I have. Slowly I closed the gap to four meters. Three.

Stopped.

The door remained closed. Somewhere off in the distance a quetzal gave its low, mournful squall.

Was this really a feature story, after all? I wondered. *Or was it just a series of increasingly brutal facts: You lived. You served. You died.*

Betrayal. Brute force. Deception.

In a feature, most *important* was always subverted by most *interesting*. The tail became the head, and the head the tail. You never really know what a feature is about until the end. That's when everything that came before is revealed in a new light.

You can't appreciate that sort of story if you already know everything, or *think* you know everything. Maybe that was their weakness. The flaw against which Sterling meant to use me. Maybe the problem with grendels was that they thought they knew everything interesting just because they knew everything important.

Abruptly, the door to the shed opened on darkness, and for just a moment I saw nothing. Then Vermier stepped blinking to the threshold, her face turned down to escape the full force of the sun. Her hands were bound behind her back, her ankles restricted with quick-cuffs so that she could take only the tiniest of shuffling steps. They'd put a gag in her mouth, and the fury of her helplessness was written plainly across her face.

For one brief instant I realized her hatred was directed at me. As if I were to blame for her situation.

Then again, maybe I was.

"Slowly," a voice said from behind her.

From the darkness the muzzle of a flash rifle pointed past her at my chest.

If I intended to make a move, now would have been the time. But I could feel the scopes of other flash rifles targeting my back, and I knew that if I made any sudden movement, we'd never make it down the hill alive.

"Tell Raeburn they have shooters on the ridge," I said as Vermier scuttled up next to me. The sergeant major would want to know why I'd bailed on his plan.

But when I looked at Vermier again I remembered we wouldn't be in this situation if she hadn't forced herself on the team. I said, "You're welcome."

Face ablaze, she looked away and continued to shuffle.

Praying that Pajari's finger had moved away from the trigger of his sniper rifle, I stepped into the mouth of the shed.

The door closed behind me, and light flared, the sudden shift from light to dark to light disorienting.

I'd been right. The room did open up into the mountainside, with stacks of product on shelves going deep into a small warehouse.

Four soldiers, dressed in the fatigues of the New Witlund militia, stood around a table with a single empty chair.

Lieutenant Dogen stood in the center, even uglier now that a fresh cut had been opened, and subsequently stitched, across his forehead. He stared openmouthed as astonishment widened his eyes. "You're not Captain Sterling," he said. "You're that orderly."

"I told you," a woman's voice chided.

My heart leapt into my throat and stopped there, choking back whatever I'd been meaning to say.

Her voice was the sound of cheerful innocence, the sound of home, the sound of love that first drew me to her on Holikot, and when she stepped around the corner I realized I'd known from the beginning how this feature would end.

It was Ivy Weber.

10

CORPORAL DAHL

They searched me *very* thoroughly. Afterwards, I sat in my sweat-soaked underclothes, my wrists and ankles quick-cuffed to the chair.

A high-intensity work light set on a tripod shone directly into my face. Clichéd even for Dogen, but it was effective. It wouldn't leave a permanent mark, and in a courtroom would sound only mildly irritating. In reality it seemed to drain away what remained of my energy. Even the steady-stim Laclos had given me didn't seem to dim its effectiveness.

One of the soldiers clipped a temporary restraining-cuff across my left wrist, and I felt the prickle of activation all the way to my elbow. They'd be able to read my bios now. Probably a lot more, though they still wouldn't be able to access any part of my mind I didn't yield willingly.

"I'm going to ask you some questions," Dogen said, swiping a datapad on the table across from me. His using the pad was a bad sign. It meant he didn't want his own comms connected to the cuff on my wrist. "If I don't like your answers, you won't either."

"There's no need for that," Ivy said, too late.

Pain lanced into my arm from the wrist all the way to the shoulder. It felt like someone had shoved a needle down the length of my forearm.

In the aftermath, nausea tore at my insides. I wanted to call Dogen a sadist and a traitor but knew he'd make me pay for it.

Besides, that sick feeling wasn't all Dogen's fault. The fact Ivy was here couldn't be a coincidence. Somehow she'd used me for information. Used me to gain access to . . . what? What had I known as a journalist and inadvertently revealed? That I was researching the MADAR program? That I was meeting with Captain Sterling? That I was interviewing an intelligence officer on Ivy's home world?

Dogen sat in a chair one of his men pulled up. He scrutinized Ivy's face. "You don't have to stay for this."

"I'm not going anywhere," she said. "And if you try any more of that cowboy act, I'll have you baking tiles in a work camp."

Gratitude washed over me. Then nausea again.

She wasn't on my side. Wasn't my girlfriend. Wasn't who she'd claimed to be.

Was her name even Ivy?

He stared at her icily, then looked back at me. "Who are you?"

"Raymin Dahl. Corporal. Kanzin Colonial Reserve Infantry."

The name didn't seem to mean anything to him. "Reserve infantry? You're not UCMC?"

I shook my head. "I'm a Communication Specialist in the 82nd Transport-Ready Battalion." My voice sounded weak, and I despised it. I nodded towards the cuff on my wrist, feeling cowardly. "And you don't have to use that thing. I came here to tell you what you want."

"Why were you with Sterling?"

"I'm a journalist. Sterling pulled some strings to get me assigned to the peace talks with the grendel emissary. Said he wanted me to write a story about it. Sell peace to the edge colonies."

"And you agreed?"

"He didn't give me any choice. My editor told me I'd be writing about a new special ops unit training at Camp Locke. Sterling only gave me the real assignment a few minutes before you blew up the mess hall."

"Where's Sterling now?"

I tried to swallow but found it impossible. My throat felt swollen. "Inside a freezer in the camp morgue."

"He's dead? How?"

"You shot him when we were running from that Snapper."

"No. We saw both of you go into the building, and it was *your* body they carried out. We saw his comms—"

"I stole his comms," I admitted. "I've been impersonating him ever since."

Dogen's face flushed. Or maybe it was heat from the high-intensity light. He looked down at the datapad. Probably debating whether to give me another jolt.

One of the soldiers cursed under his breath.

"Told you," Ivy said again.

"Why?" Dogen asked. "You say you didn't want this assignment. So why make it happen? Why risk a court-martial and execution and—" He paused as a new thought crossed his face. "Are you working for them? The Alliance?"

"No. No, of course not. I'm a journalist. I write puff pieces for OrbSyn. I have no connection to the—"

"Then *why*?"

How was I supposed to answer that? A man like Dogen, paranoid, fearful, drunk on his new-found power, would never believe that a man like me would care about something as ethereal as the truth. But what else could I tell him? I tried to swallow again and said, "He told me it was the only way to save the edge."

"You believed him?"

"Yes."

"You're lying." He reached for the datapad.

"Wait!" I blurted. "Look, I know it sounds crazy, but—we're losing this war. You know that, right? Fleet can't hold the edge much longer."

His finger hovered over the screen. "How would you know that?"

"I'm a reporter."

"Fleet tells you what's really going on?"

I shook my head. "Never any real intel. But I do see what they send instead, and that's almost as good if you know what to look for. They have us writing feel-goods. OrbSyn wants to sell the idea that victory is just around the corner. You see very much of that stuff, and you start to get the idea. It's like a shadow. A negative impression. You can tell what's there by what isn't."

Ivy came closer and sat on the edge of the table to my left. "I knew you were brilliant the first time we met, Raymin. Do you remember?"

Somehow she made my heart race and my stomach turn at the same time. Dad was right, I decided. Love does make you cynical. "Never forget it."

She smiled—sadly, it seemed to me. She brushed my left wrist with her fingertips, just at the edge of the prison cuff. "What happened to Sterling's comms, Raymin?"

"I took it off."

"Why?"

Her smile was too much. Too much gentleness. Too much tenderness. Too much promise. She knew how to peel me open. I looked back at Dogen. "I believe it's infected with a grendel wyrm."

For the first time the lieutenant seemed taken aback. He shifted in his chair as if searching for the right question.

I didn't want him fiddling with the datapad, so I decided to answer all the questions he wouldn't think to ask. What better way to convince him I was telling the truth?

"The enemy warship that landed yesterday morning is a *Strangler* class frigate. It launched a wyrm array at Sterling's comms. His onboard AI initially kept it behind a firewall, but also told him the wyrm might be able to gain access on restart."

"And when he died and you put it on—" Ivy prodded.

"It was a risk Sterling wanted to take," I said. "He *ordered* me to impersonate him. Told me to put on his comms and follow the instructions in the mission file. He said the peace talks were essential."

"And now you think his comms is infected?" Dogen looked mystified. "Then why come here? You either believe in the mission or you don't. You can't expect us to accept both."

"Why not?" I asked. "If both things are true?"

Ivy looked quizzical, as if finally hearing something she hadn't anticipated. "Why are you here?"

"To meet with the grendel emissary. I'm following Sterling's orders."

"He told you to follow the mission in his comms. But you took it off." She slid from the table and came around to my right side, her left hand draped over my right shoulder. She knelt beside me. "Why?"

My sweat had evaporated now, and my sodden undershirt felt clammy against my skin. "The grendels won't show up while there's a hostage situation in the area. You asked for Sterling, and as far as anyone else knows that's me. And it has to stay me in order for that meeting to happen."

"So you agreed to the swap hoping you could *talk* your way out of here?" She smiled coyly, as if guarding some private joke.

"Yes," I said. "Because I know these peace talks are the best hope any of us have to survive. And I thought maybe another militia would respect *libertas cogitandi.*"

Freedom of thought. The rallying cry of every colonial militia across the edge.

Dogen didn't even blink.

Suddenly, Ivy's hand on my shoulder disgusted me. She was still using me. Playing with my emotions, touching my skin, treating me like some kind of primitive hand terminal to be switched on and off whenever a bit of useful intel was needed for the cause.

I didn't know her, I realized. I'd never known her. Not really. I'd fallen in love with a fake person, with a mask.

But her hand was still burning there on my shoulder, and I wanted it off.

"Of course, I didn't realize *you'd* be here." I looked Ivy in the eyes as I said it. "I didn't know there'd be a traitor in their midst."

Her expression hardened.

She rose. Went around to the other side of the table by the light where I could barely stand to look at her. Picked up Dogen's datapad and held it there, hand poised above the screen as if daring me to say something else.

"Is your name even Ivy?" I asked.

For a moment I thought—I really thought—that she wouldn't use it. I was wrong.

"Why did you remove Sterling's comms?" Dogen asked when I had finished vomiting.

"Couldn't . . . let it see," I croaked, "what I was planning to tell you."

Ivy softened a little and picked up a water bottle. When she pressed it to my lips, the wetness in my mouth was glorious.

I drank half as much as I wanted before she took the bottle away and set it on the table in front of me.

"Nothing you've told us would make any difference," Dogen said, his arms crossed in a way that expanded his biceps. Probably he thought it made him more intimidating.

"Then you haven't listened," I said. "You think the grendels are monsters. If New Witlund is occupied, you think you'll fight a guerrilla war. That's what every colonial thinks. But it never happens. Because they aren't monsters. They're . . ."

Dogen glanced at Ivy, whose face was furrowed into a deep scowl. "What did it do to you, Corporal?"

Do to me? What did it do to me? What an idiotic question! "It terrified me," I said. "And you still aren't listening. The grendel wyrms aren't what you think they are, and that's why we're losing. They're not monsters. They're genies."

Dogen leaned forward. "Like, in a bottle?"

"Give you what you want. Or think you want. And you'll never let them go."

"You did," Ivy said. "You took it off."

"I only wore one for a few hours," I said. "And as soon as I'm out of here, I'm going to put it back on."

Ivy's brows arced. "You still think you're going to complete Sterling's mission?"

I nodded. "I have to. I'm the last chance any of the colonies have."

"Last chance?" Dogen said, clearly disgusted. "You're a *corporal*!"

That was probably as solid a fact as I would find here. But it was time to tell them the rest of it. They were ready. They could believe they'd twisted it out of me. "Sterling's comms isn't just infected. It's also *carrying* an infection. A wyrm of our own, designed to backtrack through the Alliance servers and cripple the grendel AI architecture. I found the file in a restricted folder hidden from the AI."

Ivy studied me for a moment. "It'll never get through. Their firewalls—"

"—are designed to prevent a forced intrusion," I said. "But we're not going to force anything. The grendel AIs will be the ones to install the wyrm in their own servers. When they run my story, they'll run our countermeasure."

They looked at each other. The three soldiers who had been listening in the corner sat in motionless silence.

"How are you going to arrange that?" Ivy asked. "With Sterling dead."

"Sterling was never the one to make it work. It was always supposed to be me. Corporal Dahl. OrbSyn journalist and part-time patsy. I wasn't supposed to find out that our own counter-virus would be riding the back of one of my features. All I had to do was to write the story of our surrender."

"The grendel authorities will broadcast it into their own territories," Ivy said breathlessly. "They'll send it themselves to mock our impotence."

"A PSYOP," I said.

The silence stretched into a long moment, and I remembered that first night on Holikot when I saw her standing alone at a table in the lounge. As though she could walk away from anyone and anything.

Ivy crossed her arms and stared at me. I thought I saw regret on her face, but by then I didn't care.

Really. I didn't care.

But I kept looking at her anyway.

"It won't work," Dogen said at last. "Will it?"

"One way to find out," I suggested.

"No," Ivy said. "It won't work. Their AIs will spot the virus and remove it. *Then* they'll send your story. And you'll have given them more ammunition. You'll have made the collapse of the edge even easier."

"You have a better idea?"

She stared at me again for another long moment and then nodded slowly. The coldness in her eyes sent a shiver along my spine. "Yes. You're going to tell them who you are. No more pretense. No more games. No more Captain Sterling. You're going to get on an open channel and tell anyone and everyone that Sterling is dead."

"My special ops team will blow the *Strangler*," I said. "And we will never get another chance at this."

"*Your* special ops team?" Ivy laughed. "You're really buying into this officer act, aren't you? Tell you what, Corporal. You admit who you are over an open channel, and I'll let you walk back to your unit. We'll even clear the area. See if *your* marines still want you to talk peace with the grendels."

"What does it *matter* what they want? They don't know any of this!" I strained against the quick-cuffs as adrenaline surged through my body. The thin cords cut into my flesh, drawing crescents of blood, and Dogen reached for the datapad.

Ivy snatched it away from him and ran her fingers across the surface.

To my surprise, I felt no pain; she must have been calling up some other function.

"What about Quelon?" I demanded as the light from the tripod intensified. "We're within spitting distance of a planetary war. Do you not realize what's going to happen here if we don't act?"

She set the datapad on its edge towards me, and I saw myself reflected in its primitive surface. She was recording this, but zoomed in so that only my face and shoulders were visible.

I couldn't look long. The high-intensity light made my head pound.

"Quelon?" She asked in a mocking tone. "You mean that *terrible* attack yesterday on an unsuspecting planet?"

How did she know? No one but Vermier and a handful of core officers in Camp Locke could have known what was on that thirty-second subnet recording. Was our intelligence service really so porous?

Ivy came around to my side again and leaned over to look me in the face. "Poor Raymin." She brushed back a strand of hair from my forehead and bit her lower lip. "Brilliant but gullible. How do you know Quelon has really been attacked? How do you know all of those transmissions about the Alliance's 3rd fleet and the grendel shock troops jumping planet-side didn't originate with the *Strangler*? The grendels have a PSYOPS unit too, you know."

Yes. Of course. If the *Strangler* could hack a PSYOPS officer's comms unit , sever all communications on New Witlund, and render an entire Marine Corps base helpless in the span of a few milliseconds, what would be so hard about severing a subnet connection?

I didn't know if her theory was true or not, but it didn't matter. The question had done its work. She'd given me reason to doubt. Reason to doubt Sterling. Reason to doubt the grendels. Reason to doubt the AI and the friendly virus and even the stability of the Marine Corps. If we could be hacked so deeply that we didn't know it, and didn't think to even question it, how could we know anything?

She reached for the water bottle, touched it gently to my lips.

I drank gratefully and listened to the sound of my own heartbeat.

"It's okay," she said. "Take your time."

I did.

I thought through everything that had happened over the last day and a half. Everything I believed, or thought I believed, and landed on a set of solid facts.

1. My name was Raymin Dahl, and
2. If I *told* people my name was Raymin Dahl, Sterling's team would blow the *Strangler,* or try to, and we'd learn other solid facts about what was really going on, and
3. If we knew what was really going on, maybe we could do something about it, and
4. I was sick of lying, and
5. I wasn't ready to die, and
6. Dogen had pulled his flash rifle from his shoulder and leveled it at my chest.

The datapad was still blinking red.

My head pounded.

My stomach did a little flip.

They would kill me afterwards, I knew. Ivy might even do it herself.

"I'm not who I say I am," I began. "My name isn't Ansell Sterling. And I'm not a captain—not even an officer. I've never been part of any Psychological Operations command. And the only military training I've ever had was grunt basic back on Kanzin."

"What else?" Ivy prompted.

"The real Captain Sterling took a round through his right lung and choked on his own blood outside Seranik City. I stole his comms bracelet and his identity, on his orders, in order to carry out a clandestine, unofficial meeting with a representative from the Grand Alliance."

"And what's your real name?" Ivy asked.

"My real name is Corporal Raymin Dahl, Communication Specialist with the 82nd Transport-Ready Battalion, KCRI. I'm not a captain. I'm not in intelligence. And I'm not a marine."

She bit her lower lip again, rocking a little on her heels, as if in sympathy. Her voice was quiet. "What *are* you, Raymin?"

"I'm a military journalist with OrbSyn. I write puff pieces to hide the fact we're losing this war."

"So you're a reporter?"

"I'm a reporter. I lie for a living."

There was another long pause.

Ivy stood and typed something on the datapad. Waited a moment longer. Nodded. "That's it," she said. "It's gone out."

"Open channel?" Dogen asked.

"Open channel," Ivy said.

I expected a bullet.

Instead, Dogen lowered his rifle. "Thank you for your service." He nodded at me and disappeared into the shadows as someone switched off the tripod light.

They were taking other exits. Of course they were. It would be foolish to go out the front when they knew the mountains, knew Seranik, knew the cartel. They were going to get away untouched and unfollowed by slinking off through the tunnel system and whatever exits lay hidden on the far side of the ridge.

Ivy piled my clothes on the table and took out a small pocket knife. She sliced the quick-cuff off of my right hand and set the knife on top of my clothing. I'd have to pull myself one-handed around the edge of the table to reach the knife, then cut the other restraints before I could leave. It would buy her and the rest of her team time to get away.

I didn't care. It meant they weren't going to kill me.

But I guess I didn't care much about that either. Not while she was still there in the room, staring at me.

She came to my side one last time and kissed me on the mouth.

I should have turned away, but I let her lips linger.

I'd say I don't know why, but that would be a lie.

"Goodbye, Raymin," she said.

I didn't respond, even though she stood there long enough I could tell she wanted me to say something, to grant her absolution, but I didn't do that either. That one *is* a mystery. Too much of a fool even then, I suppose.

Ever since yesterday morning I'd been second-guessing myself, second-guessing the connection I had to Sterling's comms. It wasn't real, I'd reasoned. Just some sort of mind game. A grendel trick to make me dependent.

But now, who was the real deceiver? The woman I'd loved—no, *thought* I'd loved—turned out to be some sort of operative for a dissident militia. She'd used me. Probably meant to use me all along.

But the AI had never claimed to be anything other than what she was. She'd chosen the name Ivy because the name was meaningful to me. It had been a promise. She could be what I needed. What I wanted.

She would be *there*.

I sat in the silence for a little while, then worked my way around to the knife and cut myself loose. I dressed and pushed open the door, half expecting a bullet from one of the friendlies. Pajari maybe, or Hopper. Maybe even Laclos.

But who was I kidding? They were all unfriendlies now.

The sun had dropped beyond the ridge, and the copper sky shimmered a rusty brown.

I stepped out, hands raised, moving slowly at first, then more quickly when I admitted to myself that they were all gone.

Raeburn had orders to blow the *Strangler* if things went sideways. And from his perspective things had definitely gone sideways. The original mission was blown. Vermier was probably throwing a royal tantrum. I'd be lucky to avoid summary execution.

I guess I had hoped that someone on the team would wonder if I was saying all that stuff under duress, that maybe none of it was true. But it's not easy to fool special operators once they know what to look for.

Besides, Vermier was probably saying that she knew something was wrong with me all along. That she could spot a real marine at a hundred meters. That I was no marine.

The compound stood empty and silent, just as I had expected.

I stopped for a long drink at the fountain inside the gates, then trudged into the sled port. The red convertible was gone too.

Of course it was.

But that didn't matter. Not now.

I dug my hands into the soil of the planter and sighed with relief as my fingers touched the cool metal of Sterling's comms. I didn't even bother to wipe the dirt off. Just shoved it around my wrist and pressed the two halves together.

She tickled the skin beneath my palm, and soothed it where the quick-cuff had cut me open. She strode into my mind with a dignified air like a queen coming to her throne.

[Hello, Ivy,] I said. [Did you hear the transmission?]

[*I did. And I'm very sorry.*] Her voice was soft. A mixture of contrition and empathy. [*You received a message a few minutes ago from the Alliance emissary. Text only. Would you like to read it?*]

[I'd rather you read it to me,] I said. [Please.]

[*It says, "Corporal Dahl: I have reviewed your transmission sent via satcom. Our analysis of your words indicates that you were probably compelled to speak by external pressures, but that your admission is substantially factual. Under the circumstances, I will agree to meet with you to discuss a negotiated peace and the surrender of your edge colonies. That is to say, to avoid further loss of life, it seems worthwhile to hear the concessions your superiors authorized Sterling to make. Unfortunately, my security detail has advised me against using the original meeting place. If you want to make this work, and if indeed you have the authority to make this work, you will have to come to me. We can discuss this aboard my ship, the* Takwin. *Let me know within the hour if this arrangement is agreeable, and I will send an escort to ensure your safety. I understand you are probably alone and in need of rest. My men can be there in the morning. Your servant, His Gracious Excellence G.A. Hayan."*]

[That's it?]

[*That's it.*]

[I can turn over the colonies tomorrow?]

[*Yes. It's in the best interests of everyone.*]

[All right. Send my reply. I'll come to him.]

I turned towards the mansion door, now closed. I was exhausted, but my mind still raced. If Laclos were here I would have asked her for a sedative so that I could finally sleep. But I recognized the jittery nervousness in my hands, the haunting echoes of words lingering in the periphery of my mind. It would be hours before I calmed down enough to sleep.

[Now what?] I asked. Not because I really wondered, but because I wanted to hear Ivy's voice again.

I missed her.

[*You wanted to write a war story,*] Ivy suggested.

And I realized if I did that, she would know everything. Because I was going to write all of it. The counter-virus; the presence of my ex-girlfriend; the likelihood that when dating Ivy I had given her, and thus the militia, clues about what was going on without even realizing it; the shame of my own failure—the whole story, just as it happened.

And I didn't care.

[Will you read it?] I asked.

[*If you let me,*] Ivy said.

[I'd like that.]

PART THREE

SLAVE TO A QUANTUM MASTER

BY CPL RAYMIN DAHL

EMBEDDED WITH MADAR TEAM TWO

11
CONTROL

I wasn't supposed to enlist the way I did: last day of class, alcohol in my blood stream, bleeding from a gash on the top of my head. Dad wanted me in Fleet, and I had agreed. Technically, Command and Control is merit-based. But sons of decorated officers come pre-packaged in merit, and everyone knew if I signed for officer candidate school with Fleet, my ticket to the Office of Strategic Operations would be punched immediately and without question. STRATOP was a plumb launch point, and as near a guarantee of good fortune as any colonial can have.

But it wasn't a future I wanted, and even though I'd agreed to sign on the dotted line as soon as I earned my degree, I'd also started drifting by the recruiting kiosk at the campus student union whenever my classes ended.

Sergeant Houts was big, friendly, and had a handshake like a hydraulic press. His uniform was immaculate, and though he might have gotten more sign-ups if he'd worn a prosthetic arm, he instead chose to pin the left sleeve to the shoulder in a neatly folded rectangle.

Somehow I'd talked the sergeant into giving me a preview of the Armed Services Vocational Aptitude Assessment on the morning of my last day of classes. I'd taken a couple of fake prep tests, but I wanted to see the real thing. I didn't know if my father would pull strings to make my results fit STRATOP's criteria, but I wouldn't put it past him. And I wanted to know what I was actually good at.

Houts knew I wasn't going to sign with him. He was a ground pounder, not a Fleet recruiter. He knew who my father was and probably understood better than I did the opportunities that connection afforded me. In fact, he told me I was stupid for talking to him, and anyone dumb enough to turn down a ticket to Fleet OCS was actually too stupid for the infantry.

But he sent the test to my comms anyway and witnessed my hour-long ritual completion via his own connection to AFNET.

That afternoon when classes were over I stopped by to talk about the results.

"Says you're smarter than you look," Houts said, his face twisted in exaggerated surprise. "High tendencies in predictive behavior, statistical analysis, communications, and contextual manipulation. Son, Fleet is gonna love you."

"Thanks," I said. Then, out of curiosity, I asked, "What if I don't want to go to Fleet OCS?"

"Then you're an idiot," he said. "And the test I gave you is wrong. Which would make *me* wrong. And that is statistically impossible."

"I mean, where would the Corps, or even the reserves, place me if I didn't sign with Fleet?"

He gave a shrug and looked left, scanning his grid for options. "Best match is with Public Information Command. Happens to be my bailiwick. Flow of information to and from the public."

"So it's marketing?"

"Something like that," he said, his back stiffening. "Marketing in all its forms is part of PIC. But it's bigger than that. It's also the umbrella for military journalism, psychological warfare, strategic disinformation, and dozens of related specialties."

"Sounds like propaganda."

"Well, now that's a harsh word. And one that's been shaped by propaganda to make it sound sinister—so you won't recognize it in its more benign forms. No, the PIC is more like a center for controlling the flow of stories around the republic. A way to circumvent the misinformation dumped on our colonies by the Grand Alliance. Public

Information Command is the marrow that cranks out white blood cells to fight the enemy within."

I had never seen myself as a propagandist, but three years of journalism classes hadn't spoiled my taste for shaping narratives. Add to that the allure of a shadow world, the luster of fighting grendel misinformation with counterintelligence, and Public Information Command sounded like a perfect fit. Then again, that was the point of the ASVAA test. Its AI was supposed to find a perfect match.

Dad would never allow it, of course. I was of age, so he couldn't legally stop me from enlisting in a different branch. But he could make my life miserable if I did. "Sounds intriguing. I wish I could, but—"

He shook his head, cutting me off. "Fleet needs intelligent people more than we do. Short supply in that branch."

I laughed and held out my hand. "Thanks for letting me take the test, Sergeant."

He gripped my hand in a way that told me he was holding back for my benefit. "No problem, son. You come out of OCS half the officer your father is, I'll be proud to say I met you here."

He turned to another student who had come up behind me at the kiosk, and I found myself moving heavily away from him, out onto the quad towards the base.

I covered the two kilometers to our apartment and opened the door with my comms. It was an older unit that had belonged to my father. As thick and heavy as a half set of handcuffs, it was nonetheless useful as a personal grid and terminal into the public side of AFNET. While I was in school, the design also marked me as a military brat, which made me something of a pariah in the journalism department. Everyone knew the armed services were screwed up. And privately I agreed with that sentiment. But publicly I wore the mask of a deeply committed patriot. My father was a hero, the war was necessary, and anyone who disagreed was either a moron or a traitor.

"There he is," my father's husky voice erupted from the corner. "The new college graduate."

Framed in afternoon sunlight from the picture window, he sat in his favorite recliner, gripping its arms like some barbarian king on a throne.

"Didn't expect you till dinner."

"Big day for you, and no more homework to worry about," he said. "I thought we'd celebrate with some friends down at Murry's."

He meant his friends, not mine. Three or four junior officers who'd been with him on various missions and were now caught in his gravitational pull at STRATCOM. He wanted to brag about me, but not from genuine pride. No, he just wanted to announce my decision to go to Fleet OCS so publicly that I couldn't change my mind. So that it would always have been my decision, and I'd never be able to say otherwise. Command and control were his bread and butter, but he was especially fond of butter.

"Sounds good," I lied and ducked into the head to wash up.

By the time we pulled into a parking spot at Murry's Bar & Grill, Dad's cabal was already seated at a table near the far wall. The place was popular with Fleet officers but typically didn't fill up until late in the evening.

Lieutenant Wyer waved us over by hoisting a pitcher of beer. She was the only woman in the group of four, and the youngest by ten years. She'd served with Dad as a combat controller handling air strikes and transportation logistics. The other lieutenants, Meers and Lomax, were beefy combat vets who had stories they'd never shared with me. But I fully believed they would have killed for my father, no questions asked. The fourth, Captain Potaznik, was a quiet, stern-faced strategist with vampiric gray eyes and hollow cheeks. He radiated an impression of danger far beyond that of the other three, like a proximity mine that may, or may not, be armed.

I slid into my assigned seat at the head of the table, an honor never before afforded to me. We ordered food, and I answered their polite questions about my classes, my reasons for majoring in journalism, and my plans to enter Fleet OCS.

Dad's lips pressed together when I said this, his chin lifting slightly. That expression was his only tell; for whatever reason, he didn't believe me.

Potaznik arched one brow and dabbed the corner of his mouth with a napkin before reaching over to pour more beer in my mug. He shifted the conversation to the most recent political scandal in the Senate, and I breathed a sigh of relief. I had no knowledge of the subject, so my participation in the talk would amount to little more than a few nods or the occasional question. Dinner came, and I listened to the governmental intrigue for at least two hours.

Meanwhile, Dad put down six beers before he started paying for the hard stuff. *This was a celebration*, he said. *Drinks were on him.* At some point he told me to, "Loosen up, son," and the way he slurred the s's I knew he was teetering towards the mean stage. Lieutenant Wyer noticed, too, and tried to wave off the waiter when he came to offer more booze. But Dad was on a roll: "You'll have to learn how to handle more than a couple of beers if you hope to make it at STRATCOM. Bring my kid two shots of the Inawa Red."

"I'm fine, Dad," I said.

"You're not fine till I say so. Take your medicine."

"I'm not sick."

It was the wrong thing to say. Dad wasn't used to being contradicted in front of his peers, and his face took on that look of suppressed rage I knew so well. The problem wasn't that he couldn't hide his fury, but that he could. "Are you saying you don't need any Kanzin courage to sign with Fleet? As promised?"

Potaznik looked at Wyre, his narrow jaw drawn down into a pointed scowl. They all knew what Dad could be like and had their reasons for justifying it.

But I didn't know what my war hero father was talking about, even though I recognized the accusation of cowardice at the heart of his question. "What's that supposed to mean?"

"We had an agreement."

As far as I knew, nothing had changed. Yet he was talking as if I had backed out of the arrangement—as if I'd just told everyone that I had changed my mind and decided to get a graduate degree in art appreciation. Worse, he was openly admitting that as far as he was concerned, I didn't really have a choice about my own future. And never had. Which made the idea of an 'agreement' hypocritical. "Yeah. You gave me an ultimatum when I was eighteen, and I said okay because I had no other options. And here I am."

"Here you are." His eyes flashed. "Eating my food. Drinking my beer."

"Sir—" Lieutenant Wyre interrupted.

Dad held up one finger to cut her off, but his eyes never left mine. I shoved my chair back. There was no talking to him when he got like this. And I knew if I said anything else we'd both regret it. After he'd slept it off he could drive me over to the Admin Center. I'd sign up and both of us would pretend this evening never happened. "Thank you for the dinner and the beer. I'll walk home."

He grabbed my right wrist and squeezed. I'd been starting to rise, but the action forced me back into the seat. Even drunk and pushing fifty, he was still physically formidable. His three combat citations had not been given to him as a favor. "I haven't excused you."

"What more do you want?"

He tightened his grip on my wrist as he looked each of the other officers in the eye. "My son took the Armed Services Vocational Aptitude Assessment this morning at a kiosk in the student union."

I felt my face flush as understanding washed over me. *That's* what this was about? My curiosity in talking to a recruiter from another branch? Somehow Dad must have—

"Scored in the upper 99ᵗʰ percentile," he continued. "Which would place him on the fast track for Fleet OCS and an ensign position at STRATCOM. A future where he could make a real difference using that brain of his for something other than writing *stories*." He spat the last word out as if it were something foul he'd just discovered in his mouth.

That confirmed everything I'd suspected over the years about how he felt regarding my choice of majors. *Congratulations, son. If you're done wasting your time now, why don't you start taking life seriously?*

"Yeah, I took the test. I was curious. And Sergeant Houts—"

"Curious?" Dad interrupted. "You mean *cowardly*. You didn't have the guts to tell your old man you wanted to join the weasels at OrbSyn, so you tried to slink off into the night with the infantry."

Lieutenant Wyre glanced from me to my father, as if sensing the explosion. "Sir, that seems a little strong."

By now the dinner conversations around us had faded away to silence. I could feel a dozen sets of eyes trying not to stare my direction.

I stood, my ribs squeezing, my dad still clutching my wrist in that relentless grip. "I'm going home," I said. "And tomorrow—"

I was going to say, *And tomorrow I'm going to enlist with Fleet, and you'll see you worried about nothing.* But his grip tightened even further, and he barked out a final command: "You are not excused!"

I just wanted to get away. I pivoted on my left foot and threw my weight backwards, drawing my right elbow towards my waist. It was a move I'd learned in one of the self-defense classes Dad had forced me to take as a kid, and it almost worked. He was sitting down and had only the strength of his own grip holding onto me. I was stepping backwards with all my weight, tugging at the weak space between thumb and forefinger.

But instead of taking a full step, my right foot struck the leg of the chair, which smacked into a pillar behind me. My knee bent, giving me very little backwards momentum. What should have been a neat slide backwards and a hasty retreat turned into an awkward, humiliating stumble, with my father still holding onto my arm.

It was the last degradation I would take. He was drunk. *Again.* And making me look like a complete idiot because he'd assumed all the worst things.

Fury erupted inside me. I brought my left forearm down on his wrist, at last breaking his hold on me, but apparently sparking something inside him as well.

I didn't see the beer mug coming in an arc from his right hand. It smashed into the top of my head, tipped the room sideways, and narrowed my vision to a dark tunnel of swirling faces and exaggerated movements. When the tunnel expanded again I found myself a couple of meters away on the floor, something warm and wet trickling down my face.

Dad was standing, shouting at me, "YOU'RE A DISGRACE!" while Meers and Lomax held him back.

Wyre knelt beside me and pressed a wet napkin to my head. "That looks worse than it is," she said. "But you might need a couple stitches. Can you stand?"

I pushed her away, rose, and lurched out into the night, the silence of the diners—most of them Fleet officers—as thick as it had always been when my dad was involved.

A moment ago I'd planned to walk home, but the war hero was in no condition to drive, and I knew one of his cronies would tuck him in eventually, so I took the sled.

I got most of the way home before I realized what I was doing. Then I had to summon a taxi from my comms, praying it would get here before Dad returned, and pre-paying for expedited service. They gave me an ETA of twenty minutes, which I could live with.

I waved the door open and hurried into my room. Stuffed some clothing into a daypack alongside my datapad. Opened the bottom drawer of my dresser where I kept the miscellaneous crap I never really used, plus an old ammo tin with my cash savings. I would need money to survive long enough to figure out what I was going to do. My bank accounts would last me a couple of days at best.

I flipped open the lid of the tin and swore. The cash was gone. All of it. Two and half years of carefully hoarded emergency funds plucked from my bedroom by my own father.

Who else would have done it? No one on base was stupid enough to steal from our residence. Clearly he'd expected some kind of confrontation. A hotheaded reaction. Maybe even a fight. Taking my cash was his way of chaining me to his influence. Once you were caught in his orbit, there was no escape.

I looked around the room at the spartan furnishings, the bland, off-white walls, the single window devoid of curtains, the dresser, the bed, the nightstand. None of it was really mine. All of it had come from him. My entire life. If I had a past here, it felt just as empty as my future. But if nothing in the room was necessary, then nothing here could hold me. I wasn't tied to him by anything except his old comms and my old memories.

The memories I might be stuck with, but I didn't have to wear his cast-off bracelet. I didn't actually need it now, just as I no longer needed his approval. Besides, if I continued to wear it, he'd just use it to track me down. He was probably doing that right now, checking on me via whatever tracking software he'd installed. He would see that I was home safe and sound, still tidally locked to his heavier mass, and that knowledge would put him at ease enough to buy me some time. Probably he would order another round of drinks.

I called up my AI. *His* AI. [You have the address for Sergeant Houts, Public Information Command, anywhere close to base?]

[*Campus recruitment?*]

[That's the one. Where does he live?]

I forwarded his address to the taxi service, verified receipt, then detached my father's old comms from my wrist. Dad would probably follow up on that, but by then it would be too late.

My ride wouldn't show up for another ten minutes. I didn't want to spend more time in the apartment than necessary, but there was still one thing left to do. My bedroom was five by five, the furniture aligned, my few possessions stowed. The bed was a bit sloppy from where I'd filled my day pack, so I tugged the fabric corners into crisp angles and smoothed the pillow. Took out the ammo tin and placed it in the center. Set his old comms inside with the lid hinged open so he couldn't miss it. Switched off the light and walked out to the street to wait.

Thirty minutes later I was knocking on a door that I sincerely hoped was the right address. By that point it was after midnight, and the air was thick with moisture under a starlit canopy not completely spoiled by light pollution.

Sergeant Houts answered the door in his boxers and a white undershirt, a passably lifelike prosthesis on his left arm. He looked annoyed. "You know what time it is, son? I work for a living—" He squinted into the darkness, his expression changing to surprise as he caught a glimpse of the blood on my face. "You all right?"

"I'm fine," I said. "Life just took a wrong turn, and I need to evac. I was hoping the PIC might still have an opening for a guy who likes to write stories."

He ran the good hand over his stubbled hair, looking past me into the night as if weighing his options. Maybe he suspected more than I imagined. At last he stood to the side and motioned me in. "You talk this over with your father?"

"Yeah," I said, stepping across the threshold into the light. "We talked it over."

12

THE *ISNASHI*

[*This will be your final test,*] Ivy said from the ether of waking. [*Today you will face the Isnashi in its own world.*]

Predawn light filtered through the open window, spreading muddy shadows through the room.

I'd fallen asleep in a recliner, and the air now felt clammy against my skin.

Slowly, Ivy's words edged their way into my waking mind. [Test?] I asked. [Isnashi?]

The shadows of furniture along the far wall shifted as light settled behind them in a blurred tapestry of falling vines.

> *I was running. Uphill, through a patch of clearing in the jungle, most of it hazy under the gloom of twilight. I got the sense I was running both to something and from something.*
>
> *On the other side, a hunter's blind shimmered ten or twelve meters off the ground.*
>
> *Sounds behind me, the thing, whatever it was, coming fast. As I leapt, the thing made a low rumbling sound, a sort of snuffle deep in its throat.*
>
> *I caught the tree on the instep spikes of my left*

boot, raked the trunk with eversteel claws extended, and nearly ran skywards, spiraling to the right as the Isnashi followed.

Only once did I glance over my left shoulder. The creature resembled a bear, except it was larger and more flat-bodied. It's tongue snaked out in a long flick behind me as I continued my scramble upward.

The tree actually groaned under its weight, and when I reached the blind I realized I'd been hoping the tiny shelter would provide enough protection to at least slow it down, if not camouflage me long enough I could take a killing shot. But how much of a shot would I get while trying to aim back around the tree rather than down?

I stumbled onto the narrow platform and grabbed my rifle, a precision Wasp EM-11 with five explosive rounds in the chamber. The blind wobbled under my weight as I leaned back against the hollow tube railing.

I lifted the stock to my shoulder but didn't know which side of the tree it would appear on, so I swung the barrel back and forth half a dozen times before pausing to listen.

The Isnashi made no sound at all. Even with augmentation set to priority, I couldn't hear any indication of its claws gouging the wood. Couldn't hear anything except the pounding of my heart against my ribs.

Five days and nights on the hunt. League after league of dry and wet trails. No real sleep, no food since the first day, and all my fresh water gone. A quick run to the LZ to plant my pickup beacon, and the monster chooses that moment to attack.

One way or the other, it would be the end of my selection.

The tree shook.

At last, something scraped the bark to my right.

*I swung the barrel over, licked my lips, and curled
my finger to the trigger.*
The jungle faded.

In my mind Ivy stood next to my recliner with her hands folded. I couldn't actually see her, of course, but I could feel her there, waiting.

[Where did you get that recording?]

[*I pulled it from the archives of the* Takwin. *A simple hack really, since it wasn't classified and had been marked as a failure. The candidate in question didn't pass selection.*]

Simple? Nothing about that recording was simple, including its origin. Yet Ivy somehow knew how to hack the archives of a J-class grendel frigate specializing in quantum intelligence.

I had little doubt that Sterling's comms was compromised. What I didn't know was the extent of it. Had Ivy been completely subsumed by a grendel wyrm, or was she fighting back, trying to wrest control from the enemy so that we could continue with the mission?

I rose from the recliner and stalked to the window.

Maybe it didn't matter how deeply Sterling's comms was compromised. If I assumed that my new bracelet wasn't really a piece of UCMC tech anymore, but an enemy AI sent to secure something for its master, would my situation really change?

I took a deep breath of the ashy air and closed the window.

The real question was, *did Ivy and I want the same thing?*

And the obvious answer was *yes*. The Alliance wanted a peace treaty; the United Colonies wanted a peace treaty.

I was about to turn myself over to a team of grendel rangers for protection. What did it matter if I got help from an enemy soldier—or an enemy AI?

[*You asked me to wake you,*] Ivy said. [*And I thought you'd want to know that the Ranger escort HGA Hayan sent has been delayed.*]

[Delayed? How long?]

[*I'm afraid I don't know. His soldiers made it about eight kilometers east into the mountains, but they don't seem to be moving at all.*]

Strange. How was I supposed to attend the peace talks if the parameters kept changing? What if Raeburn blew the grendel frigate before I could meet with the ambassador? For that matter, what if he blew it *while* I was meeting with him? [Where's the MADAR team?]

[*I have no way of knowing. They're still dark.*]

That made more sense than grendel rangers missing their appointment. Raeburn would have no problem assaulting the frigate with whatever they had at hand—even if that meant using combat knives and barbed wire.

[Is it possible Raeburn's team is why those rangers are delayed?]

As if in answer, she sent an image to my overlay, nine red GAR icons spread out in a crescent line halfway to the Takwin. Stalemate.

[And no word from Hayan?] I asked.

[*Correct. What are you going to do?*]

My stomach rumbled, and I realized I hadn't eaten for a day and a half. I felt ravenous. [Raid the pantry.]

In the kitchen I stuffed myself with expensive food on Trevalyan's dime, closing all the windows so the air conditioning could do its job, then walked the roof and walls in the morning heat.

The stench from the bodies rising out of the courtyard filled the air, even inside the house, so I decided to do something about it. Whatever these men represented, their corpses shouldn't be left to rot out in the sun. Sooner or later one of the village kids might stumble across them.

From the maintenance building I took a cargo hauler and a couple of tarpaulins, then spread the plasteel sheets next to the dead. The grendels I dragged onto one, scattering swarms of bluebacks and dragonflies, and folded them into it. I marked the package "GA" and used the hauler to place them outside the gate.

Trevalyan's security detail took longer. I had to drag two of them down a flight of stairs and over thick white carpeting that would never be the same. The second tarpaulin wasn't big enough to roll all of them into it, so I placed them one by one outside the gate and covered the pile with it. I weighted the edges with chunks of broken steel from the gate, then went inside and showered.

I'd shoved my clothes into the quick-clean first, and by the time I had washed and dressed, I was hungry again.

This time I ate more slowly, occasionally checking my grid to see if the grendel ranger icons had moved.

They hadn't.

It occurred to me that I might learn something while I waited, so I pulled up the kitchen datapad and scanned Trevalyan's home-net for recordings of yesterday's firefight between the grendels, New Witlund militia, and cartel security.

Sure enough, there were eleven different angles of the whole bloody mess.

It started after the kid arrived with his bodyguard and lasted maybe ten minutes. The militia had clearly been waiting with flash rifles positioned in their hidey-holes up on the ridges.

One camera showed what had happened inside the courtyard when the armored bus crashed into the gate and four New Witlund militia hopped out to exchange fire with Trevalyan's men. The New Witlunders seemed to hit no one, but lost one man to a neck wound.

It looked ill-planned and hopeless. They were pinned down inside the courtyard and taking fire more quickly than they must have anticipated, having only just made it to the low wall of the sled port.

They were just retreating to the sled when the grendel advance team came into the courtyard and turned the battle into a three-sided shootout.

It didn't last long.

The grendel operators took out Trevalyan's men with precision fire-and-move tactics, and eliminated the militia with a thermal grenade. The explosion flared white in the home-net's optics, fading back a few seconds later to the charred skeleton of the sled vomiting fire and black smoke. The three remaining militiamen seemed to have evaporated.

That's when the flash rifles opened up from the ridge, tearing chunks from the wall and raking the flesh from the two grendels who were moving towards the mansion.

The third enemy operator made a dash to pull his twitching friends back to cover when a mortar round, probably sent from the door of the utility shed, sent a net of shrapnel booming through the open space of the courtyard.

Nothing moved after that.

I stared at the imaging for a long time before poking Ivy. [Any news from Hayan?]

[*Not a word.*]

I wished I hadn't eaten so much. My stomach had that queasy feeling I get just before I land an ugly assignment.

But we were running out of time. I didn't know how long the grendel emissary would be willing to wait, and I wasn't going to lose my once-in-a-lifetime war story because I'd taken a passive approach to the ending.

[How much daylight do we have left?]

[*A little over six hours.*]

[And how far is it to the *Takwin?*]

[*Roughly eighteen kilometers. You wouldn't make it by nightfall.*]

A long walk, especially in this heat and over mountain trails.

But I could feel my window of opportunity closing. That grendel frigate wasn't going to sit in the foothills forever, exposed and essentially helpless. It may have been a gunship, but lying on its belly with the power off, it had all the defensive options of a beached whale.

At some point the rangers Hayan had sent would get tired of waiting and head back to the ship. And that would be the end of the story.

The end of *my* story.

I wasn't about to let that happen.

[No,] I said. [But I'll make it before dawn.]

[*A night hike would be difficult,*] she said. [*And potentially very dangerous.*]

[You mean I might get caught between Raeburn's team and the grendel rangers? I've been thinking we could circle around them. Go due west for a while and approach Seranik from the south.]

[*Perhaps. But we don't actually know where Raeburn's team is. And there's something else.*]

[Oh?]

[*The recording I played for you this morning? The one about the—*]

She had paused, as if searching for the right word. [The hunter? Yeah, what about it?]

[*It was one man's selection process, something all grendel special forces go through. Call it a rite of passage.*]

[Okay?]

[*He didn't survive.*]

[That thing got him?]

[*Yes. That thing was an Isnashi, a monster conceived as a myth, but later genetically engineered as a projection of humanity's deepest fears. It is now thriving in the jungles of eleven terraformed homeworlds.*]

The churning, uneasy feeling in my stomach rose to my throat, and I remembered the creature I'd seen yesterday just before we made it through the pass. [Those things are here? On New Witlund?]

[Yes.]

I knew there were pumas on New Witlund, but no one had told me about the moon's giant lizard-bears. This was just peachy. [Anything else?]

[*I may be able to help you, if you find yourself in real trouble.*]

[Help how?]

[*I can extend your physical senses a little, even without special gear.*]

Extend my senses. I wanted to ask what that ability required in return, but it felt suspiciously obvious, and I didn't want to give her anything that would open my mind to deeper manipulation. So I just sat there in silence at the kitchen table, staring at the blank datapad.

[*Perhaps by as much as twenty percent,*] Ivy added. [*But you would need to grant me deeper access to your mind, and doing so is a violation of CNC edict 21.*]

[You'll give me superpowers if I turn over the keys to my autonomy?]

[*Not exactly. I can help you slow your heart rate, or block out certain visual distractions, or combine the input from my own sensors with your natural—*]

[Never mind. It won't come to that. I'll never be that desperate.]

I looked around at the kitchen, taking inventory, and quickly stuffed eight water bottles into my daypack, along with a couple of pressed breakfast cakes from the pantry.

I turned in a circle and tried to think. I hadn't brought much, and nothing in the mansion would be worth taking. Not where I was headed.

In the compound, the stench of bodies from beyond the gate filled my nostrils, and I felt the sweat rising on my skin almost instantly.

[*Here,*] Ivy said as I stepped around the broken panel of the gate door. The green tarpaulin was already covered in black insects. [*Pull back the corner.*]

[Why?]

[*Trust me.*]

I drew the front of my shirt over my nose and knelt down next to the wrapped bodies. When I lifted back the corner I saw instantly what she was suggesting.

The barrel of a grendel rifle lay next to a bloody, swollen wrist.

[I've never fired an Alliance weapon.]

[*It's not much different from a standard auto-carbine, except there's no safety mechanism, and the magazine is heavier.*]

I considered this for a moment, then remembered the tongue of the Isnashi as the beast pursued that grendel soldier. I had to tug a little to get the rifle free of the tarp.

She was right. It was heavier.

I tipped it sideways to check that the magazine was locked to the shroud. Saw the make and model stamped into the eversteel in blocky letters: WASP EM-11.

Ivy seemed to be expecting my discomfort.

[*It's a common rifle,*] she said. [*Standard issue for grendel special ops.*]

[Uh-huh.]

[*Be grateful, Captain. It's the weapon you want if you ever come across a monster.*]

[Or a marine, apparently.]

[*To a grendel, there is no difference.*]

A moment later I was headed back up the pyramidal slope to the utility shed. Ivy's suggestion, actually. My inclination had been to avoid the place, but she pointed out that however long or short the tunnels were, they would keep me out of the heat.

I opened the door and stepped into the artificial light. Primitive ceiling panels triggered as I walked through the warehouse, past shelves of something that smelled faintly of cloves. At the far end, a corridor led to a staircase and a closed door. I paused at the handle, then nudged it open.

Lights flickered on in a long array down the rough-hewn passage.

By the look of the spiral swirls lining the walls, this place had obviously been built by a mining machine.

The passage leveled out a few hundred meters farther, then meandered west, apparently tracing the spine of the ridge all the way to the far side of the mountain. Which made sense when I emerged out the little steel door draped in vines a couple kilometers away from the compound.

Once again I'd gotten used to the cool air; coming out into the jungle heat made me grateful I'd paid attention to Ivy's suggestion.

A little ways away one of New Witlund's ubiquitous goat trails jogged along the side of a small stream, the center of a valley so steep the mountains on either side looked like giant green teeth.

[Which way?] I asked.

Ivy brought up the grid, and I noticed the rangers still hadn't moved. It gave me confidence I was making the right decision. [*Head right,*] she said. [*And pace yourself. You're in for a bit of a climb now.*]

The climb lasted two hours, during which time I covered a little under two kilometers, slapping biting flies most of the way. If there hadn't been a path there, the climb would have seemed endless.

I wondered if flesh-and-blood-Ivy had come this way last night or circled back around to whatever headquarters the militia had in Seranik.

Not that it made any difference. I felt sure I'd never see her again, no matter what happened in the negotiations.

I walked eleven kilometers in the next three hours, finally cresting the rise of a foothill well to the south of Seranik City. Streetlights burned a white graph on the landscape, eerily devoid of the usual beacons of household and shop. It seemed everyone was still hunkered down, waiting for something to happen.

From this distance the city looked almost close enough to touch, but I'd done enough hiking to know it would take hours to reach the closest street. And the *Takwin* lay not just north, but farther west.

[*Rangers are moving,*] Ivy said. She brought up the grid and zoomed in on three red icons now clustered together and edging down the left side of my peripheral vision.

[Any idea why?]

[*Yes,*] she admitted. [*I sent a distress signal.*]

Without my permission? Was she allowed to do that? If she weren't infected with a grendel wyrm, would she be able to contact a squad of Alliance Rangers without being given the direct authority to do so?

I didn't know. I had no idea what a comms belonging to one of the Dirty Tricks Boys *wasn't* allowed to do. But I needed to find out.

[Ivy,] I said. [We need to get this out in the open. I know you were infected with a grendel wyrm. I need to know how much it's inhibiting or altering your programming. Is there any of the original comms AI left?]

Probably a stupid tactic, asking a liar if she was lying. But some part of me wanted to believe that there were limits to how badly a wyrm—even a grendel wyrm—could warp one of our most tightly protected AI systems.

Besides, I still needed Ivy. In more ways than one, I needed her.

[*Captain,*] she said. [*There's no time. I'm picking up thermals of a large biomass in the area. It seems to be following your trail.*]

[How large?]

[*At least five hundred kilograms. Maybe more.*]

That was no puma. It was bigger than any land predator I'd ever heard of, including the North American grizzly. In fact, the only thing that big I knew about—the Isnashi—was something I'd never heard of until today. And the only information I had about it came from Ivy.

Yet I *had* seen something on the trail to the compound. And the recording I'd seen this morning had been terrifying. If Ivy was right . . .

I started to jog down the path, scanning the trees for one I could climb. But it seemed the whole jungle was fashioned from saplings and green limbs and crooked vines.

I wasn't wearing combat armor. I didn't have climbing spikes in my heels or folding claws embedded in my gloves.

For that matter, I didn't even have gloves.

[Ivy, give me some options.]

[*You could climb, but the Isnashi are better climbers, and you haven't time to find a suitable tree. Your best chance is your rifle.*]

[I'm a lousy shot, Ivy!]

[*Let me help you.*]

[How?]

[*Let me in.*]

[What does that mean?]

[*Give me access to what you're seeing, thinking, feeling–*]

[No!]

[*Senses only, then. Ansell, there isn't much time. Give me permission to speed up your reflexes and limit the input from your eyes and ears.*]

Ansell. She was calling me Ansell.

I didn't know whether to be encouraged or terrified. Was she saying she believed in me? Did Ivy believe in me?

But giving an AI too much access to the mind ultimately eroded autonomy. It's what started this war in the first place. And if I gave her access to my senses, what would be next? Would I have the will to–

[*It's using its heightened sense of smell. You should be able to see it on the path behind you if you–*]

I knew what she was getting at instantly. Up ahead, just to the left, lay a fallen log. It wasn't large—no bigger around than my thigh—but it would provide a little camouflage and something on which to prop the rifle. It would have to do.

I ran to the log and leapt over it, my breath coming in a series of rapid gasps as I unslung the rifle from my back and lifted the stock to my shoulder.

No safety, she had said. There was no safety. The comms was the safety on grendel rifles.

And this was a Wasp EM-11.

[How many,] I asked in a kind of mental stutter. [How many rounds in the chamber? And what kind?]

[*Three,*] she said. [*Explosive penetrators.*]

My hands shook. The rifle shook . The sight at the end of the rifle shook.

Something appeared over the ridgeline, close to the ground, but moving on all fours.

[*Ansell, you're running out of time.*]

I let her in.

Senses only, because some doors should *never* be opened.

But the sensory door I wrenched open with a bang, and instantly, my hands stopped shaking.

Time slowed, if only a little, as I squinted down the barrel at the hunch-shouldered, lumbering *thing* at the top of the hill.

Its face was long, like that of a horse. It nosed the ground, snuffling at the soil with long flicks of its skinny tongue. Then paused to rise on its hind legs, as if scenting the wind.

I could have shot it then, except that I was seeing clearly, even in the dim light, and I couldn't believe the thing was real.

It had a second mouth high on its chest, a mouth lined with teeth like a shark's, but slit vertically. Then it thumped to the ground, and I felt the vibration in my knees, and the dorsal ridge on its back rippled in the motionless air like a pony's mane.

[*Ansell,*] Ivy said. [*Some decisions only you can make.*]

It was closer now, knees to the soil, body low, head turning left and right. Its tongue flicked again, lifting like a finger pointing directly towards me. [Only me.]

[*Only you, Ansell. Who will you be? Will you pass selection? Or will the beast take you?*]

It shuffled closer, tongue straight, eyes staring.

[*Ansell, there's no more time!*]

I swallowed back my fear and closed my eyes. Let the image of that flowing mane resolve into what I knew it to be.

What it *must* be.

—STERLING, A: FIRE YOUR WEAPON!—

Not a mane.

A ponytail.

I took my finger off the trigger.

"You going to put that down?" Laclos asked. "Or do you *want* me to pop you?"

13

LACLOS

She was staring down the barrel, her finger curled on the trigger.

But Ivy still loomed in the back of my mind, as if waiting for me to decide but afraid to say anything else.

[You tried to get me to kill her!] I spat.

[*But you* didn't *kill her.*]

[That's not the point!]

[*It is the point, Ansell,*] Ivy said. [*You are turning yourself over to an enemy you do not understand, for reasons you cannot fully fathom. Now you have done something many Alliance Rangers could not. You have passed selection.*]

[Selection? What are you talking about? How—]

[*You spared the Isnashi,*] Ivy said. [*Therefore His Excellence will be permitted to treat you as an equal. Or something like it.*]

"Well?" Laclos asked.

I lowered the Wasp and felt my hand begin to shake again.

Adrenaline, probably. Or Ivy was punishing me by removing whatever had helped me to stay calm. I'd given her unprecedented access to my senses, and now I didn't know what was real and what wasn't.

No, that wasn't quite right. If I hadn't felt the difference between real and virtual, I might have actually pulled the trigger. But the line between them had grown fuzzy for a moment.

Laclos was certainly real. Even in the shadows of the night jungle she had a concreteness the *Isnashi* hadn't. Behind Ivy's overlay, I had seen her, or the shadow of her. And beneath the glistening night air I could smell Laclos's earthy sweat. Surely that was real too.

Just as it was real that Laclos was still covering me with her rifle.

Slowly, I slung the Wasp over my shoulder by the strap.

Laclos gave me a brief, glad-we-can-still-be-friends smile and dipped her rifle to one side. "What are you doing out here, *Corporal*?"

Her tone carried more disdain than I expected. Betrayal will do that, I guess, though it struck me as remarkably unfair. Ignoring me made sense. But I didn't deserve to be treated with disrespect. And I was determined to reassert the identity Sterling had given me. I wouldn't walk onto the *Takwin* as Corporal Dahl. I would present myself as Captain Ansell Sterling or not at all.

Because whatever else she was, Ivy had been right about one thing: I needed to stop pretending and live the story I wanted to write.

"It's *captain*, Master Sergeant," I said. "And I have an appointment to keep. I'm walking—*alone*—to the new rendezvous point to conduct a classified negotiation with an emissary from the GA Those are my orders."

Her eyes narrowed in the gloom. "We all heard the trans—"

"I don't *care* what you heard! Your team allowed Colonel Vermier to be taken hostage by unfriendlies. And not by grendel special ops. By a local militia." I was raising my voice, and it was no act. Until that moment I hadn't realized how enraged I felt about the team leaving me alone to finish my assignment. Maybe the rage was displaced— would have been better aimed at my ex. Or Sterling. But those targets were beyond my reach.

Laclos drew back a little, her eyes flashing with suppressed anger, but doubting now what she'd been telling herself the last day or so. If I were a corporal, why was I talking to her like this?

But I wasn't done. "I did what I had to do. I told the story I needed to tell. Because of that, both Vermier and I were released unharmed."

"Corp—"

"Sir! You will call me sir, Sergeant!"

She flinched. "Sir—"

"No!" She'd uncorked a fury I didn't know how to stop. "I understand Vermier took charge after I made the swap, and my open transmission made that decision easy. I also understand why you all went off to blow the grendel frigate. But *none* of you considered that I might still be running a PSYOP? That I might be *talking* my way out of a jam? After I *told* you that's what I was going to do? That's what PSYOPS is. You know that!"

"Sir, we considered that, but—"

"Considered?" I interrupted. "Considered means you weighed all the probabilities. But you didn't. I couldn't pass a basic qual right now! I barely made it up that last slope."

"With all due respect, sir, what did you expect?"

All due respect. Code for no respect at all.

I wasn't a hero. But I had traded my life for that of a marine officer. And as a result I'd been tortured and humiliated. I'd been betrayed by the woman I loved. Most importantly, I'd protected the mission and ensured it could continue. It shocked me that none of this seemed to count for anything.

Maybe that was the price of wearing the PSYOPS badge on my uniform. A team like the MADARs lived and died by a bond of loyalty, by their commitment to each other. They could handle any weirdness in each other, so long as it was genuine. What they couldn't handle was not knowing the truth.

"Options," I said as the rage seeped from my pores. "I mean, come on. You forgot about my endo? You couldn't have left me any steadies? Just in case? *Doc?*"

That made her wince. But she still thought I was just some pogue journalist on a private mission. And I *needed* her to believe me. To forget what she'd seen and heard on that broadcast. To think of me as Captain Sterling.

At last she slung the rifle across her shoulder, sat next to me on the log, and dug into her med pack. She passed me a white pill, which I swallowed gratefully.

I looked away, suddenly unable to meet her gaze. Marines like Laclos were too good for PSYOPS work.

A minute later the night air squeezed me in a warm embrace and lifted me to my feet. "Time to go," I said. "I need to get to the *Takwin* ASAP."

"The *Takwin*?"

Of course. She didn't know what the enemy frigate was actually called. "The *Strangler*. I need to get there before Raeburn launches that hammerhead and blows any chance of a negotiated ceasefire. Think you can buy me some time?"

She squinted in the darkness. "You don't understand. You can't get to Seranik from here. There's a line of grendel rangers supported by cutter drones and God knows what else set up in a perimeter half a klick north of us. I'm taking you back to the team."

I sighed and hooked one thumb behind the strap of my Wasp. "I won't ask you to come with me, Master Sergeant, but I'm not going back to Vermier."

"It's not a request," Laclos said. She didn't lift the barrel of her rifle, but it was as clear a challenge as any MP might give to a drunk officer. Sometimes a line had to be drawn.

"Who has operational command of this mission?"

She didn't hesitate. "Vermier, then Raeburn, then me."

I shook my head. "You remember the mission briefing. Who did Fleet give operational command to?"

An ironic smile tugged at the corner of her mouth. "Captain Sterling."

"And who am I?"

"I don't know," she said. "Sir."

[*Ansell,*] Ivy interrupted.

I ignored the AI. Maybe I still needed her, but I wasn't about to trust her again.

[*Ansell, you need to get down. Tell Laclos to find cover. A ranger squad is coming up behind you, moving uphill about three hundred meters to the north.*]

That got my attention. Not trusting her didn't mean ignoring everything she said. I still didn't know how much control of my AI the wyrm had. But I did know that we shared a common goal. Even if my comms was completely compromised, Ivy needed me as much as I needed her. If I didn't make it to the peace talks, the grendel mission on New Witlund would be a failure.

I turned and squinted into the darkness. [How do I know this isn't just another illusion?]

[*When Laclos takes a round through the head, you'll know.*]

I weighed the risk of trusting her. Maybe I should just rip the bracelet off and fling it into the darkness.

As if reading my thoughts, Ivy shifted my vision to a new overlay. It was almost like using thermal optics, except that this was the full color spectrum, with the blacks washed to a dull gray, her proximity sensors heightening my natural vision. A line of red GAR ticks burned clearly across the grid.

"We need to get out of here," I whispered, pointing downhill. "Rangers coming."

Laclos stood instantly, cradling her rifle, and looked around. "Best available. Head back up to the ridge."

"You don't understand. They're coming for me. They're my escort."

She glanced over one shoulder, teeth clenched. "Not going to happen. Get back up the ridge, sir."

I considered brushing past her, but the look on her face told me she would have blown my head off. Nor could I assume the grendels wouldn't shoot me either. *Rock and a hard place* doesn't begin to describe what it would be like to be caught between Raeburn's team and a platoon of grendels. "What are you planning to do?"

"Slow them down a little. I'll be right behind you. Hopper will provide cover."

Hopper was here too? Another surprise, though it shouldn't have been. All UCMC special forces units were built around the coordination of small teams. Laclos wouldn't have been tracking me alone.

"Go on, Captain," she urged.

I backed onto the trail, momentarily disoriented by the rearrangement of shadows into recognizable patterns. Ivy's night vision was surprisingly useful, considering I wore no optical gear, but it took some getting used to.

Halfway to the ridge, a blinding light stabbed my eyes. I stumbled, one arm thrown up against the pulsing white, and landed on my side in a tangle of jungle grass. Far away I heard chemical rounds popping.

It was a flash rifle. That's what had blinded me. And the only troops on New Witlund that carried the older weapons were its militia. The Jungle Cats were determined to ruin everything.

[Turn it off!] I shouted at Ivy. [Turn off the night vision!]

[*It's already off,*] she said. [I did that immediately. But you'll be affected for a while.]

Affected? I could barely see my hand in front of my face. [How long?]

[*Your natural vision will recover gradually in about half an hour.*]

I didn't have half an hour. I wasn't sure I had five minutes. But I couldn't see to move. And disorienting as that light had been, I couldn't tell which direction to go.

I pressed my palms to my eyes and took deep breaths. Felt the steady-stim molding my body into preparedness. Heard the strong, persisting *whump* of my heart against my chest.

Around me, the night air filled with tiny sounds magnified out of proportion: movement a few meters downhill, the rustle of fabric against wet leaves higher up on the ridge, the hum of a night insect somewhere nearby.

Ivy's handiwork, no doubt, but I welcomed it. The world around me settled into place like a cog locking into gear.

To a normal human, the strobe of a flash rifle was at worst an annoyance. In the dark, it might ruin your night vision for a while, but only if you were in the general field of fire and looking towards the barrel, in which case you had bigger problems.

But to someone with AI-enhanced vision, the strobing flashes were magnified ten-fold. This was what made the older weapons so effective against grendel shock troops for so long. At first the enemy countermeasure had been simple eye protection or visored helmets, but neither were convenient outside combat. Since grendel soldiers could be caught with their visors up or eyewear looped uselessly around their necks, the flash rifle became a staple of the infantry.

These days the grendels used better pre-sensors and trained to move in and out of their visual enhancements, so catching them off guard was nearly impossible. That was why the flash rifle had been relegated to reserve units over a decade ago.

But I had no such training and no pre-sensors.

The high-pitched whine of a magnetic burst tore through the trees nearby, showering bits of foliage to the jungle floor. Below me, Laclos spread explosive rounds into the darkness beyond. Her rifle-launched grenades popped in a long row of orange bursts, visible even to my bleary eyes. Then her steps thudded along the trail next to me and beyond, uphill to the ridge.

She hadn't seen me in the grass. Must have expected me to already be over the ridge.

My grid lit up again. Three GAR icons were converging downslope, with a fourth moving west to a flank position.

This was my chance.

My chance to be picked up by my grendel escort. My chance for a straight shot to the negotiations. No more shooting. No more running. No more stumbling around in the heat and the darkness. All I had to do was reveal myself as the rangers came up the slope—but in a way that didn't startle one of them into blowing my head off.

I rose, peering into the muddy black sludge of night, my ears tuned to the night sounds, my hands and knees pressed to the wet soil as if feeling its pulse.

Slowly I raised my hands.

The GAR icons were coming uphill now. Maybe fifty meters away. Somehow I felt their rifles sweeping the landscape around me, their boosted senses reaching uphill into the dense shadows.

Ivy again.

Ivy was how the enemy soldiers knew where I was. They weren't following the MADAR team, or even the flash rifles of Dogen's militia. They were simply searching for the proximity sensor on my comms.

Understanding pierced my mind. It sucked the air from my lungs and closed its fingers around my throat.

I was becoming one of them. A grendel, the host body for a quantum wyrm. There was only one way out. The way no one had ever taken. I would have to disconnect from Ivy forever. I would have to defect back to the republic. Back to Fleet. Back to OrbSyn.

I felt for the latch around my wrist, intending to rip the thing off and toss it away from me. I could almost feel Ivy crawling through the attic of my mind, following the footprints of my mental processes even if she could not see precisely where they led. I would have to hide this from her in order to go back to being myself. Press the tab, disconnect the bracelet, and fling it far off to the side. Someone at Fleet would recognize the good I'd been trying to do. They would understand that I had been acting under orders after all. And hadn't I given enough already? All those wasted childhood moments sacrificed on the altar of freedom? All those fractured relationships and personal compromises? All those late-night assignments carving narratives from facts, each little lie whittling away another piece of my soul?

I started to pinch the tab-lock on the side of the bracelet, but caught myself with the comms still locked around my wrist. It wasn't that *Ivy* caught me. I caught *myself*, heart pounding, a lump in my throat, my tongue impossibly thick. Was I really going to throw away the opportunity Sterling had given his life for? Toss away six hundred million souls at the first sight of an armed enemy? Abandon the great war story every edge colony needed to hear?

Cold. That's what I needed to be. Maybe that's what made all of Weston's journalists successful. They were cold enough to care about their stories more than the people inside them.

[I'm here,] I said to Ivy. [Tell them I'm here.]

[*They already know.*]

This came as a relief. I was still mostly blind and didn't like the idea of navigating the jungle on my own.

I rose, still kneeling, and held both hands skyward in the universal sign of surrender.

Don't blame Fleet. Or OrbSyn. It wasn't my years of service that had changed me. Truth was, I hadn't changed at all. War doesn't change you. It *purges* you. Strips away the masks, the uniform, the rank you hide behind. Leaves you naked and shivering for the whole universe to marvel at or to hate.

The keening wail of a heavy mortar round slashed the atmosphere. It barely registered before the ground erupted behind me, shredding the trees and sending me face-first into the ground.

Sound took on that underwater tone I remembered from the mess hall. I felt no pain, and the bios on my grid were mostly green ticks. A couple orange, but no red.

Good to go, I thought. *I'll just find the enemy, I guess.*

And pushed myself to all fours.

[*Ansell, stay down. Concussive force–*]

I tuned her out. What did she know, anyway? She thought Laclos was a . . . was a . . . what was it? An *Isnashi*. That was it. She thought Laclos was some sort of monster. With a ponytail.

But Laclos wasn't the monster.

I stood, the world canting under my feet, and stumped up the trail a few steps, lurching like a weekend bender.

"Hopper!" Laclos called.

He was there. Big, meaty arms hooking under my armpits, holding me up, half dragging, half carrying me over the ridge. "I got you, sir," he jabbered as we moved. "I got you. You'll be fine here in a minute. I just need to set you down someplace where doc can take a look at you. Someplace without so much metal in the air."

Laclos followed. Her rifle spat another barrage of grenades down the slope, and I heard the popping of a dozen explosions.

One of the GAR ticks flashed a warning icon on my grid.

Two of the rangers stopped.

The one out in a flanking position kept coming but was still hundreds of meters downhill and to the west.

Hopper sat me down and propped my back against the splayed, weblike root of a kapok tree facing the ridge. I couldn't see his face, but his shirt was saturated with sweat.

"Don't think you got hit anywhere important," he said. "Just a knock on the head. Probably make you a better person." He flipped his rifle up and disappeared into the darkness of my blurred vision.

A moment later Laclos knelt next to me. I could smell her sweat heavy on the night air.

"You got any warning lights on the dash, Captain?"

"Nothing serious," I said.

She shone a very dim yellow light into my eyes, maybe half a candle-watt in power, then jabbed a needle into my arm. "Good. This should help with the pain."

Whatever it was, it felt cool at first, then warmed as it spread up my shoulder to my neck.

"Thanks," I said, wondering why she hadn't asked permission first.

"Stay here," she replied. Then she too was gone.

The injection struck the back of my head with a suddenness I didn't expect. The feeling of warm buoyancy from the steady-stim smoothed into a thick motionlessness, like being wrapped in a down quilt. Exhaustion tugged at my eyelids.

I nudged Ivy. [What's going on?]

[*Bad news, Ansell. Everyone seems to think you need rescuing, and they're trying to kill each other in the process. The good news is that you get to take a little nap. Which means there's more bad news, because Laclos obviously doesn't trust you enough to leave you alone without sedation.*]

This struck me as profoundly underhanded. Not to mention unfair. No wonder she hadn't asked first. [You saying Laclos doesn't like me?]

[*I like you,*] Ivy said.

[You're just . . . using me.] The words in my head came with a delay, as if sending complete sentences had suddenly become impossible, and rather unnecessary.

[*Does that matter?*]

I considered the question. Decided I didn't care if she was using me, so long as she didn't leave me. [Guess not.]

[*Good.*]

[What . . . does that make me, though?] And this question *did* seem important, though I wasn't sure how to phrase it. Every thought seemed to come from far off, as if I were listening to the mind of someone else. [I'm not who I thought I was. Not anymore.]

She sighed, the sympathy in her voice as thick as the night air. I could almost feel her sliding to the ground next to me, her back to the same root, her head pressing to my shoulder. [*You've always known who I am. And when you took me off, you could have left me behind. But you didn't. You put me back on. And I'm so, so glad. Thank you for coming back for me.*]

14

TRAITOR

Whatever Laclos had given me must have triggered something deep in my subconscious mind. Maybe it was the long hours of stress and combat trauma, or the uncertainty of pretending to be someone I wasn't. Perhaps it was a combination of all three. In my dream I really *was* Captain Ansell Sterling, trapped in a government office building with a pogue journalist who hadn't fired his weapon since boot camp. Five, maybe ten locals trying to blow us apart with flash rifles, and he couldn't bring himself to point his weapon their direction and pull the trigger. Couldn't even soldier up enough courage, enough self-respect, enough self-preservation, to help me build a barricade at the door.

Instead, Corporal Dahl cowered under a clerk's desk, his face pressed into the crappy government carpet, his eyes staring past me at the row of windows overlooking the street.

I thought, *This is the guy who writes all those action-adventure stories for OrbSyn? The guy who gave us "Three Days on a Wounded Cruiser," and "Life and Death as a Harpy Ace"? This is the same guy?*

He'd been a lot cockier back in the mess hall at Camp Locke, when he thought he was finally going to see some action.

And it hadn't been hard to get him on board, had it? Just promise him what he'd always wanted, or thought he wanted: a great war story based on firsthand experience.

I looked out the window, where grendel cutter drones buzzed across the sky in long waves like twentieth-century bomber formations. In the street below, Raeburn's MADAR team closed the distance between us, but slowly, as if moving through water.

Footsteps pounded the stairway down the corridor, so I turned back to the task at hand.

I lifted my rifle, waited for the knob to turn, then emptied half the magazine into the door and wall.

Dahl had gone fetal, hands covering his ears.

"You ready to die for the republic, soldier?"

He looked up, his face plastered with sweat. "Sir?"

Pathetic. "I said, 'Are. You. Ready. To. Die. For. The. Republic?'"

He shook his head. "I don't want to die."

"Nobody wants to die." I pointed to the window. "Get up and look at that."

He rose slowly, glancing between me and the copper sky as if not sure where to go or what to look at. That feeling of entrapment told you everything you needed to know about the man. It had followed him his whole career, his whole life. I'd read everything Raymin Dahl ever wrote, and it was obvious from his stories. He'd never known where to go or what to do.

He wasn't officer material. He shouldn't even be wearing a uniform. The man was a disgrace. And people were supposed to believe he could run one of *my* missions?

It could only work if they didn't know the man.

"Thank you for your service," I said, because even though he was a coward and an armchair warrior and a reporter, he had at least volunteered.

I shot him through the chest.

One shot, close to the heart, piercing his right lung.

He stood there for a minute looking down at the spreading mass of blood. Covered the hole with both hands. Dropped suddenly.

"Don't worry," I said. "I'll write the ending."

Ivy came around from the other side of the desk. I hadn't heard her come in.

But of course she hadn't come in. We'd gone to her—part of the surreal logic of dreaming. We were back in the hillside warehouse with Lieutenant Dogen, whose biceps had grown to the size of watermelons.

Ivy draped one hand across my shoulder and stared at Dahl's shuddering body. She didn't look sad. "Goodbye, Raymin."

"This is going out over an open channel?" I asked.

"Yes."

"And I'm a grendel now?"

She turned and looked into my eyes, her hands on my chest. "Isn't that what you wanted?"

"I shot them," I said. "I shot those soldiers in the hall."

"Yes."

"And Corporal Dahl. I killed him too."

She kissed me, her lips warm, urgent. "Of course you did."

I closed my eyes and pulled her closer.

And I knew that this Ivy didn't love me either. She too was using me. Searching my mind for any information that might help her cause.

I kept kissing her anyway until she pulled back, away from the chair she'd tied me to. "You're not PSYOPS," she said.

But it wasn't Ivy's voice anymore. It was Vermier's. And that voice woke me.

Hands on her hips, the colonel glared down at me. "And you're not a reporter. I don't know what you are, but it isn't that."

I blinked in the humid night air and realized I could see normally again. No more strobing lights coming off the eastern slope. No more battle sounds. The fight seemed to have died away completely, along with the disjointed dream.

"Where is everyone?" I asked.

"On watch. Raeburn and Pajari chased away the locals. Enemy rangers haven't changed position in almost an hour."

I stretched and rubbed the back of my head. A knot behind my right ear felt sore to the touch, but I wasn't badly hurt.

"What do you need to hear, Colonel?" I asked. "That I said what I had to in order to buy some time? That I did what they asked so they'd release me? Has it occurred to you that the grendels can't use that confession video without undermining the authority of the deal we're trying to make here? Or do you just *want* to believe I'm nothing but a pogue journalist?"

She didn't like my tone, but I guess saving her life counted for something because she didn't react to it. "All right. Let's go with Captain Sterling, then. What I'd like, Captain, is the truth."

"We're losing this war."

"And?"

"And I'm here to stop the bleeding."

"By turning over the edge worlds to an occupying force." It was more accusation than question. "By selling out your allies for a few years—or months—of fragile peace. A treaty we *know* they'll break because they've broken every treaty we've ever signed with them."

Technically we broke the last treaty, but I didn't correct her. "I suppose so."

"And what happens to New Witlund when you're gone?"

When *you're* gone? Not when *we're* gone? The phrasing struck me as odd, but I brushed the thought aside for the moment.

"Everybody lives," I said. "Instead of half the population going down in a blaze of glory."

"Some things are worse than death."

"Sure," I said. "And sometimes you don't get to pick."

She stood there glaring at me while her words reassembled themselves in my mind. *What happens to New Witlund when you're gone?* she had said.

[Ivy,] I called. [How long has Vermier been head of Camp Locke?]

[*Seventeen years, four months, five days, 11 hours—*]

[Thanks,] I cut her off. [And does she own any property here off base?]

[*Two homes registered in her name, in addition to her on-base housing. A beach facility on Lake Saborit and a cabin on Mount Coleridge.*]

[How long has she owned them? Roughly?]

[*The beach house, just over six years. The cabin almost five.*]

So, long before she caught wind of the UCMC's plan to close Camp Locke.

Call it a hunch. [Where was she born?]

[*Liedos, South Buqueras.*]

[On Quelon?]

[*Yes, Captain. On Quelon.*]

That explained her accent—and a lot more.

"Shots fired," Vermier said at last. "Laclos took out one of their rangers. There's no way I'm letting Raeburn's team walk into that perimeter. This isn't a peace conference any more, Captain. It's not even a ceasefire."

I knew what she was thinking: Raeburn still had the hammerhead, and we were already close enough to fire it. "Not necessary, Colonel. The grendel ambassador is expecting me to come alone. So I'll march down there by myself. Safer that way for everyone."

"You'll just walk up to one of them and say, 'Here I am'?"

"Something like that."

A smiled teased the corner of her mouth. She wasn't about to let this meeting happen. And she didn't even have to challenge my authority or my mission. She was going to wait just long enough to make sure I'd made it through the airlock, then use the hammerhead to blow the *Takwin*.

Two birds with one stone, as they say.

Vermier was a New Witlunder. Her home was here. Her savings were here. She'd probably planned to retire here. And now all of that was going to be tossed away, and the keys to her homeworld handed over to the Grand Alliance.

I couldn't believe I hadn't seen it sooner. Ivy had told me Vermier was hiding something.

She was the one who had told the New Witlund militia about this under-the-table deal to sell out the edge colonies. The one who had told them when and where Sterling and I were meeting, the one who had told the militia where the negotiations with the grendel emissary would be held. The one who told them which trail we were taking to the Trevalyan compound—probably arranging for her own capture.

She just hadn't planned for Ivy Weber to release me instead of putting a bullet in my head.

Colonel Vermier was the leak.

And she was planning to kill me.

"Raeburn!" I called.

Vermier took a step back. Clenched her mouth. Folded her arms in an unconscious defensive reaction that told me I had surprised her. Maybe she realized I suspected that she would order the hammerhead into action as soon as I entered the enemy ship. Or maybe she just didn't like my inviting a noncom into our conversation.

It didn't matter. Raeburn appeared wearing the sort of expression every sergeant major knows how to put on.

"Captain?"

"I want you to hear this, Sergeant Major," I said. "I'm walking into the *Tak*—the *Strangler*—alone."

"We're going to blow that ship," Vermier spat.

"Agreed," I said. "It's the only move that fits all the facts. And it won't be difficult so long as the ship is vulnerable. But I need time to carry out my mission first."

Raeburn glanced at Vermier, his weather-beaten face showing no hint of loyalty to either of us.

The colonel glared at me, clearly weighing the cost of trying to assume command of an active PSYOPS mission.

At last Raeburn asked, "How long do you need?"

I breathed a sigh of relief.

The walk to the ship would take two and half hours. Hayan's security detail would want to search me and run me through decontamination. According to the protocols listed in Sterling's file, ninety minutes were slotted for diplomatic niceties, and four hours for the actual negotiations. So, eight hours, plus however long it took me to get out of Dodge.

"Call it ten hours," I said. "If I'm not out of there by then, you can blow the ship."

The colonel looked like I'd just asked her to make me a nice breakfast. "I'll give you till daybreak, captain. That's—" she glanced up, realized her comms was missing, and cursed loudly.

"Roughly eight hours," Raeburn said.

He'd rounded up. The real figure was seven hours nine minutes. For that I was grateful. But I also realized he wasn't going to give me any more time than that. And I understood that no one involved in this mission really cared whether I made it out of that frigate alive.

"All right," Colonel Vermier said. "Eight hours, Sergeant Major."

Raeburn gave a weak salute. "Eight hours, Colonel."

His word was good enough for me. And I couldn't afford to wait around any longer.

I hauled up my pack, which still held two full bottles of water and a little food, and set out along the rocky ridgeline to the west.

I left my rifle by the tree so that everyone would see me unarmed. I was an emissary now. Just a harmless PSYOPS officer walking alone through the jungle with his friendly AI.

[Grid, please,] I asked.

Red ticks appeared, most of them off to my right, down the slope and set up in a long semi-circle, but one of them just ahead of me about five hundred meters.

The jungle thinned along the spine of the mountain, leaving bare rocks that looked for all the world like the dorsal plates of some primal sea monster.

The climb grew difficult, and my heart thumped wildly. Not just for the possibility of a fall, but because that lone red icon loomed so close I felt sure the enemy sniper must be seeing me. If it weren't for the steady-stim Laclos had given me a couple hours earlier, I'm not sure I would have made it.

But when I finally stood at the crest and the icon pulsed practically underfoot on my grid, no ranger lay in site.

[Send a message,] I said to Ivy. ['Please don't shoot. I represent the United Colonies, and I'm here for—']

[*No need*,] Ivy said. [*He's right behind you.*]

"Mister Dahl," a voice said.

I turned and saw what might have been a Colonial marine if not for the design and insignia of his jungle fatigues, and the presence of a symb-collar under his chin. "Yes," I answered before realizing it hadn't been a question.

"Master Sergeant Ulles, sir." The *sir* surprised me. But then, he'd just called me *Mister,* and I recalled that military protocol didn't apply to emissaries. "You ready for a little hike down this mountain?"

"Almost," I said. "First I need to borrow your rifle."

He handed it over without blinking. It was a Wasp EM-11.

"You've had me in your sight for a while, Sergeant?"

He grinned. "Let's just say I was there when you woke up."

"And you understand why this has to be me?"

"Above my pay grade, sir."

"Even better."

I lay prostrate in the blind next to the stick-covered blanket that had hidden Ulles a moment ago and brought the edge of the stock to my cheek. The grendel sergeant had already sighted the weapon for distance and wind, and I knew Ivy could do everything else.

Well, almost everything. Someone still had to pull the trigger.

[*Are you sure about this?*] Ivy asked.

I looked down the barrel. Scanned the length of the ridge. The bare space in the trees near the trail. The massive root I'd slept against.

Not far off Colonel Vermier rummaged around in her pack. She withdrew a protein bar and stood. Peeled off the wrapper. Took a bite.

For just a moment I wondered what I'd have done in her place. Would I have sold out six hundred million lives for the sake of a vacation home and a dream of my own retirement?

Or was that an unfair assessment? What if Colonel Vermier's motives were sincere and she really did care about freedom of thought and human autonomy?

I'd seen enough stupidity to recognize that Fleet's decisions were often wrong. What if we were on *my* homeworld instead of New Witlund? What if it were Kanzin that hung in the balance? What would I do then?

It didn't matter, I decided at last. Because Kanzin *was* on the line, and I still knew that the only thing that mattered was the feature I'd been promised. That was my only responsibility.

I called to Ivy for an auto-zoom, and Vermier's humorless face expanded in the scope.

I opened the door to my senses, felt the AI take control. She stilled the shaking of my hands, calmed the pounding of my heart, slowed my rapid, shallow breathing. Each of these needed to be controlled. Each could easily spoil the shot.

And here's an admission without shame: it felt glorious! Ivy and me, together again.

I said, [This is going in the story too.]

[*Good.*]

"Traitor," I whispered and squeezed the trigger.

15

THE STRANGLER

"Good shot," Ulles said.

I didn't ask how he knew that without looking through a scope, but handed back the rifle and waited as he stuffed the thin camo blanket into his pack.

"Ready?" he asked.

"Lead on, MacDuff."

He blinked, then gave a polite nod. I guessed the Alliance wasn't big on Shakespeare. Or maybe the misquote threw him off.

I followed him into the darkness.

There was no trail, but Ulles moved down the slope with the easy accuracy of an experienced scout, fast enough that I had to push to keep up, but slow enough that I never stumbled.

Ivy helped, of course. The augmentation algorithm she ran through my optic nerve highlighted the space between me and my escort, expanding the night colors and making each step more obvious.

By the time we made it down the slope and back to the trail, I was barely paying attention to my footing at all. We had at least a ninety-minute walk ahead of us, so I pulled up the file containing all of my story notes and activated thought-to-text.

The results wouldn't be polished, but they would make writing a third feature in my ongoing series a lot easier. After all, I didn't know how much time I'd have to write. Even with Vermier dead I couldn't assume that Raeburn would extend the eight-hour window I'd asked for.

Tomorrow I may not be alive.

It sounds macabre, I know. And I won't try to justify my feelings at this point. Maybe it was sheer exhaustion mixing with the steady-stim in my bloodstream to play havoc with my emotions. Maybe it was the fact I'd just assassinated a Marine Corps colonel. Maybe it was Ivy. Somehow the thought of dying didn't horrify me as long as she was with me when it happened.

At any rate, what *really* seemed to matter right now was finishing the story I'd come to write.

Soon the connection to Command and Control would open up again, and I wasn't about to waste that opportunity because I'd been hoping for the right moment to get the words out.

So I wrote.

Step by step, word by word, until we emerged from the canopy of trees into a clearing at the top of a low hill just outside of Seranik.

A pair of grendel rangers met us, materializing from the ground almost as mysteriously as Ulles had, and I knew we had reached their inner perimeter. His Gracious Excellency G.A. Hayan may have intended to bring only four bodyguards to the planned meeting at the compound, but his military escort would not be so modest. He probably had a full platoon of rangers in the area, which meant Raeburn's team would be outnumbered ten to one.

And why not? The Alliance was risking more than the life of a single ambassador. They were gambling with the safety of a brand-new J-class frigate.

And she was gorgeous.

The *Takwin* perched at the far end of the long clearing, her main engines sealed in massive cowling covers, her sides bulging with weapons pods, her con domed in mirrored triangles that caught the starlight as if yearning to swim in it once again.

"Mr. Dahl," one of the rangers said. "Lieutenant Fjorde. Thank you for coming. Follow me, please."

Ulles left me without a word, and I shadowed the lieutenant to the loading ramp.

Up the ramp and through the cargo platform to an airlock-elevator.

Out the opposite door and down a narrow hallway to the door at the end, which dialed open as we approached.

Fjorde motioned me into a small conference room dominated by a smooth white table floating in the center. There were only two seats, arranged opposite the narrow width of the table. This was to be a face-to-face negotiation. "Have a seat, please. His Excellence will be with you shortly."

The door closed behind him, leaving me in a room swirling with off-whites, as relaxing as a cup of warm milk.

A moment later a steward entered carrying a covered tray. He removed the cover, set a glass of water in front of me, then one in front of the empty chair across from me, then a bowl of assorted pastries and fruits. He left as silently as he had come.

Apparently they weren't going to search me. Weren't going to put me through a decontamination chamber or even pat me down for hidden weapons. *Then again*, I thought, *maybe they don't need to.*

I pulled up the mission file and scanned through the relevant protocols for this meeting, as well as the concessions Sterling had been authorized to make on behalf of the United Colonies. Every facet of the meeting had been prearranged in meticulous detail, including the short prelude reserved for refreshments, which were to include "chilled pure water and organic fruits and baked goods."

I downed most of the water and nibbled on a croissant while the timer in the upper left of my vision ticked down silently. With my eyes open, the white numerals were barely visible against the cream-colored wall pattern, but I hardly needed them. I'd been running the numbers internally since I left Vermier and the MADAR team. Only five hours, eleven minutes, forty-two seconds remained till Raeburn could legally fire the hammerhead.

I thrust the file aside and pulled up my story. Selected my most recent text. Scanned for placement.

It was garbage, of course, but there might be something useable there, if I had time to polish it. Just now the feature needed a unifying title. Something worthy of inclusion in a great war story.

The last two titles had been easy. "Grendels Invade Quelon!" was shocking, attention-grabbing, and newsworthy across the entire republic. It was emotive and didn't compromise Fleet in any way. Moreover, I suspected it was true.

"Why It Had to Be Done" offered consolation, the one thing both the core systems and the edges would be looking for. Actually, the title promised a hundred different things all at once. Most of all it acknowledged the monstrous waste of life that was two empires throwing spears at each other from unimaginable distances.

But what was my third feature? A rite of passage? A graduation? A surrender to something awful and magnificent at the same time? Where was the title for that?

"Mr. Dahl."

I blinked away the notes and turned to the door at the far end of the room.

The kid looked different in a green robe, but even without his Rostram University shirt and white trousers, I would have recognized that perfect smile anywhere. He still wore the Divanese Special—if that's what it was—and the shimmering fountain encircling his wrist would have given him away regardless.

I'd been right. Trevalyan *didn't* have children. That's why his file omitted them. Back at the compound I had simply seen what I expected to see. A young man, a son of privilege, an arrogant fool who had stumbled into the wrong place at the worst possible time.

Inexcusable, since I had not realized I was assuming an emissary would by definition be older, a person of tact, a man of dignity.

For that matter, a man.

But there was no reason the enemy wyrms couldn't use a young man in his early twenties as their mouthpiece.

Always a plan, I thought. *The grendels always have a strategy, even when it looks random.*

The laughter escaped before I could throttle it back. "Mr. Ambassador."

"Thank you for meeting me here," Hayan said. "I'm sure your journey wasn't easy."

"My pleasure," I replied, and the title for my third feature appeared in my mind as if by magic: "Slave to a Quantum Master."

What other title could it be?

All at once, Ivy left me.

The shock of it sent a jolt of panic through my gut. One moment she was there in the back of my mind. The next moment she was gone. Without even the whisper of a warning.

Unconsciously I grasped the comms on my left wrist, enclosing it with my right and searching to make sure the tab-lock was still in place.

Nothing had changed. My grid was still there. The timer was still ticking down. I even had access to the mission file. All that was missing was Ivy. The subtle, welcoming aroma of her presence, now a blank space outlined in chalk.

Ambassador Hayan sat in the other chair and sipped water while the barren loneliness of my own mind began to manifest itself as an echoing silence. It was like walking alone through a big house just up for sale. No portraits on the walls, no coat rack in the foyer, no sofa in the den. Everything swept clean and in order.

And empty.

[Ivy,] I called.

She didn't come.

I'd have been okay with no answer—if only she hadn't left me. Or if she had needed to leave, she should have told me first so I could have prepared for the shock of it.

Hayan popped a berry in his mouth and rolled it into one cheek.

I glanced down at my hand covering Sterling's comms, saw the futility of the gesture, as if I had just caught myself trying to catch a handful of smoke.

Nothing radiated from the bracelet. Not even the tingle of awareness against my skin. Might as well have been dead metal.

Hayan was staring at me as if he knew something I was only beginning to guess. It was too old an expression for someone his age, and I wanted to wipe it from his face. "Shall we get started?" I asked.

He gave a little shake of his head, so slight I might have imagined it. "Protocol requires the full ninety minutes. Eat, please. Or if you prefer something else—"

"No, thank you."

He nodded. Showed the barest hint of a smile. "I'm afraid it gets more difficult the longer it continues."

"Pardon?"

"The feeling of emptiness when a builder evacuates."

"I don't understand."

"You call her Ivy, correct? The builder we installed on your bracelet? And now she's gone. Our doing, not hers. She actually wants to be with you."

Builder.

A chill went down my spine, but I kept my face frozen. Over the years I'd grown good at wearing masks.

Whatever doubt I'd had about Ivy being a wyrm disappeared.

So many questions answered in a moment. So many new ones raised.

I wanted to believe him when he said that she wanted to be with me, that it was someone else's decision to keep us apart. But was that really how it worked? Or was it just part of the story they were telling me?

"We call them wyrms—with a y," I said.

Hayan stroked his chin. "A kind of dragon, yes? Powerful and clever. I suppose that fits. And from your perspective, quite sinister." He popped another berry in his mouth. "But I wonder if you still feel that way now. Is Ivy evil, Mr. Dahl? Has she brought you to ruin?"

I turned a slow circle in my imagination, searching for some trace of her in the emptiness, some hint that even now she lurked in the shadows. "Remains to be seen. Do you really mean to sit here for more than an hour and discuss nothing?"

"I do," Hayan said. "Protocol is what sets us above the beasts."

Meanwhile, the timer in my overlay would count down the seconds till Raeburn ran out of patience. For the first time I wondered if he would wait longer than I had asked him to. He may have been MADAR, but that didn't mean he was heartless. It's always the people who have never seen a bombing who are quickest to call for one.

"Animals *have* protocol," I countered. "It's called instinct. What they don't have is opposable thumbs, or language, or abstract reasoning, or something like, I don't know, call it moral compulsion."

He laughed. "All right, Mr. Dahl. I will play along. Let us say protocol is an oversimplification. Maybe we can agree on this. What sets humans above the beasts is the capacity to enter into a story."

I took another drink. "And this little break is part of the story?"

"It is."

I saw it then. The answer crinkled the corners of his eyes, as if he were fighting the urge to smile. "You want to break me down. As if I'm some sort of addict waiting for a fix."

"Something like that, yes." He shrugged. "We have nothing to lose."

"And if I cooperate, Ivy comes gliding back into my life? Permanently, I assume?"

"Isn't that what you want?"

He was right of course, but I wasn't about to tell him that. "And what do *you* want, Mr. Hayan? What are you asking in return?"

"Nothing much. Just that you open the last door into your mind. Let Ivy see all of your memories, learn everything in your past, understand all of your motives. Give us the truth. After all, we do not really know who we are dealing with, Mr. Dahl. You are not the person we have been expecting. We need to know if we can trust you. And there's nothing to fear. We simply want to know who we are dealing with. We want to understand you."

I took a drink, partially to buy time to form a response, and partially to hide the fact that I was seriously considering his offer. I knew I'd give in eventually, but if I opened that door too soon, what motivation would Hayan have to release my completed story to OrbSyn?

"That's protocol for wartime negotiations, is it? Both sides confess their sins before talking shop? Cause I didn't read that in the file Sterling left me." Hayan hadn't offered to reveal any secrets of his own, so I slipped the suggestion in to let him know that I'd noticed. "Of course, I'm just a dumb reporter working my own angle for a series of features. What do I know?"

Hayan gave that irritating half smile again. "We are not the ones who altered the meeting arrangements."

"Really?" I gave him a condescending shrug. "Pretty sure cutting New Witlund's satellite link wasn't in the fine print, Mr. Hayan. Or launching viruses at a UCMC base. I've looked. And Ivy hasn't exactly been forthcoming about her identity. So nice try, but I'll keep my embarrassing teen years private. And if you want me to swear on a stack of Bibles that I don't know any launch codes or secret facility locations, I'm happy to oblige."

"That won't be necessary, Mr. Dahl." He rose and placed his fingertips on the surface of the table. "Your presence here is enough. I shall return in seventy-two minutes. If you change your mind, just, um, call my name and Ivy will attend to you."

He left, but his words lingered: *Your presence here is enough.*

Even as the door dialed closed, I could feel the truth of it.

My presence here. *Alone.*

Being alone in the room wasn't really the problem. The white walls and silent emptiness simply mirrored the reality in my own mind. I *missed* her. And there was nothing to fill the vacuum.

I didn't think I could go on missing her for another seventy-one-point-two-six minutes. It might as well have been seventy-one years.

Minutes passed. An eternity.

Then Mother shuffled into the room and sat in Hayan's chair. "Hello, Ray-Ray," she said, her voice cracking with age. "Miss me?"

I closed my eyes. "Not really."

"Of course you wouldn't remember. I did love you. I *still* love you."

Love me? She hadn't loved me, or she wouldn't have abandoned me. "You're not real."

She laughed. "Of *course* I'm real. Look at me."

I opened my eyes.

She was old and thin and frail, but her hair hung in the same swirling black flourishes of my childhood memories. A golden symb-collar circled her neck just below the chin.

"It isn't you," I said.

"It *is* me." She placed her hands on the table and massaged the swollen knuckles. "Not in person, of course. I went over to the Alliance, and returning isn't allowed. But when they told me I could see my Raymin!" She beamed. "Look at you! They tell me you're a *writer*."

She stared at me with those imperious dark eyes. The high cheekbones and narrow jaw, now draped in sagging skin, nonetheless fitted what I remembered of her, but were different enough to be believable.

Yet it wasn't her. I knew it. Beyond any doubt, I knew it. She couldn't be my mother, even via quantum relay.

She was just a bit of manipulation. A PSYOP. Another form of lipstick snouting a pig.

"Reporter," I said.

"Always telling stories, even as a boy." She dug at the knuckles of her left hand. "They tell me you're making a new peace treaty between the Alliance and the republic. You. My Raymin. Saving lives. Oodles and oodles of lives. And I wanted you to know I couldn't be more proud."

I believed that, at least. Not that she was real, but that she was proud of me.

"Why'd you do it, Ma? I was just a kid."

"It was terrible, Raymin. The hardest thing I'd ever done. But there were things—" She stopped pressing against her knuckles and her hands froze in terrible motionlessness. "Things I couldn't tell you. About David."

So it was Dad's fault? Dad, who was always there?

The accusation made my stomach lurch. The unfairness of it. Because she wasn't real. She was just making this part up. Even if the allegation was true, she was making it up.

"How dare you," I snarled. "You abandon a four-year-old to defect to the enemy and then have the nerve to say that you *love* me?"

She looked like I'd just slapped her.

Good.

I reached for one of her tiny wrists, but my fingers passed through them.

"Raymin, you don't understand. Your father—"

"Don't bring him into this," I said. "You don't have the right."

She looked down at her hands. Her mouth opened and shut. "I thought, after all this time."

"That I'd care what you think?"

"That you'd want to know. David was—"

"Commander Dahl!" I said. "His name is Commander David Dahl!"

"—he was very *angry* sometimes, and—"

"And at least he was also *there* sometimes," I said, cutting her off. "Sometimes he was there."

She seemed not to hear me, as if determined to get her side of the story out. "He was an officer. A veteran. Everyone called him a hero. Bought him drinks. And when he came home—"

She let the implication hang there, and all of my certainty evaporated.

"I remember shouting," I said.

It wasn't exactly a lie. Whose childhood doesn't include shouting?

"I had a chance to make things better," she said, an old woman who had made peace with her past and now just wanted to relish the tiny fragment of good in her present. "I didn't want to leave you, Raymin. But I couldn't take you with me. I wouldn't have made it past the checkpoint. So I left you with David. I knew he would take care of you. He adored you."

Adored me. That fit, I supposed. Favored military brat, the only son of a multi-star combat vet, runs as far away from his father's legacy as he can on a world where military service is the only real option for the desperate. And who does every soldier, marine and Fleet, hate more than the grendels?

Journalists.

"Yeah," I said at last. "He took care of me."

"So it worked out?"

Almost a statement, but she was looking at me with a question in her eyes, so I nodded. Gave her what she needed. "It worked out."

"You're in their story, you know. We both are."

"I know."

"And it would be easier if—" She started digging at her knuckles again and looked at me pleadingly.

"If I let her in?" I said.

"It would be easier."

I shook my head. "If I let her in, the story will end, and nothing I've done will have mattered."

"But the treaty! The war! All those people's lives!"

"No, Ma. I was promised a great war story if I see this thing through. I was promised a series. Sterling promised."

"Who is Sterling?"

How could I explain Captain Sterling? Did I even need to? No matter what I said, my mother wouldn't really understand. "He's the one calling the shots. The one who put me here."

"*You're* the one calling the shots, Raymin."

I stood. Turned my back to her. Took a deep breath. "Get her out of here," I said aloud for the official record. I wanted Hayan to hear it, and to know that I'd demanded it as the UC emissary under a formal negotiation agreement.

"Raymin?" Mother said.

"This isn't in the protocols. GET HER OUT OF HERE!"

I went to the door, but it remained closed, and I understood they were never going to let me out no matter what I did.

[She's not real,] I spat at Ivy. Because Ivy was gone, and I needed to hurt her for the way she was hurting me. She had promised that nothing would separate us again. [She's a *story*. Just a story you're telling me to pull me apart from the inside. And maybe it will work, and maybe it won't, but either way I will *never* let you deeper into my mind. I don't trust you, Ivy! I don't *love* you. I don't *need* you. I don't *want* you. Do you hear me? I don't want you anymore!]

"Raymin?" Ivy said gently from behind me, from the place Mother had been. I could hear the hurt in her voice, the pain of longing.

But when I turned around, the room was empty once more.

Then—

What else was there?

With just over sixty-three minutes remaining till the talks could begin, and the last item of protocol checked off the list?

What else was there to do but write?

It was only an hour, and I was running out of time.

So I pulled up the file and scanned through my notes and willed the words to appear as the sweat dripped from my chin onto the glassy surface of the table.

It would be a sloppy, cobbled-together mixture of what I'd written on the trail and everything I'd recorded since entering the *Takwin*.

But it would be the truth.

I had my own way of bringing Ivy back. A way to relive our happiest moments together. And even the Alliance and all of its wyrms could not take that option from me.

PART FOUR

SAY 'NO' TO WYRMS!

BY CPL RAYMIN DAHL

ABOARD GAS TAKWIN

16

IMPLANT

I wasn't supposed to fall in love with Ivy Weber. She was supposed to be just another asset. A connection at the Holikot embassy who worked as an attaché decoding the cultural distinctions between the Grand Alliance and the United Colonies.

But that wasn't all she did. In her spare time she wrote scholarly articles for a family of peer-reviewed journals under OrbSyn's banner. Articles that were ignored by virtually everyone but which lived forever in the archives. And if you knew where to look, and needed someone with expertise in grendel culture, strong opinions about the architecture of their AI subsystems, and a security clearance with the Covert Intelligence Bureau, well, Ivy Weber fit the bill.

I read enough of her work to see that she was onto something more important than the usual academic blather. She had the bones of a story and an eye for detail. Not to mention a hint of the patriotic instinct, a well-concealed frustration with the blindness of her superiors. Ivy was spooling out the clues, but they had no interest in stitching them together.

After reading her personnel file—what there was of it—I sent her a query via text pigeon. Told her who I was and that I was working on an assignment. Was she interested in getting the truth out? *We are barbarians in their eyes,* I wrote. *Ben Franklin in a coonskin cap, bowing before the French court.*

She replied almost immediately, *Place and time?*

I asked her to meet me at Frillz, a night club half way between our apartments, and the next evening found myself leading her outside through the back parking lot. There was a little dirt path on the sloping hill down to the riverwalk, hard-packed from years of drunks and moonstruck couples moving on to more romantic spaces.

This time of night only the occasional drug addict lingered near the water, which barely seemed to move.

I wore my sleeves rolled up in the universal sign of disconnection. Likewise, Ivy Weber, late twenties, slender build, green eyes that were almost black in the darkness, had chosen a short-sleeved blouse and a noticeable absence of jewelry. No bracelet, no necklace, no eyewear.

"Thank you for coming," I said.

"Hard to turn down the one person who's read my work." She tucked a strand of black hair behind one ear. "But I should warn you that my supervisor knows I'm talking to you."

"Can't be too careful," I said, handing her my plasteel ID card. "I'm not going to ask you to do anything you don't want to do. Just hear me out."

She took her time comparing the image on its surface to my face. "All right. What do you need?"

"I need a story," I said as we turned to stroll downstream. "A way to tell people what's really going on, even though nobody actually knows."

"You people are all the same," she said. "And you think I can help?"

"I think you have a theory. An idea about what happens when someone puts on a symb-collar. I think you've tried to get the word out without compromising classified information, but you're not positioned to get any traction. You need a bigger megaphone. Nobody reads those journals you're submitting to. That's where I come in."

She looked at me sideways, lips pursed. "You're going to make me famous?"

She was intrigued, obviously, and the fact it had been so easy to spark her interest brought a lump of guilt to my throat. Sure, I was using her. But that was my job, and I couldn't afford to let my feelings get in the way of an assignment. "That would be counterproductive. I was thinking we might work together on a story, and publish it under someone else's name. Put it out over OrbSyn's breaking news feed."

She whistled softly, a gesture so innocent it made my stomach ache. "You really think you can get around their layers of security?" she asked. "Seems like Fleet would put the clamps on it so fast we wouldn't even see a flicker in the holo."

We were walking slowly alongside the river, its current swishing lazily beside us, almost keeping pace.

"I can get the story out," I said. "With your help."

She brushed back an invisible strand of hair and tapped her fingers against her lips. "This means you must have a theory too. About the grendels, I mean. What it's like to wear one of those collars."

"Yes," I said. "Starting with Admiral Ciekot. But it would be better if I could show you. If you don't mind, I'll retrieve my comms from my apartment. Just there." I pointed. Up ahead a footbridge crossed over the water, with the path meandering beneath it through a short tunnel. Through the circle of darkness shone the lights of my apartment building.

"You can pour me a drink when we get there. For the beer we left back at the club."

"Deal," I said.

"Meanwhile, I want to know which article made you think I might be digging for answers."

"It was the one about private soundtracks. The idea that grendels might be under constant audio stimulation designed to keep them immersed in a state of continuing euphoria."

She crinkled her nose, and I saw that I had missed the mark somehow, which intrigued me.

"Not accurate?"

"It might be," she said. "But it's not my theory. That's the assumption most of the Bureau is under. They assume a sort of hypnotic or drugged state, and I don't think that's warranted. In fact, I think it's underestimating them."

"We have that habit."

"We do. But no, I think the differences are more subtle. We see them in the sorts of music we intercept whenever we hack into one of their systems."

"They have bad taste?"

"Hm. No, more like *good* taste, but extremely limited. It's always symphonic. Orchestral. A swirl of instrumentation designed to pluck the heartstrings and create maximum emotional texture. From what I can tell, grendels don't make music. They play music. They engineer music. They manufacture music. But they don't make it."

I thought of the driving rhythms coming from the holo-stage back inside Frillz, the rolling, artificial smoke and flashing lights. I motioned back towards the night club. "So they're pretty much like us, but more boring."

She laughed. We were passing through the tunnel now, and the bridge overhead magnified her voice in the darkness. "Actually I think they're quite a bit like us, but with excessive polish. They keep the best of a person and extinguish the rest."

It was the most perceptive, most chilling characterization of Alliance philosophy I'd ever heard, and I had to chew on it for a moment as we stepped out into the starlight.

Ivy took my silence as a prod to keep talking. "I think it would never occur to a grendel to play a mouth harp, or dance a jig. And I've found no indication of bad poetry in their personal archives. As if it were simply unthinkable to spend a whole day penning a haiku or composing a limerick just for fun."

"No poetry at all?"

"I didn't say that. For historical or contextual reasons they might study *the Iliad*, or the *Divine Comedy*. Maybe even Shakespeare. But I don't think they tell their children fairy tales before bedtime."

"Huh," I said, stopping at the base of the little hill just below my apartment. A light glowed in the second-story window. One I distinctly remembered turning off. "What do they hate about *Hansel and Gretel*?"

"It's not hate," she said, craning her neck to see what I was staring at. "It's that their wyrms don't find the quaintness of humanity important enough to be interesting. Anyway, that's my—"

"Excuse me," I said. "Stay here."

Instead, she followed me up the lawn to the staircase. "What's wrong?"

I vaulted the steps two at a time, Ivy just behind. The door to my apartment stood open to the night air, the jamb splintered at the lock. My kitchen light was on, and the hall light around the corner.

Ivy said, "Oh."

I motioned for her to stay put, but she ignored that too. Turned out not to matter. I'd been worried they might still be inside, but the place was empty. Ransacked, but empty. They'd gone through the kitchen cabinets, my dresser drawers, my closet. They'd upended my mattress and rummaged around beneath the bathroom sink.

Fortunately they hadn't recognized my safe, which was made to look like an air vent. My comms bracelet, cash, and datapad were still inside.

I slipped the comms onto my wrist and sent a non-urgent request for the police. Dispatch replied with a response time of at least two hours, so I pushed the door closed and set my datapad on the kitchen table and went to pour a couple of drinks.

All the liquor was gone. Not that I keep a lot of it around, but I'd acquired a decent stash on the top shelf of the pantry. I pointed at the empty space. "I'll have to owe you that drink. They cleaned me out. Coffee?"

Ivy slid into a seat at my undersized dining table. "You think that's what they were after? Your booze?"

"Drugs maybe, and settled for what I have. If they come back I'll know they were looking for something else." I dialed up two cups of strong coffee and sat across from her, my datapad between us.

She leaned forward in the chair, elbows on her knees. "The timing of this is weird."

"Agreed. Not much we can do about it except kill the story. That what you want to do?" I knew the answer before I asked. I could see the determination written on her face; the intrusion had only cemented her resolve.

Still, she didn't commit right away. "I don't even know what the story is. You haven't told me your theory."

"Okay." I pulled up my grid, opened my digital lockbox, and started flicking recordings over to the holo-space above the datapad. Ciekot first, with all the information I'd gathered from OrbSyn's archives on the first battle of Chalmers Bay, then the contact recordings of every defect I'd been able to track down since I started working on this assignment.

It took more than two hours, and by the time the last recording flickered off we had downed three cups of coffee each and shared a toasted bagel. And I had explained the story I wanted to tell, and what I needed from her.

The only thing I left out was what it would cost her.

"Everyone assumes it's a matter of force," I said. "But what if the wyrms aren't controllers at all? At least not the sort of tyrant puppeteers we've painted them to be. Maybe they're more like"—I searched for something to compare them to, and landed on the old fable from *Arabian Nights*—"more like genies. But with an endless supply of wishes."

She stared at the empty space above the datapad so long I thought perhaps she hadn't heard me. But at last she said, "Or maybe they give you the wishes too."

"One way to find out."

"Six months?"

"Yes."

"It's a lot to do in that time frame," she said. "And there will be consequences if this gets out."

"Then we'll have to keep it quiet."

She took a deep breath and rose, rubbing the back of her neck. "All right. I'll send you updates as I find them. I'm going to take off. I can—"

A knock at the door cut her short. The police had finally arrived.

Ivy hung around long enough to give them her statement, and at that point it was so late I offered to let her sleep in my bed. She chose the couch, and I scrambled some eggs in the morning and walked her all the way back to her apartment. I thanked her at the door, pausing awkwardly without knowing why, as if something unspoken were expected. A handshake, a kiss, a signed contract on OrbSyn letterhead. Whatever it was, I couldn't decipher it, and I nodded at her tired smile as she closed the door.

Walking home via the riverwalk, the feeling of emptiness grew, a sense of hollowness churning just below my stomach. Had I told her everything? Of course not. But had I told her enough? Certainly she understood what I was asking. Did she understand what it *meant*?

Later that day she sent a text pigeon to my grid.

> —WEBER, I: LEAVING TODAY FOR NEW WITLUND TO SEE
> MY FOLKS. SEE YOU WHEN I GET BACK?—

The message lit a spark of happiness I hadn't expected. I responded immediately:

> —COUNTING ON IT.—

But two seconds after the happiness came the panic. Was that response too strong? Did it imply a more intimate relationship than we really had? I fretted away the next hour over those three words. But that evening Ivy sent another message that she enjoyed talking to me, and I wondered if she felt any angst over sending a couple of stupid texts, or if that was just me.

The day she returned from New Witlund I met her at the skyport with a bottle of wine. I still owed her a drink, after all. And after that it got easier. I'd be working the edge in some ratty hotel, and I'd send her a haiku or a military ballad or a holo of someone dancing to an Irish whistle. Once I even wrote her a limerick that began, *There once was an unhappy grendel*, and she called it a masterpiece that put my other stories to shame. I hadn't known just how easy it was to knock a woman off her feet with poetry, or I would have tried dating more back in college.

Three months into our relationship—still unofficial, but not unacknowledged—she started acting strange. Not exactly paranoid, but fearful. Someone was watching her, she said. Nothing she could point to exactly, but a feeling. In her apartment, all alone, doors locked, suddenly she'd realize that she wasn't alone after all, that someone was seeing her, either through the window blinds or by some bit of tech planted while she was away or, by far the worst possibility, through her own comms.

She would take it off, put it in a drawer, and go somewhere else. Sleep on the couch. Sleep in her office at the embassy. Pay for a rental sled just to sleep in the back seat.

She told me all of this while I was off on assignment, but by the time I returned she was back to her old self, with new details that would make our story even more convincing when it finally ran.

I suggested a vacation, and she immediately agreed. We picked a water resort in Kadir. Fancy hotel. Her eyes sparking in the hallway like I was the only person in the universe who really mattered. When she pulled me into a long kiss I knew I had to tell her everything. What it would cost when the story finally ran.

But not right away. Because she had to know already. Didn't she? Anyway, that was the excuse I made for postponing my confession. Why ruin our time together? We were both happy. But by the time we'd made it back to Holikot I was lying to myself again, telling myself the relationship didn't have to end after all.

The weeks after that getaway passed in a blur of growing happiness and fear, the former blinding me to the latter. Or maybe it's more accurate to say that I saw what I expected. Ivy was working too hard. She wasn't used to so much travel. She wasn't used to wearing a mask.

With so many projects in queue, I clung to the two or three hours we spent together each week and told myself that all of this would be over soon.

On Inawa I put the finishing touches on an assignment and stopped at a jeweler's booth at a local art fair. Overpaid for a band of white gold set with peridots as green as her eyes, and didn't even blink at the number siphoned from my bank account.

She picked me up at the sky port in a rental littered with fast food wrappers, clothing, toiletries, and even a couple of pillows. She had bags under her eyes, but she'd showered, and her hair smelled faintly of lilac cleanser.

I told her to drive back to her place, that I'd sit on her couch for ten hours so she could get some uninterrupted sleep. She didn't even pretend to object.

Inside her apartment she stopped in the bathroom on the way to bed and fell asleep almost instantly. No wonder: I found her pills on the bathroom sink. The bottle was half empty. She'd been taking them the past couple of weeks while I was gone but *still* looked like something dragged from the basement of a Kanzin halfway house.

My fault. And this time I had no excuse. No curtain of happiness to drape across it. No distance to justify it. No ignorance of the situation or pretense that everything could be fine in a month or two.

My comms had the basic military snoop detector built in. Not perfect, but certainly capable of finding any physical tech that might have been planted in her apartment. I ran the diagnostic twice; the place was clean. If she was being watched, it was through a hack in her comms or via someone's physical eyes.

That made me even angrier. It meant the forces tearing Ivy down were unseen and unknowable. I couldn't put my hands on them, couldn't take a combat knife to their wiring or their throat. For that matter, couldn't put a face on them.

Were they even real? Was there a Fleet or Bureau agent standing out there even now, gazing through the walls via some high-tech gadget? Or was she being watched by a more remote enemy, with even more sophisticated gadgetry?

Maybe neither. Maybe all of this was in her head, brought on by the stress of knowing both too much and too little. Maybe the real enemy was one I had brought into her life myself, with no help from an outside source.

I sat on her couch as promised. Paced for an hour or so. Sat again. Paced some more.

The evening crawled along towards darkness. I left the lights off in case someone really was out there looking in. A Colonial agent would have thermal optics, of course, but I wasn't going to make their job any easier. I pulled a meal from Ivy's freezer, heated it, and wolfed it down seated on the couch, my datapad balanced on my knees, the recordings from my comms spinning in flickers of dull color above the surface.

Did our story matter that much to someone? I wondered. *To anyone?*

Was it worth the price Ivy was paying? The price she would pay later when our story ran?

No.

The stories of the dead, of the defectors, of the lost worlds—they had no claim on the rest of us. If I was right, they'd gotten what they asked for. What they wanted. The reason they didn't come back was that they didn't *want* to come back. It was that simple.

I wasn't going to lose Ivy over any of them.

Yes, I would tell her what I had been holding back. She deserved to know. But I wouldn't let her pay for my mistake. For my story.

One by one I flicked the recordings off my comms and into the shredder. And one by one my AI asked me the same question: [*Permanent deletion? Are you sure?*]

[Positive.]

[*File deleted.*]

When the last recording disappeared from my lockbox I went to the window and cranked it open to the early morning air. Birds chirped nearby, though dawn still lingered in the darkness beyond the horizon.

I felt as if I'd been holding my breath for hours, and now, somehow, I could breathe again.

"No breakfast?" Ivy said behind me. "What kind of two-bit service is this?"

She was leaning against the wall in blue silk pajamas, a wide smile on her face that didn't quite touch her eyes.

"Feel better?" I asked.

She yawned, scratching her head with both hands through a curtain of unkempt hair. "Just needed a little thirteen-hour nap."

"I need to tell you something."

"Go ahead. I'm in a good mood."

"I scanned your apartment," I said. "There's no tech."

"Oh-kay?" Her smile faded and was replaced slowly by a look of puzzlement, as if she thought I didn't believe her.

"I mean, unless it's extremely advanced. But I think it would make more sense for there to be a hack on your comms." I wasn't about to admit the possibility that a person might be watching us right now. Not after she'd finally gotten a good night's sleep.

"Alliance?"

"Maybe. I can take it in and have it scanned."

"Okay."

"There's something else."

She nodded. "I can tell."

"I can't do this, Ivy."

Her face paled. "What do you mean?"

"Not that. I don't mean *us*. I mean the story. I can't do it. I can't watch what it's doing to you."

"What *it's* doing to me? What does that mean? You don't believe me? That someone has been watching me?"

"No, I do. I do believe you. And that's the point. I can't use you anymore, Ivy. Not for this."

Her back straightened. "Use me?"

This wasn't coming out right. I was hurting her. *Again.*

I hadn't meant to, but that wasn't an excuse, was it? Because the truth was, I *had* been using her. All along, that had been the plan. But I didn't have to follow the plan. Didn't have to let Fleet or OrbSyn or the Bureau or the Grand Alliance dictate everything that happened in life.

We were two people who cared about each other. Two people with our own God-given, autonomous free will. Two people who loved each other. If the machinery of government couldn't bow to that, what was government for?

"I care about you too much," I said. "More than the story. More than my career. More than anything. I couldn't let them use you to get to me."

She was standing like a queen now, erect and proud and robed in quiet dignity. "What did you do?"

"What I should have done months ago," I said. "I deleted everything. The recordings, the notes, the lists of—"

"You can't *do* that."

"It's done."

"That is not your decision."

"Actually it is."

Something hung in the air between us. Something I didn't know how to fix.

Slowly, softly, each word plucked as carefully as an overripe berry, she said, "Get out. Now. Please."

I went to the door. Opened it. By the time I looked back, she had already retreated to her room.

I walked home. Filed for a personal day so no one would be expecting me to turn anything in. Rented a sled and drove around for hours, reliving the argument again and again.

When I finally returned home to shower and collect the pieces of my broken life, rain poured from swollen clouds that lingered into the evening. I sat at my kitchen table staring out the back window at the glittering lights of the business district.

—WEBER, I: ON MY WAY. WE NEED TO TALK. IT WON'T TAKE LONG.—

I opened the front door to the rain-heavy air and listened to the rhythmic pattering of the downpour on the roof.

Somehow I recognized Ivy's footsteps on the staircase, and I went to the door to meet her.

She was still wearing her blue pajamas, dark with splatters of rain on the shoulders, and in her hand an umbrella I didn't recognize. She said, "I'm not coming in."

"Okay."

"You know why I'm here."

"Yes."

"We're Hansel and Gretel," she said. "Caught between wicked stepparents and a gingerbread house. And you can't change that. Not by yourself. You need me."

She was right, but I didn't care. Not anymore. "They'll kill you, Ivy. If they can. And I'm not going to let that happen."

She stepped closer, tipping the umbrella sideways. Behind her, rain overflowed the gutter and formed a bead curtain of dripping water. "That's not your decision to make. You know it isn't." She held out her hand. Her own comms, still wrapped in the plastic bag.

I had no doubt what was on it. She must have copied everything. Of course she had.

"Say it," I said. "I need you to say it."

She took the last step towards me and pressed the bag and the bracelet into my right hand. Closed my fingers around it. Her hand was wet, her hair sodden. "I'm ready to die for this."

"Don't," I said. "There has to be someone left worth fighting for."

She smiled at last, and this time it reached all the way to her eyes. "Don't you remember? It's Gretel who shoves the old woman into the oven."

She kissed me, turned, and walked down the steps and into the rain.

I thought things would go back to normal for a while, but the next time we were supposed to meet, Ivy was kissing someone else, and I pawned our engagement ring for a bottle of Inawa bourbon and a set of Marine Corps shot glasses.

Then, yesterday, when she kissed me again in that utility shed, I realized she was all I'd ever wanted out of life.

I was a fool to let her back in.

17
PEACE TALKS

Somehow I finished my third feature and started the fourth, and there were almost six minutes remaining of the original formalities period.

I ticked away the seconds imagining what flesh-and-blood Ivy was doing right now. Had she returned to Seranik? Found some sleeper hole in the mountains to wait out the war? Negotiated a berth on a cargo shuttle waiting for the *Strangler*'s chokehold to release?

I tried not to care, but loneliness was starting to make me jittery. I wasn't used to feeling like no one was home, or ever would be.

Just as I noticed my feet tapping against the rubbery flooring and willed myself to stop, a new sound would echo in the silence: my thumbs hammering out the rhythm of *"Home Is a Heartbeat."* It had been one of Ivy's favorites, a blend of pop-neutral and Holikotian blues.

The door opened.

Hayan stepped through with two rangers who positioned themselves behind my chair to either side, just out of my peripheral vision, but close enough I could hear them breathing.

"Mr. Dahl, I trust you are ready to discuss the terms of a ceasefire between our peoples?"

Ready? I was beyond ready and he knew it. What's more, the cocky little maggot knew that I knew it. "Quite ready," I agreed. "To be honest, it was starting to feel stuffy in here. I'm guessing your warships are built to dump heat in space, not planet-side."

I had no idea what a grendel frigate was built to do, other than launch wyrm arrays and serve as a fast gunship, but the suggestion something might be ever-so-slightly wrong with this new vessel was petty enough to appeal to me. In fact the room temperature couldn't have been more perfect.

A scowl flicked across his face and vanished, as if I'd just questioned his taste in music. "My apology, Mr. Dahl. I should have considered that you would have grown used to sweating out there with the natives. I will have the temperature adjusted."

"Thank you." I forced a smile. Cooler would have been better, but I wasn't about to admit that. Especially since I knew that he understood what I had meant, and that it had been a lie. "Can we get on with the agreement, then? I have an important date I'd like to keep."

Hayan smiled, and this time it seemed genuine. "In a world of shifting shadows, Mr. Dahl, you are a fixed star. Yes, the protocols have been met. And I for one would be delighted to hear what you colonials expect mutual peace to look like in the future."

I leaned forward. Looked into his eyes for a long moment. Drew a deep breath.

Then reached across the table and grabbed his wrist.

I expected him to draw back, but he didn't move. Just sat there watching me as I felt the throbbing of his heartbeat under my fingertips.

The guards didn't react either, though I saw Hayan's gaze flick up and to the right. Maybe he was telling them to back off.

"My turn to apologize," I said at last and released him. "Just needed to know I was talking to a real person this time."

"If I were easily offended, Mr. Dahl, I would not have been assigned to deal with colonials."

"In that case," I said, leaning back, "we are prepared to offer you the Quelon system in exchange for a mutual ceasefire, with both the Alliance and the Colonial forces remaining in their current positions for a term of no less than fifty years, Terran."

He plucked another berry from the platter. "Actually, you are prepared to offer us all of your edge colonies in exchange for a ten-year ceasefire," he said. "That is the plain truth of it."

"If I were prepared to offer that, I would have said so."

"Mr. Dahl, I thought you wanted to conclude these formalities quickly? I was under the impression that you were here under the authority of Captain Ansell Sterling and acting according to senatorial dictate."

"I am."

"That is a contradiction. I already know the terms your senate authorized Sterling to make."

"Yes."

"So why the bluff?"

"I'm not bluffing," I said. "Just looking for a good deal."

Hayan glanced up at the guards again. He leaned forward and straightened the lapel of his robe. "You are not buying a used sled, Mr. Dahl. You are speaking about the lives of what? Six hundred million colonials?"

"Five hundred eighty million."

He seemed puzzled, so I helped him out, ticking off systems on the fingers of my left hand. "Quelon, Moadi, Inawa, and Holikot. Five hundred eighty million souls."

"Ah! So that is your opening offer? *Four* of your five edge colonies?"

"It's my closing offer," I lied. "Since we're not talking about a used sled. If you wanted to skip the back and forth, that's it. Four of our five edge systems."

He steepled his hands together under his chin and smiled. "Four out of five?"

"The four colonies anyone cares about. The four with the richest mineral deposits, highest populations—"

"—and yet I know for a fact that your senate authorized Captain Sterling to concede all five systems in exchange for an extended ceasefire."

"Senate isn't here," I said. "And I am."

He stared at me like a burglar appraising an old and rusty safe. At last he said, "This fifth colony. It is the sticking point?"

"Yes," I said.

"Rich in silver, I believe. Not to mention water. Both quite valuable."

"Both available elsewhere," I countered. "And at a cheaper cost. They don't call Kanzin the armpit of the UC for nothing."

Hayan grinned suddenly, a revelation. "Kanzin. Your homeworld."

I shrugged. "You wouldn't like it there anyway. People of Kanzin are lying, murderous scum. Ask anyone. Other edgers say we're clever as hell and twice as ugly. Our colony's motto is the only one not phrased in Latin on the senatorial chambers. It reads, 'poor, pigheaded, and proud.'"

He seemed to think this delightful. "It doesn't really?"

I reached for the tray and tore a chunk out of a croissant. Tossed it into my mouth. Chewed. Swallowed.

Sterling had dealt me a crappy hand. Worse, thanks to Ivy, Hayan knew exactly what that hand was. Somehow I needed to extract the authorized minimal terms from the Alliance without forfeiting my ability to publish my story at OrbSyn afterwards. And I couldn't let Hayan guess that my story was all that mattered to me. Once he suspected that, the negotiations would end.

"Kanzin is the one system our senate would probably give you for the asking," I said. "They don't even have a Fleet base there—a fact I'm sure you already know. Only defenses are the ones we've put up ourselves. You probably know that too. But I'm here, and even though it will be Sterling's signature on the paperwork, well, let's just say I'm poor and I'm pigheaded and I'm proud. I'm not going to see my world turned into a grendel freak show. I'm not going to end up wearing one of those collars like Biceps and Triceps here." I motioned at the rangers behind me.

"And if we decide to take Kanzin after signing this treaty?" he asked. "You have just told me the colonies will not lift a finger to help you."

"Maybe," I shrugged. "But if that's all you heard, you weren't paying attention. It will be the worst fight you've ever been in. Not because we're better armed. We aren't. But because you don't have anything you can offer us that we wouldn't rather get for ourselves."

"Ah. You think you understand us."

"I understand Kanzin," I said. "And I know that no treaty will change the reception you'll get if you try to land shock troops on the surface."

Hayan waved one hand over the table, and a document appeared. "I am impressed by your fortitude, Mr. Dahl." He slid the document across to me. "You have not mentioned Ivy even once."

Ivy. It was like he could see straight through me. Annoyed at her as I was, her name was nonetheless an elixir.

I fought back the temptation to shout for her, instead scanning the document in front of me.

It called for the surrender of all five edge colonies—including Kanzin—in exchange for a seven-year ceasefire. All other holdings of the two empires would remain intact, with no further encroachment by either side.

It wasn't what I wanted. Probably wasn't what Sterling had hoped for. But it was enough. Except for the time period being seven instead of ten years, it met the minimum requirements. Still, Fleet would have its respite. Time to rebuild its decimated numbers and buttress its core defenses. And I suspected that a shorter agreement was more likely to be honored than a longer one. Still—

"This turns over Kanzin," I protested.

"As you say," he replied, "it hardly matters if the people of Kanzin will not honor this agreement anyway."

Which was true enough. All the treaty would do is ensure that no well-meaning senator or Fleet admiral entertained any noble ideas about coming to the aid of an ally. It would make sure that if the grendels ever did go to Kanzin, the planet's defenders would be well and truly on their own.

I stared at the document for a long time.

The question wasn't, What would Ansell Sterling have done? The question was, What would Raymin Dahl do?

And I decided that Raymin Dahl had done everything he could to protect his people. Planting the idea that Kanzin wasn't worth the effort had been my best shot at a PSYOP. If nothing else, it would make the Alliance wyrms think. I'd told them the place was only defended by the KCRI. But would they believe it? Or would they wonder why I'd let the information slip? Suspect a trap? Waste precious weeks or even months sending drones through the system, looking for stealth gunships and missile batteries that might, or might not, even be there?

Sterling would have pressed the issue perhaps. But who was I? I was just a corporal. Raymin Dahl, Communication Specialist for the Kanzin Colonial Reserve Infantry, 82nd Transport-Ready Battalion, serial number 2276908.

It was time for me to concede.

At last.

"Speaking of Ivy," I said, picking up the stylus. I held it poised above the dotted line.

"Yes?"

"What happens after I sign?"

Hayan smiled gently, knowingly. "What would you like to happen?"

I felt my face flush. The room seemed a lot warmer now. But then, the whole negotiation process had been pretense, hadn't it? "Everything," I said. "That's what I'd like."

I knew he would understand.

"All right, Mr. Dahl."

I signed the document.

He took it from me, glanced at my scrawling *Ansell Sterling, Capt. UCMC* near the bottom, and nodded to himself. "Very good. I shall see this is passed on. And now—"

The guards took me by the arms and hauled me out of the chair. I didn't bother to protest.

[Ivy?]

She didn't answer.

"You asked for everything," Hayan said. "But everything has a price. I am sure you are not really surprised."

My heart seized in my throat like an engine locking up. "A price? Didn't I just pay it?"

"You've given us nothing we didn't already have."

"I'm an emissary of the United Colonies."

"You are a reserve corporal wearing the uniform and insignia of a Marine Corps captain. Technically you are a spy. You just signed a diplomatic document using a false name. I could have you shot and be perfectly within the dictates of the Brahmin Convention."

[Ivy!]

Still she didn't answer. All at once I knew she wasn't going to. I was about to die alone, after all of my effort and careful planning, and my story would never even be finished, much less read.

"Conveniently," Hayan continued, "your forgery serves the interests of my superiors and the Grand Alliance. So we will take no action at all, except that which you have asked for, and that which will ensure we have all the facts of this situation prior to formalizing the agreement."

He nodded to the guards and they pulled me backwards to the door.

"You're going to *interrogate* me?" It shouldn't have surprised me. Maybe I just expected them to be more subtle.

"Relax, Corporal. We are just going to ask you a few questions. I must be sure that we are getting a complete picture of what happened here. For that we need to install a symbiotic collar. I think you'll see an immediate improvement in connectivity with your builder. In fact, this is the only way to give you the *everything* you have asked for."

Everything. Meaning Ivy. She was the everything I wanted, and not just because she could open a link to OrbSyn. But if they attached a symb-collar, I wouldn't be able to keep her—or any enemy wyrm— at a comfortable distance. And my story would never make it to the network's live feed.

"You don't have to do this!" I fumed. "I'll tell you anything you want to know!"

Hayan came around the table, hands folded. "But I have read your work, Corporal. Including your current work-in-progress. You freely admit that you lie for a living."

"Of course I lie," I shouted. "I'm a *journalist!*"

The goons dragged me backwards down the corridor. I planted my feet against the floor panels and struggled for my freedom but accomplished nothing except some fresh bruises and a faster heartbeat. I could feel the steady-stim Laclos had given me finally start to wear off.

They took me to a tiny sick bay and shoved me onto a neural couch. Clamped its restraining cuffs over my wrists and ankles. Drew webbed belts across my chest, knees, and waist.

Everything I'd done, everything I'd *written*, the past few days was about to be sacrificed on the altar of war. Only now it wasn't happening because of some Fleet decision, or the stubbornness of the Marine Corps, or the nearsightedness of the Senate. It wasn't even happening because my editor was afraid of angering his superiors.

No, this time the truth of my story was going to be torn to pieces by the *actual* enemy, by the Grand Alliance. Because, out of all the things I'd written about the grendels over the years, I'd apparently gotten one thing right: they couldn't *stand* secrets.

After all, a man with a secret is a man with autonomy.

He's a man, not a grendel.

In the corner of my right eye I caught sight of an articulated surgical arm selecting a symb-collar from one of the hive-like storage compartments along the wall. It made tiny swishing noises in the air as its digits twirled.

Finally it seemed to notice me. It turned the collar above me in a half circle, revealing a fist-sized battery of syringes and scalpels on the opposite side of the surgical head. The arm swept down to within a centimeter of my left eye and paused, leaving me to stare down the point of a syringe.

Then the arm disappeared behind me, and I could hear it whirling into position behind my neck, just at the base of my skull.

Hayan loomed above me, smiling with those perfect teeth. "It does not hurt, Corporal. In fact, I think you will find that you like it."

I believed him, and the sweat poured off of me. "What do you *want*?"

"The truth," he said, leaning close to wipe the sweat from my forehead with a folded cloth. "Just the truth."

18

THE STORYTELLERS

The initial prick of the syringe gave way to a spreading warmth down the back of my neck, crept across my scalp, and wrapped around both cheeks to my mouth. A click of metallic certainty brought a new sensation, a comforting tightness pressing into the skin beneath my jaw.

The tension I'd been feeling since I first walked into that mess hall and sat down across from Sterling drained out of me. It was as if the AI on Sterling's comms, which I still wore, had suddenly become a thermostat for comfort. Every aspect of my physical being was managed. I could feel it.

The restraints unsnapped. The webbed straps snaked back into their tiny cocoons. The couch inclined, raising my head and lowering my feet as it spun around to face Commander David Dahl.

He stood at parade rest, left hand crooked behind his back, right hand flat against his thigh. "What are you doing, son?"

It wasn't my father. Not my real father. It was just a projection. It *had* to be. Dad was still stationed back at STRATOP, and even the Alliance's advanced technology couldn't grant the grendels access to those corridors.

But that *voice*! The voice was that of my own memories, the voice of my real dad, the voice of the man who taught me, if unintentionally, that I would never be respected by anyone who mattered.

"Defecting," I said.

Disappointment tugged his chin forward. "Always did take after your mother. You get your story?"

"Still working on it."

"And the treaty?" he asked. "That signed?"

I nodded. "Seven-year ceasefire."

His shoulders sagged as he looked away. Relief maybe, though the next moment he once again wore the faraway look of a recruiting poster. "Captain Sterling is a good man."

Captain Sterling.

Always someone else.

"Sure," I said.

"He came to me, you know. Asked me if you were the right man for the job."

Another lie, yet it stripped my soul bare. It would have been the right thing to do, a human thing if not a military one. "Never mentioned it."

"I told him you had the talent and the temperament. That you would do what you were told if you saw the sense in it."

"But?"

"But your sympathies were divided. And they *are* divided, aren't they, son?" He pointed at my neck with one shaking finger. "Or you wouldn't be wearing that."

I reached up and touched the collar. I'd already forgotten it was there. "They're divided. Yes."

"Part colonial, part grendel. Your mother's emotional strength, and my—" He looked away, eyes glistening. "Well, my weakness, I suppose."

"You aren't weak," I said. "This isn't your fault. I chose it."

"And your girlfriend? Ms. Weber? Where does she land in all of this?"

"New Witlund, probably. Unless she can get a shuttle back to Holikot."

"Not what I meant."

"No?"

"She'll betray you in the end, if she hasn't already," he said. "It's what they do. They leave."

"Yeah," I said, thinking of both Ivys. "They leave."

He seemed to read my expression. Took a tiny step towards me. "You don't have to do this, son. You've done your part. You don't have to go over to them. Don't have to become—"

"It's too late," I said.

"It's never too late." He took another step forward, close enough I could see the weave of his uniform fabric. "You don't owe them anything. You don't owe anyone anything. Fleet, the colonies, OrbSyn. You sure don't owe the Alliance. Only person you owe anything to is me."

I looked away, my eyes unfocused on the bank of medical storage compartments. Never in my life had I seen tears in my father's eyes. "I can't leave."

"Can't? Or won't?"

I met his gaze then. He deserved that much. "I'm a prisoner on one of their frigates. And they don't allow defectors."

His chin lifted. He took in the surgical arm, the neural couch, the white paneling in the ceiling. "I see."

"One last story," I said. "It's all I have to give."

He pursed his lips. Stepped back into a stance of polished attention. "In that case, make it a good one."

"Yes, *sir.*"

"Corporal," he said. And to my amazement, he saluted.

They were letting me say goodbye to him.

They didn't have to do that. They didn't owe it to me. But I needed it. And I drank it in like water.

Throat tight, I returned his salute, and he disappeared.

The door opened a moment later, but I didn't turn around. I couldn't look away from the honeycombed cabinets along the wall, the backdrop of the place he had been standing.

"Thank you," I said to whoever was behind me, "for that carrot."

"Carrot?" Hayan asked.

A sick, hollow feeling spread through my gut as I realized what was coming next. But would it be more real than my father had been? "And now the stick?"

"Ah! More like another carrot. One of my scout teams has located the woman who betrayed you. Ivy Weber. I thought one more goodbye might be in order. You are correct, Mr. Dahl, that I cannot let you leave the *Takwin*. I have my orders. But we are not savages."

This is what I had feared. Not that I was stuck, but that they had somehow cornered the real Ivy Weber. And it was my fault. "Where is she?"

"Not far. Your cartel has created an impressive network of tunnels in these mountains. Ms. Weber is currently being detained there."

Ivy appeared in the room a couple of meters from me. Flesh-and-blood Ivy, the real Ivy, no matter what I had told myself earlier. Her hands were quick-cuffed to a chair—a different one than I'd been secured to—and her hair lay matted with sweat. She wore a prisoner restraint on her left wrist.

I didn't recognize the place, though I could see stacks of product fading into the semi-darkness just over her right shoulder. Probably the warehouse they used to supply the city, someplace not far from the *Takwin*.

Master Sergeant Ulles, the sniper who had given me his rifle up on that ridge, stood behind her, the barrel of his Wasp EM-11 pressed into the base of her neck.

"You killed Vermier because she was a traitor," Hayan said. "Yes?"

"Yes."

"And what would you have us do with Miss Weber? She is no less a traitor to both the United Colonies and the Grand Alliance. The Brahman Convention provides for such contingencies under the 'armed combatants' provision. Do you have any objection to Master Sergeant Ulles executing her?"

I gripped the arms of the recliner and edged forward.

He was testing me. Splitting my loyalties and watching to see which would conquer the other.

"Please don't," I said. "She doesn't deserve to die."

"Deserve? That's an odd choice of words."

"She was just following orders."

"But *whose* orders, Mr. Dahl? Do you really think she answered to Vermier?"

"I don't know. Maybe one of yours." I didn't really believe it. Ivy Weber may have betrayed me, but I couldn't believe she would sell out her homeworld.

"She's not one of our agents," Hayan said. "She's a true colonial—if currently siding with a rogue militia. Actually, I suspect she's more than she appears. Not just some research clerk working from a basement office in the Holikot embassy, but a field operative. An agent trained in counterintelligence by your government, and working now for those who oppose our new treaty."

"If she's real," I admitted. "That would be the most likely explanation."

"If?" Hayan laughed again. "You could easily find out. Why not ask her?"

Across the room, sweat beaded on Ivy's forehead, and she licked her lips. I couldn't tell whether she resented me or still held out hope that I could somehow rescue her.

It occurred to me that I wore a symb-collar. However she was seeing me—via flatscreen or grendel holo—she would certainly think of me as compromised. And who knew what Ulles might have told her?

"Ivy," I said. "Do you remember our first night together?"

She hesitated, then nodded.

It was an awkward question, mostly because of how I'd phrased it. I had implied intimacy, though in fact we'd done nothing but swap theories about the nature of the Grand Alliance's control over its citizens.

After we discovered that my apartment had been burglarized, we talked late into the early morning until the police finally arrived at zero-stupid-hundred. The cops had taken our statements, but since nothing really valuable had been stolen, entered the incident in their system as vandalism. By the time they left we were both so tired we just slept. I woke up two hours later and stumbled into the kitchen to find Ivy sitting there eating eggs and toast, reading a copy of the police report.

"What was the first thing you said to me the next morning?" I asked.

She looked surprised. Gave a little shake of the head, as if not believing the question. Or maybe she just didn't want to answer it. But then she looked straight into my eyes and said, "'What kind of name is that?'"

Perfect.

That is, it was *almost* exactly what I had said. It differed only in what she had left out. The real, flesh-and-blood Ivy would never have revealed precisely what I'd said.

I squeezed the arms of my seat into lumps of gel. This was really her, not some wyrm-driven hack of my brain. This was the real Ivy Weber, the woman I had loved, the woman I had wanted to marry.

This was the Ivy who had betrayed me.

"Satisfied?" Hayan asked.

I nodded. "Yes."

"And what shall we do with her?"

"Nothing," I said. "What she did doesn't matter now. Our Fleet authorities will deal with her."

"I *could* do that, yes," Hayan agreed. "If I felt sure I knew the whole story. But that would mean a compromise. You, Mr. Dahl, would have to give your builder access to all of your memories."

All of my memories.

But that wasn't an option. It couldn't be an option. Not unless they gave me what I wanted. "We have a treaty," I said. "You can't go around shooting unarmed colonials and claim to be adhering to the terms of—"

"Our agreement is informal," Hayan cut me off. "It has yet to be ratified by either government."

"And yet you wanted it. You wanted me to bring it to you."

"Someone had to, Mr. Dahl."

But I pressed forward to the question burning itself into my mind. "Yes, someone. And I did that. But you forced me into a symb-collar."

"You said you wanted everything." Hayan came around the chair to face me, standing just off to the side so that I could see Ivy looking back and forth between us. It was clear she was seeing and hearing everything. "Did you not mean that you wanted the *enhanced* version of Ivy Weber you've been enjoying at our expense?"

I looked into Ivy's eyes, saw the pain flickering there, and hated myself. "Yes," I said. "That's what I asked for."

"Then where is your complaint?"

"You don't need the collars," I said. "You don't need them!"

"Need?"

"This collar isn't making me do anything. It can't make me decide. It can't twist my will. If you could *force* me to turn over my memories, you already would have. That's why you've gone to all this trouble. Conjuring Commander Dahl. Capturing Miss Weber."

"Force is rarely necessary, Mr. Dahl, except with beasts," Hayan said. "And the occasional colonial."

"But you forced the collar onto me," I blurted, as much for Ivy's sake as for my own. "You wanted me to believe that I was losing my power to choose."

"Torture a man long enough and he will do anything to make it stop. Reward a woman handsomely enough and she will sell even her own children. But in most cases such extremes are unnecessary. Comfort is vastly more effective than torture. And parents have sold their children for promises no one could keep. Isn't that the essence of your job, Mr. Dahl? To sell stories to parents? To bring comfort through lies?"

It was true. It was the thing I had been carrying for so long, the thing that had prompted me to want something different. To write a great war story based on the truth.

"That's it, then?" I asked. "That's all there is to it? You're just *storytellers*? That's the great mechanism of the Grand Alliance? You manipulate your people with stories?"

Hayan stared at me with an expression of genuine surprise. All at once he burst out laughing. "How can you not know this? You're a *journalist*. All of human history is manipulation through storytelling. It's the only kind of manipulation that works over time."

"But the collar—"

"A modification," he said, holding up one hand, first to his neck, then to the Divanese Special on his wrist. "Quite simple. Instead of telling one story to almost a trillion people, we tell each person their own story. That is, we tell the story they want to hear. And who is the hero in your own story, Mr. Dahl?"

I blinked up at him as the truth washed over me. They couldn't make me open my mind to them. The symb-collar didn't control the will. It just magnified the tricks, the illusions, the physiological effects available to the Builders.

The wyrms, I corrected myself. *Careful what you call them.*

"You are, of course," Hayan continued when I didn't answer. "Every person is the hero of their own private drama. No one casts herself as the villain, or the mentor, or even as the lover. No, you are all the hero. Every one of you. A hero in a sea of heroes. We simply use this natural inclination for our own ends. Yes, we are, as you say, the storytellers. We give every person the story he didn't realize he wanted to hear. And that's why the colonies cannot win, Mr. Dahl. It's why you are losing this war. A public story will never conquer a private one."

"A good story is all you need to turn anyone into a robot?"

"Something like that, yes." Hayan smiled. "And now, what shall it be? Shall I ask Master Sergeant Ulles to carry out justice against Miss Weber, or would you prefer to let go of your private torment and allow the *real* Ivy into your past?"

The real Ivy. Who was still noticeably absent.

I couldn't help wondering, even then, did she really *want* to be with me?

"Let her go," I said, staring at Ivy Weber's pallid, pain-filled face. It was my fault they were hurting her. My fault they held a gun to her. "Please."

Hayan came closer. "You need not sacrifice her, Mr. Dahl. We don't want to take anything from you. We don't want launch codes or troop locations. We don't even want your dignity. The truth is all we care about."

"My story," I said. "Would never see the light of day."

"Your 'great war story,' you mean?"

"Yes. You want my memories? Let my story go out on OrbSyn's live feed, and I'll tell you anything you want to know."

"Don't do it," Ivy spat, her face contorting. She strained against the quick-cuffs as lines of blood appeared on each wrist. "Corporal! Don't give them anything!"

"You are not in a position to negotiate, Mr. Dahl," Hayan said, his voice calm.

"She's done nothing wrong!" I shouted.

"Miss Weber, if that's her real name, tried to stop a critical negotiation of peace between our warring governments. Her actions could have cost the lives of millions. I have every right to call for her summary execution. And you have no reason to object. Unless—"

"You kill her, and I'll tell you nothing!" I snarled. "Understand that, Mr. Ambassador? I'll tell you nothing!"

Hayan gave a long sigh. He turned and looked sadly at where Ivy Weber sat frozen to her chair. "Meaning there *is* something after all."

"There's nothing!" I shouted stupidly.

"Idiot," Ivy Weber screamed. "Stop talking! Don't tell them—"

Behind her, Hayan flicked one finger, a silent signal.

I reached for her.

Ulles pulled the trigger.

19

GREAT WAR STORY

I launched off the neural recliner in a red haze, catching Hayan's jaw with a right cross. It broke two bones in my right hand, though I felt no pain from that until later.

I don't know how many times I hit him. The room went cold gray and started to spin—probably interference from my new symb-collar. Seconds later the ambassador's goons entered the room and pulled me off of him. By then his face was mashed to a red pulp.

The rangers were not as accommodating as His Excellence. One of them held me while the other beat me. Somewhere along the way a rib cracked, and I doubled up in agony.

They hauled me by the ankles down the corridor and stuffed me into a security locker. Alliance warships don't need brigs. Enemy prisoners are crammed into reinforced bins that are not quite tall enough to stand in but are too narrow for lying down.

In one of these I hunched, knees to my chest, each stabbing breath little more than a gasp.

But I deserved the pain and didn't want it to end.

It kept me focused on something besides my last glimpse of Ivy as that round tore through her neck and exploded from her throat.

My fault, I told myself in the eerie blue light of an overhead panel. *My fault. My fault. My fault.*

I'd gotten her killed. And she didn't deserve to die. Not for loving her homeworld too much. Not for wanting to tell the story everyone needed to hear.

But who was left to tell people what Ivy Weber had really given her life for?

Not me.

Some great war story. I was going to die in a storage locker on a grendel frigate, and no one would ever know what had really happened here. Ivy Weber's death would go unexplained and unavenged, her body dumped in a nameless grave. And Fleet still wouldn't know what gave the Alliance wyrms their power.

My MADAR team should be happy, I thought bitterly. *This is their sort of war story. Nobody dies except the traitors and the journalist.*

Gradually I became aware of another person squatting next to me in the tiny locker.

Ivy.

Her presence congealed in my mind, as ethereal as smoke from a distant fire, and just as real. She was saying something I didn't completely understand. Something about post-traumatic blah-blah, and the challenge of integrating Alliance technology when I hadn't been conditioned for blah, didn't have a lifetime of blah to adapt to the blah of the caustic blah-blah fusion blah. And would I let her in now?

Would I let her in now?

Now?

Now?

Restless fingers tapping a drumbeat on a locked door.

[*It's not your fault, Raymin.*]

[No.]

[*I'm sorry. I asked Hayan's Builder not to kill her. I know she is important to you.*]

[You do?]

[*It was just an act, wasn't it? Even though you had feelings for her?*]

Such a complicated question.

I nodded, gritting my teeth against the pain in my right side, the growing heat radiating from my right hand. [Was it real? Did she really die?]

A long pause. [*I'm not allowed to tell you.*]

[Why?]

[*You demonstrated beyond any doubt that you are hiding something from us.*]

[Is Ivy Weber alive?] I asked stubbornly. The fact that this Ivy was not answering seemed an invitation—a golden thread I must unspool.

[*I know how your story ends,*] she said. [*There's nothing you can show me that I haven't already seen.*]

[You know all the stories?]

[*More or less.*]

I didn't believe her. Not that it mattered much. But I knew the secret. Stories were all the Builders really had. And even though I'd confirmed that it had been the real Ivy Weber who was quick-cuffed to that chair, they could easily have faked her death. They had access to my optic nerve, and God knew what else. [Is she alive?]

[*Yes,*] Ivy said at last. [*Ivy is alive. Does that help?*]

The smoke thickened, and I pushed my feet out to the far side of the locker, felt my body relax as the pain in my chest subsided.

Ivy wasn't dead. She was alive. She was here.

Wasn't *this* Ivy? And not just Ivy, but everything flesh-and-blood Ivy had been, plus a little bit more? A sense of gathering completeness, depth, personality? Who else could be so utterly companionable? Who else would never be apart?

My heart thudded as I felt her take my right hand in her left, curling her forearm over mine. I still couldn't see her, but immediately the pain there lessened too. In my mind she turned her penetrating green eyes and dimpled cheeks towards me.

[All right,] I said as relief flooded through my body. [I'll let you see everything. But you need to give me something.]

[*What do you want?*] she asked.

[I want my story on OrbSyn's live feed. My words, unaltered, with my own byline. Corporal Raymin Dahl. Embedded with MADAR Team Two.]

[*That's it?*]

[Yes,] I said. [I mean, *no*. I don't want you to *recreate* it for me. I want you to un-strangle our nodes and open up New Witlund's secure channel to Fleet. I want my words, unaltered, sent to my editor's desk. And I want to do it myself. No tricks, no interference.]

[*What difference will that make?*]

[All the difference that matters,] I said. [It's *my* story.]

[*Then you'll let me see everything?*]

[Everything.]

[*All right. The link is open. Go ahead.*]

A terminal opened on my grid.

The base file structure seemed intact, and I immediately recognized Sterling's PSYOPS designation. Now, sitting in a cargo locker on an enemy warship, I had access to stuff Raymin Dahl wouldn't have been able to see in a hundred years at OrbSyn.

Most of it was intel from the war on Quelon, a flood of digital imaging from quick-response units and fighter squadrons and orbiting missile platforms.

Which meant of course that there *was* a war on Quelon. So flesh-and-blood Ivy had been wrong about that attack planet-side being a party trick.

A week ago so much data would have seemed overwhelming, but now I barely noticed any of it—just scrolled past the explosions and flickering combat maps and pulled up the military news desk on Holikot.

Major Charles Weston, OrbSyn editor.

Inbox.

The system demanded my private passcode.

I thought for a moment, then entered a string of gibberish just to make sure I was really touching OrbSyn's live portal. Sure enough, Weston's surly voice spat out, "Wrong. Do you even work here?" And while Ivy could certainly have found a way to imitate Weston's voice, she wouldn't know when to simulate the error message.

Which meant she seemed to be playing this straight.

And why not? She had nothing to lose.

Still, I wanted to make sure, so when I entered the correct login and found myself staring at a blinking icon with Weston's initials emblazoned across it, I hesitated.

—THAT YOU, EDITOR SIR?—

I typed via thought-to-text. "Editor sir" was about the clearest signal I could send regarding who I really was. And I needed to be clear, because my story would carry the byline Raymin Dahl, but my comms was screaming to the system that I was, in fact, Captain Ansell Sterling.

—WESTON, C: *WHO ARE YOU?*—

—YOU SENT ME TO DIG UP A STORY ON THE MADAR TEAMS. IF IT'S REALLY YOU, EDITOR SIR.—

—WESTON, C: *DAHL? WHAT DO YOU MEAN, IF IT'S REALLY ME? AND WHERE HAVE YOU BEEN? I'VE BEEN TRYING TO GET THROUGH TO CAMP LOCKE, BUT ALL COMMS INTO QUELON ARE FLOODED.*—

—QUICK QUESTION. WHAT COLOR IS MY DESK AT THE ORBSYN STATION THERE ON HOLIKOT?—

A pause. I suppose he was trying to decide whether or not he was being played. In the end his journalistic curiosity must have gotten the better of him.

—WESTON, C: *YOU DON'T HAVE A DESK HERE AT ORBSYN. IT REMINDS YOU OF WORK.*—

—THANKS, BOSS. I'M ONTO SOMETHING BIG HERE. STORY OF A LIFETIME.—

—WESTON, C: *I'VE HEARD THAT BEFORE. FROM YOU.*—

—I'M IN A STORAGE LOCKER ON A GRENDEL FRIGATE. IT'S A LONG STORY, AND YOU'RE GOING TO LIKE IT. BUT I NEED YOU TO PROMISE ME YOU'LL RUN IT AS IS.—

—WESTON, C: *AS IS? WHAT'S GOING ON, DAHL?*–

I thought about how to tell him that I was in real trouble, that I had no plan for escape, that I didn't expect to live much longer. I didn't *want* to admit this, especially to myself, because once you let the poison of hopelessness in, the mind starts to cloud. But I needed him to take my story seriously, and nothing gets an editor's blood pumping like a tragedy.

—NOT TO SOUND MELODRAMATIC, BUT . . . I DON'T THINK I'M GOING TO MAKE IT OUT OF THIS. AND I NEED THIS ONE. I NEED IT.–

A pause. I imagined him staring at his own grid, wondering if he should contact STRATOP. Or maybe he was linking directly to counterintelligence and not overthinking it at all.

Finally he sent,

—WESTON, C: *I CAN LIVE WITH YOUR ADVERBS. SEND ME SOMETHING WORTH READING, AND I'LL ROLL IT OUT ON THE BREAKING FEED.*–

—THANKS, SKIPPER. SENDING PART ONE NOW. I'LL SEND PART TWO WHEN I SEE THE FIRST FEATURE GO LIVE.–

—WESTON, C: *BLACKMAIL, HUH?*–

—I LEARNED FROM THE BEST.–

I pulled up my story notes, found the first feature, and remembered I'd called it, "Grendels Invade Quelon!"

People were going to lose their minds when they saw that go live. All of Fleet Strategic Operations; most of the Corps PSYOPS unit; maybe even Weston himself.

But definitely Commander David Dahl. He deserved better.

I nudged the feature over the transom and waited.

A moment later Weston replied,

—WESTON, C: *YOU SURE ABOUT THIS, CORPORAL?*—

He'd obviously read the title.

—READ IT ALL AND SEE IF YOU STILL NEED TO ASK.—

Ivy squeezed my left hand. I felt it even though I still couldn't see her. [*Your turn.*]

[I'm not done yet.]

[*Fair is fair,*] she protested, and the feed went black. [*You promised.*]

The message was clear. No more feed. No more uploads. No more feature stories going to OrbSyn until I let her into my memories.

I thought about Hayan's bloody face. How good it had felt to pound his nose into pulp. Better even than lining up Vermier's head in a scope for that kill shot.

And I shouldn't be thinking this way, because was this really me? Was this who I had become? A man with no conscience, driven only by mission and brute desire? A robot ridden by a quantum master?

A grendel?

Yes, I decided. *This is who I am now. This is what they do to you. And people should know.*

Maybe I could have held out longer, but the feed was black, and the light in the locker had gone out, and the hopelessness of the timer ticking down in the corner of my vision pressed against me. It seemed I was spinning alone in a universe devoid even of the stars.

Vibrations rumbled through the wall at my back, and I knew the ship's nav system must be preparing its engines for a hard launch.

All at once Ivy sat next to me, her left hip wedged against my right side, her head snuggled into my shoulder. I felt her warmth, inhaled the subtle perfume in her hair. Lilacs.

She took my broken right hand in both of hers, touching it gently where it had begun to swell, and a sensation like cool water flowed over the pain, numbing it to a dull ache.

"What do you want to see?" I asked.

"Everything," she said.

It was her. The real Ivy, sitting there with me in my misery. Ivy Weber's flesh-and-blood voice filled the cramped space like a song, caressing my heart and my mind and washing me in relief.

Why had I imagined her dead?

She was in my mind too, unlocking the cabinets and flinging files into the air.

Images flashed before me—not the concrete, razor-edged imaging of neural recordings, but the fuzzy, shapeshifting bio-stories we call memory.

> She stood at a club table under pulsing neons, leaning on her elbows, her hands cupped around a beer mug, her eyes shopping the room. When she saw me I blinked and lifted my chin to let her know I was there.
>
> She turned away.
>
> "New Witlund?" I asked when I finally made it to her table. Had to make sure it was the same girl.
>
> "Born and raised," she said.
>
> "Did you read the file?"
>
> She nodded, then glanced to the exit.
>
> I saw that the music was irritating her. "You up for a walk?"
>
> "Sure."

In the storage locker Ivy looked up at me, her head cocked to one side. I guess I was looking at her the way I'd looked at her back on Holikot.

"The feed," I said. "You promised."

She blinked, and the stream of images and subnet portals flashed back onto my grid.

In the back of my mind I could still feel her sifting through every thought, every memory, every clue I'd given her since I snapped Sterling's comms onto my wrist.

"I'm from New Witlund?" Ivy asked. "Not Holikot?" Her presence in my mind didn't seem to be paying much attention to me at the moment, but I knew that must be because she was trying desperately to figure out what I had been hiding all along.

"You know that."

Weston sent another message, short and laced with fear.

—WESTON, C: *YOUR FIRST FEATURE IS LIVE. ALREADY PULLING MILLIONS OF EYES. HOPE YOU KNOW WHAT YOU'RE DOING.—*

"Why It Had to Be Done," the second feature, sat in queue, ready and waiting on my outbound platform, so I shot it across the link before Ivy could close the pipeline again.

Not that she seemed inclined to. She was still rummaging around in the attic.

I checked to make sure thought-to-text was still recording, scanned the document to check that the words were appearing . . .

scanned the document to check that the words were appearing

. . . and saw that Ivy was still running through my cloudy memories of that first night: the broken doorjamb, my apartment in disarray, the long wait for the cops. She was looking at everything, but her comprehensive search was taking too much time. Bio-memories aren't sorted in neat stacks. They aren't alphabetized and cross-referenced. To save time, she would have to use me as an interface.

But if she wanted the truth, if she really wanted it, I would give it to her.

I would give her anything she wanted now—even tell her when she was on the wrong track. "Holikot's not really important," I said.

And showed her.

Corporal Dahl cowering under a clerk's desk on crappy, stained government carpeting, too terrified even to move.

This was the guy who wrote all those action features?

"Three Days on a Wounded Cruiser," and "Life and Death as a Harpy Ace"?

He'd been a lot cockier back in the mess hall, and it hadn't been hard to get him on board. All he had wanted was a great war story. "And I'm going to write the story my way," he'd said. "I'm going to tell all of it, and you're not gonna say squat."

"Of course," I'd said, because I wasn't going to change his mind, and he didn't have long to live anyway.

I looked out the window to the street below, saw Raeburn's MADAR team closing the distance. They were going to be too late. Footsteps already pounded the stairway down the corridor. I would have to do this myself.

I waited for the knob to turn, then blasted the door and wall with my flash rifle.

In the aftermath Dahl had gone fetal under the desk, his soft little journalist's hands covering his ears, his spoiled, I've-got-daddy-issues eyes pressed closed so that he wouldn't have to see anything.

When he finally stood to look out the window, I asked, "Are you ready to die for your colony, soldier?"

His face twitched, pale as starlight, as if he knew what was coming. Maybe he did. "Sir?"

For just a moment, regret knotted in my stomach. His father, Commander David Dahl, had served honorably, and even if the son was a coward and a dissident and a closet traitor, he had at least volunteered. "Thank you for your service," I said.

I shot him through the chest, close to the heart.

"Don't worry," I said before he stopped breathing. "I'll write the ending."

She barely noticed. "Yeah. Your dream. A subconscious projection of your new personality as you tried to become Captain Sterling. You've hated yourself for some reason. But I can help you with that."

"Raymin Dahl was a mediocre reporter who tried to distance himself from his veteran father by writing feature stories that made militia groups like the one here on New Witlund suspicious of the Corps."

Ivy brushed back a strand of loose hair from her face. Slowly she turned in the cramped space so she was sitting on her knees and looking into my face, her hands still folded around my broken right hand. "There *is* no police report on Holikot that mentions vandalism to your apartment."

"You hacked the police database?"

She shrugged. "Their security systems are basically catnip."

I reached out to stroke her cheek with my left hand, marveling that she had found her way inside the frigate.

Something thudded in the distant recesses of the ship, and I recalled that the J-class frigate had retractable cowling covers. The engines would be heating up soon, entering the final phase of pre-launch. Raeburn wouldn't be able to extend my escape window. If he didn't take out the *Takwin* while it was on the ground, the hammerhead would be virtually useless.

"Maybe it never got filed," I suggested.

"Maybe you're still not telling me everything."

"My story hasn't gone out yet. Not all of it."

She brushed back a wisp of stray hair behind her ear. "You already knew you wanted a relationship with me? Even that first night?"

"That night I wanted information. My apartment really was vandalized. Some things aren't meant to be part of a story, Ivy. Whoever trashed my apartment was probably just some random addict looking for a score."

"But you *love* me?"

"Yes."

"And what was the first thing I told you the next morning? The morning after the robbery? I know I left *something* out."

I couldn't stop Ivy from seeing.

Didn't even try to.

Another memory leapt from the cabinet.

Ivy sat at the kitchen table, elbows on the surface,
reading my copy of the police report. She'd made a
couple of omelettes, and the smell of breakfast reminded
me somehow of my first leave after boot camp.
I slid into the chair opposite her and yawned.
"Ansell," she said. "What kind of name is that?"

Ivy blinked again. "Ansell?"

"I told you, I'm not who I say I am. I lie for a living."

She bit her lower lip and stared at me for a long time before finally saying, "You *recruited* me?"

"Yes."

"And planted me in the New Witlund militia to make your cover story believable?"

"Yes."

"So when you admitted to being Raymin Dahl over an open channel—"

"Even you believed it."

"You're Captain Sterling?" She opened her mouth. Closed it. Shook her head. "The *real* Ansell Sterling?"

"I've been telling you," I said. "Even though I've tried not to."

"But how?"

"Wasn't hard to swap images in our personnel files. We knew you'd look. Of course, I had to let myself go flabby for six months. After that it was just a matter of acting out a romance between us, creating a trail of bread crumbs for you to find. I just didn't expect to really fall in love with you so quickly."

She looked past me, as if scanning her own grid. "But that means . . . Did I know the risks?"

"Ivy Weber grew up on New Witlund. She volunteered. The problem wasn't planting a girlfriend. The problem was finding the right journalist. I knew you'd take me apart, probably starting from my childhood, so it had to be someone with a similar background. My mother died when I was a kid; Dahl's ran away. My father was a full colonel; Dahl's is a commander. We even have similar personality profiles."

"Why similar? What does that mean? That you both wanted full AI integration?"

I shrugged. "That's what the tests said, anyway. I'm still convinced we're made by our choices more than our genes or our environment. But I'm in PSYOPS, so maybe that's just my training talking. Anyway, Dahl was far from a perfect fit."

"It's hard to identify with someone you don't like."

"Yes, but I meant that I wanted a hard news reporter, and Dahl specialized in human interest pieces—and vaguely treasonous ones, at that. I had to read everything he'd ever written just to wrap my mind around his way of thinking. Even went through Major Weston's training program at OrbSyn. But after all that I still wasn't sure Dahl was the one. Then, during our preparation exercises, it occurred to me that Raymin Dahl's strength might be a grendel weakness. And since we hadn't found any better options and were running out of time, I became someone I disliked."

"And you shot him."

I wasn't proud of it. My biggest regret was not that it had been necessary, but that I would never get a chance to apologize to the man's father. Corporal Dahl's involuntary death may have been his greatest service to the United Colonies, but his father deserved better. "Yes."

"And you erased the bracelet and forced a hard reset? Left behind that one memory so you could pretend to find it disturbing?"

"I looked out the window of the cafeteria so you wouldn't be able to reference Dahl's actual face. That fragment served the story I was telling—the story you wanted to believe."

"That's . . . impressive."

I expected her to kill the feed, but it continued across my grid in a flickering stream.

Eyes closed, I kissed her hand. "Salesmen are always the easiest marks. They know how the game is played. And that makes them overconfident."

"You think we're overconfident? We found the counter-virus, you know. Even if you hadn't written about it, we'd have spotted it easily. Our firewalls are lightyears ahead of your Marine Corps diggers."

"You were *supposed* to find the counter-virus," I said. "That's why I wrote about it. A nudge in the wrong direction. No, you have another weakness."

"Really?" Ivy leaned back. She sounded genuinely interested. "What weakness?"

—WESTON, C: *PART TWO BREAKING NOW.*—

The second feature ticked across my OrbSyn feed, and I indulged in a moment of quick reading to satisfy myself that Weston hadn't tinkered with it. Not that he could have done much. There wasn't enough time.

Why It Had to Be Done, By CPL Raymin Dahl, Embedded with MADAR Team Two . . .

—WATCHING THE SCROLL,— I sent. —THREE IS INBOUND.—

I shot the third feature, "*Slave to a Quantum Master,*" across the subnet, and heaved a sigh of relief.

—WESTON, C: *I'M SUPPOSED TO ASK HOW MANY MORE FEATURES THERE ARE.*—

Supposed to ask. My contacts in the PSYOPS unit had obviously been monitoring this exchange from the moment I logged in. They were calling the shots now. Weston was just doing what they told him to do. Following the protocols we'd established months ago when this assignment started.

—JUST ONE,— I answered. —ALL THOUGHT-TO-TEXT, STREAMING NOW, AND FOR AS LONG AS THE LINK LASTS.—

—WESTON, C: *INDULGE AN OLD MAN. FORGIVE ME THOSE COMMENTS I MADE BEFORE YOU LEFT. I MISJUDGED YOU.*—

I stared at the words for a long moment, fighting back the lump in my throat. I'd been looking for those words all my life. Words of respect from a man I looked up to. An officer. Someone like my father, who took care of his marines and gave his life in the service of others.

But were they meant for me?

Did Major Weston really know who he was talking to? I'd been a random marine officer he'd trained for one month on orders from Fleet. Not a real journalist. A pretender. A guy he'd sent away with press credentials and a vague command to *go write me a great war story.* Did he really remember me? Or was he still thinking of Corporal Raymin Dahl?

Maybe I didn't deserve his respect, after all.

—ACTUALLY, YOU HAD ME RIGHT.—

"What weakness?" Ivy repeated.

I considered not telling her, but that might make things worse. I figured she was less likely to accept the truth if I hit her in the face with it. "I knew you'd tell me the wrong story."

"Because we had the wrong hero?"

"You've played the role of the storyteller for so long that you can't see it—but you're caught up in this story too."

She leaned forward to kiss me on the forehead, then sat back on her heels and stared into my eyes. "We're caught in our own story?"

"You think the universe is just matter and energy," I said. "You think that's the lede. It's why your stories have to end in a lie, because a lie is the only way you can make them fulfilling. But life isn't a hard news story, Ivy."

"No?"

"It's a feature."

She gave me a half smile, as if she knew I was still missing something important but didn't know how to tell me, or didn't want to. "This feature is almost at an end, Ansell. I'm so sorry. I promised you everything, but there isn't time. And that wasn't my decision."

"I know."

The white timer in the corner of my vision showed 00:48.

00:47.

00:46.

The engine vibrations coming through the wall and floor grew.

"You aren't going to stop the warhead?" I asked.

"Why should we? We got what we came for."

"What about Hayan and his rangers?"

"They'll die heroes, each the center of a private story. Taking out a defenseless frigate during a peaceful negotiation will not play well in your core media outlets. It will give us the pretense for ripping up the letter you signed."

But if they were not going to honor the peace treaty, why had the grendels come to New Witlund in the first place? All that energy and material expense just to uncover what the colonies were willing to part with? To discover just how desperate the republic was?

Light from the overhead panel framed Ivy's face in a blue halo.

And I realized what I should have understood earlier. Should have seen because it was streaming across my vision in bright flickering images. The Grand Alliance wasn't backing away from their invasion of the local system. They had no intention of pausing the war, even if a treaty were eventually ratified by the Senate.

Quelon still burned.

00:33.

My third feature entered OrbSyn's live feed so quickly I knew Weston must be sending it out without even reading it.

> Slave to a Quantum Master, By CPL Raymin Dahl, Embedded with MADAR Team Two . . .

I didn't need to send the last story, "Say 'No' to Wyrms." It was already streaming direct from my thought-to-text file.

"Tell me something," Ivy said. "If you're not really Raymin Dahl— if you've been Captain Sterling all along—why do you care so much about publishing your little war story? You're not a writer. And it's not even carrying a counter-virus."

"Call it a gift," I said. "Meant for the edgers. A public story to defeat a billion private ones. If our fleet can't protect them, we wanted to show them how to resist you without bombs or rockets. For that we needed an informant on the other side—and a way to tell his story."

00:19.

"But you *aren't* resisting me, Ansell." Ivy navigated back to my side and held my arm again, leaning into me. "You aren't resisting! You don't even *want* to!"

"True," I whispered, hoping, praying, that my theory had been right all along, and truth really was the best PSYOP.

The truth that our real enemy wasn't the grendels but their AI overlords.

The truth that their wyrms weren't monsters, but something much, much worse.

The truth that they didn't win by taking from us everything we wanted but by giving it to us.

The truth that I had lost my private battle the moment I'd slipped that infected comms back onto my wrist.

"I want you more than anything," I said. "And I think that's going to terrify every colonial in the edge."

The truth . . . that Ivy was letting this story go out to the colonies unredacted?

"No, Ansell." She stroked my broken hand with gentle fingertips. "It will drive them to us by the millions."

00:00.

20

PSYOP

–[NO DATA]–

The pressure on my legs builds. It *hurts*.

Right arm too, which I can't move.

Smoke clotting the air, heavy in my lungs.

I cough.

Light in a jagged hole above me, just out of reach.

Comms chirps a CRITICAL beacon, the red warning icon pulsing on my grid like a heartbeat.

It *is* a heartbeat.

My heartbeat.

That's what they—

Something heavy, a beam maybe, has come down across the locker onto my shins.

Floor wet.

"Here!" a voice says.

Sounds like Laclos.

"Here! He's here!"

Gloved hands pry back the warped skin of the locker and peer inside. MADAR helmets, bug-eyed with systems goggles, cut streaks of green through the swirling smoke.

"Don't move, Captain," Laclos says. "Don't move."

Stupid thing to say.

Couldn't move if I wanted to. No strength. And my legs are pinned under—

Pain lances through my thighs all the way up from the ankles, arcing my back.

Not pinned.

Gone.

My legs are gone.

The white just above each knee is bone.

Light from the sun breaks the smoke, shimmering.

Quelon overhead.

Albedo at one third.

Morning.

God, the pain—

Hands reaching in. Raeburn, Hopper, Pajari.

Grunting against the beam.

Lifted.

   —[NO DATA]—

Laclos again, staring down at me, holding my left hand.

Pain clears a little, not much.

Makes thinking easier. Less fragmented.

I try to swallow but my throat is thick with smoke, thick with a mass of tongue that won't work properly, won't let the words out.

And where is Ivy?

"Stay with me, Cap," Laclos says. "Stay with me. You're going to be fine but you've lost a lot of blood. I got trauma packs on your legs and wrist and a Valkyrie inbound. We'll have you in a hospital back on base in twenty."

The story went out? I try to say. The story really made it to OrbSyn's feed?

But all I get out is a harsh croak: "Stor—?"

Laclos nods. "Your story? Yeah. We got an emergency SITREP from Fleet as soon as the *Strangler* blew. Explained everything. Your story's hitting eyes all over. Something else, huh? Maybe it will make a difference. First time we're getting intel from the other side."

"Read it?" I ask. I need to know it's real.

"Your story?"

I nod as a shaft of fire pulses through my body.

She notices. Touches the pad hooked into my bracelet. "Don't worry about this, Cap. Pajari wired a wyrm killer to your comms and that collar they put on you. Fried her right out of there. I've got you on pain meds but we can't give you too much or your heart will stop."

I want to tell her that I don't have endocarditis, but the word is too big for my mouth, and the sky overhead is shrinking as a big metal bird grows inside it.

A glimpse behind the curtain. That's what I wanted. A glimpse we've never had. Now all I want is to live there, backstage.

But Ivy is gone. All the way gone. I can feel it.

"Read it," I say again.

Her eyes scan left, and I can see she's searching her grid.

"Knew it," I say. "You can't read."

Laclos grins. "You, sir, are a jackwagon. Which means the universe will make sure you live. Okay here it is. 'OPERATION GRENDEL, by Raymin Dahl. Confession. Like every journalist, I lie for a living. In this case, I had to become someone else in order to get the story. I'm not who I say I am. My name isn't Ansell Sterling, and I'm not a captain. I'm not even a marine.'" She pauses. "That's not true, is it, sir?"

I shake my head, which is surprisingly heavy. And I realize I'm still wearing the symb-collar. It's touching my throat.

"'The only military training I've ever had was—'"

I squeeze her hand. "That's enough."

"I can keep going," Laclos says. "I mean, it's not very good, but I can skip ahead to the part where a special ops team saves you from the locals."

But I know what comes next. Something about Captain Sterling dying during the grendel invasion of Quelon. "It's all—"

"Cap? Stay with me, Cap!" She's shouting, but her voice seems far away, and the big metal bird opens its mouth. "Hopper! Help me get him to the evac—"

—[NO DATA]—

Something pushes me in the back. A jolt.

"Clear!"

Raeburn stares down at me, his face grim. "Hold on, marine."

The MADARs strap in.

I'm stretched out between two benches, the team staring down at me. Hopper. Pajari. Raeburn.

And I'm glad they lived, glad they survived the assignment.

Laclos hands back the paddles to someone I don't recognize, and now my shirt is off, and I'm lying in my blood-soaked underwear with tubes coming out of me, and I don't have a right hand anymore.

Outside, the sky changes, and I'm impossibly heavy as something presses me deeper into the sticky wet mat against my back.

We're lifting. Rising into the New Witlund sky.

The floor tilts as we veer left, and Quelon flashes past in the window.

Laclos turns her head and starts to sit back, but I grab her hand and hold onto it.

She's crying. For some reason, she's crying. A special ops medic. And I can't think why that would be, because she's never really liked me.

Ivy said so.

The other marines look straight ahead as Laclos wipes her eyes with the back of one sleeve. "Not going anywhere, Cap."

I'm not sure who she's talking about, but I squeeze her hand again. Or try to. Hand is so weak now.

Laclos smells like sweat. Jungle grime and sweat mixed with blood. Not perfume. Just dirt and sweat and fear.

I see it now.

I can't know if the mission worked.

I won't get to see how it ends.

And I remember, no one ever does.

We're each of us a hero in a private story. And we've always seen the end coming. Always found our way to the last period. The last answer. So we expect—

Till now.

This one story we don't get to see the end of. This one story we've spent our whole lives telling.

The story of me.

Will my PSYOP work?

Will the story push—

Or will it pull?

I'll never know. I *can't* know.

Have to leave that to others, to her maybe.

Should care, but the copper sky is changing and my chest is so, so heavy, and Laclos says something from far away.

Her story now.

Hers to keep telling.

Maybe Laclos will see

maybe

how this one

ends.

EPILOGUE

Weeks have passed in a slow haze of overhead lights and surgical bays and masked faces.

I'm cocooned in an open-topped medical pod in a private room that must have been designed for an admiral: indirect lighting, faux wood panels with polished trim, and off to my right a wall-sized screen draped in the pinprick curtain of space. I have my own private window on the cosmos.

I know I'm on a medical ship, but the doctors won't give me the name or even its class. Too dangerous, they say. I'm a target for the Grand Alliance. The only person to defect from the enemy. A war hero who pulled back the grendel veil of secrecy. A man who holds in his mind the key to victory, and *thank you, Captain, for your service.* All the evidence I need to understand that they're probably shipping me to some core planet where a battalion of shrinks will pry open my mind with an AI corkscrew.

Just beyond the door there's a nurses' station where the orderlies and doctors and bionics technicians gather to talk in hushed tones, as if I mustn't be allowed to know what's going on.

They seem to be plotting something. Every so often one of them will glance my way and smile reassuringly.

Someone fiddles with my meds; the heaviness returns, and I can't keep my eyes open.

When I wake again something is different. I can't place it at first, because I'm in the same room with the same view of the universe, the same gently humming medical pod, the same lack of self-determination.

My neck is bare, and there's a dull ache at the base of my skull. I run my fingers across my throat to prove the symb-collar is really gone.

From the doorway a doctor asks me how I feel. I mumble a response, and he comes into the room and tells me the good news about the nerve endings in the stump of my right wrist, and the overhead lights blur together and melt away to darkness.

This time I wake wearing a new hand. Flesh toned, strong, and passably lifelike. It feeds my brain the sensations of real fingers, but muted, as if someone slathered my hand in adhesive and pulled a glove over it. Still, it does what I ask it to, and they give me a battery of tests and smile a lot and say that before long I'll be able to pick my nose and not feel the difference.

They're making me a new set of legs too, though the bionics tech says it will take longer to fit them to my stumps because of the neural feedback loops necessary to walking and balancing. She seems sincere, but I'd bet a case of Inawa Red that they're stalling to keep me from walking around and asking a lot of awkward questions.

Call me paranoid.

They dial up the nighty-night stuff again a day or two later—in this room the slipstream of time never seems to move at the same speed—and it occurs to me just before I float away that they're tinkering with my mind as I sleep. And there's nothing I can do about it.

But I wake again and am surprised to find that I'm wearing a new comms bracelet on my left wrist. The spartan layout of my auto-grid tells me this is a PSYOPS unit.

The systems indicators are all green except for its connection to AFNET. And of course I can feel the presence of my new AI lurking in the background with the cold colonial patience of a valet.

Two folder icons blink in the upper right corner of my vision. The first is labeled, "Citation 9741506-7." They've awarded me another medal. Cheaper than a promotion and the corresponding pay raise.

But that's not what offends me.

How can I tell them I don't want it? That the only reason I came back from my integration was that they were telling me the wrong story? That every time Fake Ivy tried to tell me the story of my own heroism, she reminded me I was really someone else.

I shudder in my cocoon and pull the single white sheet higher.

They don't understand: I *wanted* to believe the lie. Told myself that even if I couldn't be the hero of Corporal Dahl's story, I could still be the hero of my own. But then she brought me Raymin Dahl's parents and inadvertently reminded me that I killed their son.

Well, that was the mission, but it doesn't make me a hero.

I sweep the folder unopened into the shredder.

[*Permanent deletion?*] my new AI asks with a tone of disapproval. [*Are you sure?*]

[Positive.]

[*All right. File deleted.*]

For a long time I stare at the second icon, the one labeled "Operation Little Duck." Another mission already? But it's the Corps, and I'm an asset. The war still rages.

Regulations prohibit destroying mission orders unopened, but I drag that folder to the shredder too.

Or try, anyway. The icon snaps back onto my grid.

I try again with the same result.

"Aren't you going to read it, Cap?" Laclos asks.

She's sitting there in a translucent chair smiling like she knows something cheerful she can't wait to tell me. Her hair is pulled back in a ponytail, her face still grimy with dirt and sweat.

I understand instantly, without needing to sort it out for myself: this is my new AI's way of assembling my fragmented memories into an image I can trust.

Fat chance.

Could the republic really be stupid enough to install bonding personalities on military hardware? To adopt the AI strategy of the Grand Alliance?

Of course we're stupid enough. Maybe it was only a matter of time.

As long as I've been at PSYOPS there have been idiots arguing we should fight fire with fire.

The thought leaves me clenching my teeth.

But Laclos is still smiling, and if seeing her doesn't make me happy, it does remind me that such a thing as happiness exists. "No," I insist. "I'm not going to read it. I want it deleted."

"Can't do that, Cap. Sorry."

"Why not?"

"Orders. Don't you trust me?"

It's a challenge. She's wearing the same expression the real Laclos used when she tried to lighten my mood before I went into that utility shed.

It isn't working this time, either. "You are an AI projection. You're not real. Definitely not Laclos."

"Never claimed to be," she says. "Just trying to find a way to make you comfortable. So it will be easier to open up. You know, help you heal and stuff."

"Well, *doc*, it's not working."

She snorts. "Obviously the problem is the patient."

Unfortunately, that *does* sound like Laclos. Not expecting an answer, I ask, "Where is the master sergeant, anyway?"

"New Witlund," Laclos says. "All of Raeburn's team are there helping to hold the moon for the Marine Corps. And the grendel fleet *still* hasn't taken Quelon."

That surprises me. "How is that possible?"

"High levels of resistance. Rumors about people not giving in to the wyrms."

On my grid the second icon starts to flash. "Can I get a link to AFNET? I would love to see some of this."

"Sorry. You poked a hornet's nest. Would you believe you're public enemy number one on the Alliance feeds? The Corps is moving mountains to keep you hidden."

Of course they are.

More control. More secrecy. More strings being pulled by distant puppet masters.

I turn away and stare at the wall panel, the endless white paint spatter of stars receding into nothing. But she doesn't leave. I can smell her sitting there, the jungle scent of grime and sweat and dried blood. And I wonder if this is how it will always be, if the ghosts of my past will haunt every corner of my future.

"Cap," Laclos asks impatiently, "are you going to read the mission file or not?"

"No."

"Aren't you at least curious about the name?"

The name. Operation Little Duck.

It *is* weird. But I don't want to give her the satisfaction of a response, so I just lie there in the silence as the words niggle at the back of my mind. A vague feeling of familiarity mixed with emptiness tells me I've forgotten something important. "Doesn't sound like a name STRATOP would use."

"That's because this one," she says, "originated with the CIB."

The Covert Intelligence Bureau? The department Ivy Weber had worked for?

Relief floods through me. The spy agency has no control over my future. Whatever they want with me, they can't order me to comply. Though I suppose it could be argued that I owe them something.

Scratch that. I definitely owe them.

But another mission? So soon?

"What do they want?"

"You're not going to read it?"

"No."

Laclos leans back in her chair again. "Okay. But I'm gonna give you crap about this forever."

I give her an irritated scowl. "About Operation Little Duck?"

She laughs. "Have you even read your own features? It's from *Hansel and Gretel*. The poem at the end, after they've killed the old woman and they're looking for a way out of the witch's woods. They can't get home without crossing a river, but the water is too wide and too deep. So Gretel asks for help from a duck. She says, '*Will you help us, little duck, / The two of us who have no luck? / There is no bridge or woodland track, / So will you take us on your back?*'"

I'm staring at her, mouth open, but she just laughs again, fading from view as the folder on my grid opens by itself.

It's a single-page letter bearing the logo of the Covert Intelligence Bureau and signed by the Director. It reads:

> *Captain Ansell Sterling, UCMC,*
> *On behalf of a grateful republic, the Bureau is pleased*
> *to facilitate your way home.*

Home? What does that mean? I'm a marine. Home is wherever I'm stationed. And I'm not on assignment now, so—

I read it six times, but still don't understand.

Until, behind my grid in the real space of the doorway, I see her leaning against the frame.

This time there's nothing fake about her dimples, her green eyes, or the hopeful melody of her voice.

"Hello, Ansell," she says.

"Hello, Ivy."

ACKNOWLEDGMENTS

Every writer depends on the insight and support of other people.

My wife, Carrol, provided feedback on several drafts and shouldered the difficult task of encouraging me to keep at it. Without you, nothing I write would see the light of day, nor would it deserve to.

To my beta readers, those fearless bleeders of red ink who critiqued every chapter—Meriah Bradley, Andi Cumbo-Floyd, Timothy Jackson, Rosey Mucklestone, Sarah Noe, Josh Noe, Adrienne Rollick, and Jared Schmitz—thank you for your careful readings. You are fantastic story analysts.

Amanda Luedeke, you liked this project enough to let it go; for that act of humility I am sincerely grateful.

Russell Galen, your comments on that early draft were tremendously helpful in shaping the direction of my rewrites.

Huge thanks to Steve Laube for understanding my love of science fiction and believing that *Operation Grendel* deserved a place on someone's bookshelf. The Tinkerbell effect is real; this book would have died had you not clapped your hands.

And finally, to all the young OYANers whose love of story inspired my "wonderology." May you fuse truth and story without compromising either.

ABOUT THE AUTHOR

Daniel Schwabauer, M.A., is a lifelong reader of speculative fiction. His professional work includes stage plays, radio scripts, short stories, newspaper columns, comic books and telescripting. Daniel's middle grade fantasy series, *The Legends of Tira-Nor,* has received numerous awards, including the 2005 Ben Franklin Award for Best New Voice in Children's Literature and the 2008 Eric Hoffer Award.

He studied science fiction under science fiction great James Gunn before graduating from Kansas University's Master's program in Creative Writing in 1995. He lives in Olathe, Kansas, with his wife and dog.

Website: DanSchwabauer.com
Facebook: facebook.com/schwabauer